TED TAYLER

BURIED SECRETS

By Ted Tayler

The Freeman Files

Red Herring Season

Gathering Clouds

Still Standing

Vinci Books

vinci-books.com

Published by Vinci Books Ltd in 2025

1

Paperback ISBN: 9781036704971

Chapter One

Wednesday, 21 May 2008

ALAN DUNCAN LEFT his home in Cuttle Lane, Biddestone, at six-thirty in the evening. His partner, Madeleine Mills, known to those who knew her as Maddy, watched him walk to the gateway. She turned away as Alan eased into a steady jog and set off on his regular midweek run. She had their two-bedroomed semi-detached home to herself for ninety minutes.

The couple had met in Chippenham four years ago at a leaving party for one of her call centre colleagues, Anna Phillips. For eleven years, Anna and Maddy had shared a desk. That party had been the last place Maddy wanted to be, but Alan had arrived with Wayne, Anna's husband.

Maddy suspected Anna and her husband had planned this so-called chance encounter for several weeks. As the evening progressed, however, she relaxed and enjoyed Alan's company. In his own words, he joined the Royal

Navy at eighteen to see the world. But, unfortunately, the magic had worn off after a dozen years. So on his thirtieth birthday, he moved from the high seas to work for a Corsham firm as a draughtsman.

"What on earth attracted you to Corsham?" she had asked him.

"I was born there. My parents still live in the town, and my father, Bob, spotted an advert on the work's canteen noticeboard. It was pure luck. I had many skills they were looking for, and the family connection didn't hurt. Dad has worked there for over thirty years. Finally, his firm agreed to give me a shot. Wayne suggested I come with him tonight to celebrate. I heard this afternoon that my three-month trial was successful. I'm official as from Monday morning."

When Alan kissed her goodnight at the end of the evening, he'd asked to see her again. They hadn't spent more than a day apart in the past four years.

After Maddy finished her chores, she caught up on one of her favourite TV shows. She reminisced that any thoughts of avoiding a new relationship had disappeared within weeks of that leaving party. The couple had moved here to Biddestone together after four months. Village life, a handful of miles from their workplaces, suited them down to the ground.

Maddy's friend, Anna, had had three enjoyable years with her new job in Swindon, but Joshua's arrival last December had put a temporary hold on her career. Maddy and Alan had agreed to be the boy's godparents if Wayne and Anna ever got around to arranging a christening. Maddy had already driven to the Phillips's home in Cepen Park, Chippenham, to babysit frequently. For Maddy and Alan, there was still time, but they were enjoying life as a couple. There was no pressure.

Maddy had worked at the same company on the Bumpers Farm Industrial Estate on the outskirts of Chippenham for fifteen years. Alan was plodding along at his job in Corsham. It might have seemed an ordinary existence to many, but Maddy had learned from experience that wild fluctuations of highs and lows were overrated.

Alan had kept fit during his time in the Navy. As he told Maddy, he had little choice, and in the past four years, her partner had maintained a regular exercise regime. Alan loved to run around the village lanes but had never attempted to persuade Maddy to join him. She told him the housework she did while he ran kept her figure trim.

Wayne and Alan were still firm friends and shared a common interest. But, in Anna and Maddy's opinion, it was more of a passion. Their men were keen cyclists with high-spec bikes, helmets, and the ubiquitous lycra clothing that accompanied it. So on weekends, Wayne drove across from Cepen Park with his bicycle on a frame attached to their car's boot. Then he and Alan disappeared for three hours.

Maddy and Anna reckoned that the distances they covered were like the fisherman's tale about the size of the one that got away. There was no escaping the facts; they were both fit individuals for men in their mid-thirties.

Maddy finished watching her programme and checked her watch. Almost eight o'clock. Alan would soon be home. Before joining her in the lounge, he would shower and don a fresh t-shirt and shorts. It was rare for Alan to wear long trousers at home, except in the dead of winter. He told Maddy that wearing a suit during the working week was bad enough. He'd had his fill of uniforms.

Alan Duncan jogged along Church Road and turned the corner towards home. He usually enjoyed his weekly run, but tonight something had unsettled him. As Alan reached the Crown Inn at Giddeahall on the outward leg, a man sat in the beer garden pointed at him. Then he tapped his nose. As Alan turned back into the village, he was sure he heard the man say, "You can run, but you can't hide."

The man was a stranger. Alan didn't look back to confirm that he'd heard the comment. Instead, he dismissed it as the ramblings of someone who had been sitting in the beer garden since lunchtime, and was drunk.

Alan closed the garden gate behind him as a Vauxhall Zafira cruised past. He watched as the car disappeared along the lane. Alan couldn't recall their neighbours driving a Zafira, but why did the driver look familiar?

As he ran upstairs to the bathroom, he tripped on the last step, ending up on all-fours on the landing.

Maddy appeared in the lounge doorway.

"Are you okay, Alan?" she called.

"Yeah, don't worry, sweetheart. I forgot there were fourteen stairs. Give me ten minutes. I'll be with you."

Maddy returned to her seat, and Alan took his shower. As the water cascaded over him, he realised why the driver seemed familiar.

Saturday, 24 May 2008

"WHAT TIME IS Wayne picking you up today?" asked Maddy.

"He wants to be on the road by one o'clock," said Alan. "I ate a good meal last night and plan a high-carb breakfast to get me through today's session. What will you be doing?"

"Can you come with me to do the weekly shopping this morning?" asked Maddy.

"No problem. We won't need anything for tomorrow, don't forget. We promised to go to my Mum and Dad for dinner. I can rely on Mum feeding us until we're fit to burst. I don't think she believes we can cater for ourselves."

"I remember. As for later, Anna might appreciate a visit," said Maddy.

"No doubt you'll offer to give Joshua a cuddle to ease her burden."

Maddy had pulled a face, thrown Alan the car keys, and he'd driven them to the Morrison's supermarket on the A350.

"Is this the route you took on Wednesday evening?" asked Maddy.

"Mmm," replied Alan. "I doubled back at the Crown. This supermarket is brilliant for us, isn't it? Only a ten-minute drive from home, and we never get snarled up in those interminable traffic jams through the centre of Chippenham."

"Hark at you," laughed Maddy. "I've got the devil of a job to get you to come shopping with me most weekends. Or did you want to change the subject? What happened, Alan? Did you decide to stop at the Crown for a crafty pint on a warm evening?"

"No, nothing like that," he replied as he searched the car park for an empty space.

An hour later, they drove home. Alan kept checking his mirror but saw nothing.

Wayne sounded his horn as he drove past the house at a quarter to one, turned his car around in a gateway and idled back. Alan was in the lane with his bike, waiting. He stood and watched his friend detach his bike from the rack.

"A good day for it," said Wayne. "Are you sure you're ready?"

"Warmley via the Cotswold Way and then back on the A420," said Alan. "You bet I'm ready. It should take us two-and-a-half hours. I can't think of a better way to spend a Saturday afternoon."

"It's a route we haven't tried before," said Wayne. "We must be ultra-careful on the busy main road. Don't worry; I'll look after you."

"Yeah, right," laughed Alan. "Let's get going."

Alan checked the Crown's car park and beer garden as they cycled past. There was no sign of the Zafira or its driver.

After two-and-a-half hours of steady cycling, Wayne followed Alan back into Biddestone. They were both tired but satisfied with their afternoon's work. Wayne noticed a man by The Green standing by his car, waving. Ahead of him, Alan cycled harder. Wayne puffed out his cheeks.

"Give me a break, Alan," he called, "I'm shattered. Who was that guy, anyway? Did you know him?"

"I saw no one," Alan replied.

That was odd, thought Wayne. He looked straight at us.

Maddy had just arrived home when they pulled up outside the house. She watched as Wayne re-racked his bike.

"How was Joshua?" he asked.

"He slept most of the time I was there," said Maddy.

"Never mind, sweetheart," said Alan.

"Typical," said Wayne. "He'll be awake half the night now."

"You love it, really," said Maddy.

Wayne grinned, and with a cheery wave, he drove home.

"Someone's going to sleep well tonight," said Maddy as she watched Alan wheel his bike up the garden path.

Alan wished that were true. As tired as he was, he

couldn't stop wondering what the guy in the Zafira wanted. He'd imagined that Wednesday evening could have been a random event. How did the guy know to be in the village this afternoon as they returned from their cycle ride?

Sunday, 25 May 2008

MADDY DROVE them to Corsham for Sunday lunch with Alan's parents. Bob and Elizabeth were always pleased to see them. Alan was an only child. Maddy had a brother, Darren, and her parents lived in a village outside Leeds. Maddy had left home at eighteen and wasn't in a rush to return. She kept in touch with her family members with a few words in a Christmas card. Years ago, the family had decided they had their own lives to lead.

Alan and Maddy knew what to expect when they came to the Duncan family home. A Sunday roast with all the trimmings, plus a long list of questions about work, marriage, holidays, children, and did they want the second helping of rhubarb and custard now or after their tea?

When they left at seven o'clock, Alan was glad to escape.

"Sorry if they went on a bit, Maddy," he said.

"I don't mind," said Maddy, "they care about you. Your Dad will retire at sixty next year, from what he said. So it's only natural they want to see we're financially secure. Any spare cash they have will get spent on foreign holidays; they won't want to dig deep to get us out of a hole. As for any wedding, your Dad probably thinks that because of the distance I've put between myself and my family, they wouldn't be much help. He's right, but we're happy as we are, aren't we?"

"Happy as pigs in the proverbial," said Alan.

Wednesday, 28 May 2008

"I'LL SEE you at the usual time," called Alan as he left the house.

Maddy walked through from the kitchen to watch him start his weekly run. He'd been quieter than usual these past few days. Perhaps the mundane routine was getting to him. Maddy promised herself they would arrange something different this weekend. A trip to the coast on Sunday, maybe. That was it. She started her chores and thought about where they might go.

As she returned the ironing board to the cupboard under the stairs later, Maddy wondered how far Alan had run tonight. It was a quarter past eight. She switched on the television and tried to concentrate on a quiz show. It was no good. Alan was never this late. What could have happened?

At half-past nine, Maddy rang Anna Phillips.

"Is Wayne home, Anna?" she asked.

"He's just got in from five-a-side football. Hang on, do you want a word?"

"Alan's not home from his run," said Maddy, "I'm getting worried. Did he tell Wayne which route he might take tonight? I'll drive out to search for him."

Anna handed the phone to her husband.

"Alan mentioned nothing to me, Maddy," said Wayne. "He was fine on Saturday. I saw him in Corsham yesterday, but something preoccupied him. He didn't respond when I called across the road."

"Where in Corsham? What time?" asked Maddy. That

didn't sound like Alan. "He was at work out at the Industrial Estate at Leafield."

"Well, he must have needed to go into town to the High Street. Alan was on the pavement outside the bank in the middle of the afternoon. Do you want me to drive over to you? We can cover two routes that way. He could have twisted an ankle or something. Did Alan take his mobile with him?"

Maddy frantically searched the house for Alan's mobile, but it wasn't there.

"Why didn't I think of that," she cried. "What a dummy. I'll call Alan to see where the hell he is. The air will turn blue if he's sat in that pub out at Giddeahall."

Wayne laughed.

"Give us a ring later, Maddy, to let us know. Please don't ground him for Saturday. I've got another new route for us to tackle."

Maddy ended the call and rang Alan. It went to voicemail.

She collected the car keys from the hall table and checked her watch. Nine forty-five. Which route should she take? Sunset was over half an hour ago. Maddy set off along Cuttle Lane towards the centre of the village. She returned an hour later after a fruitless search. Her heart sank as soon as she rounded the bend and saw the police car parked outside their home.

Maddy stopped the car, got out, and ran towards the two officers who stood beside the car.

"What's happened?" she screamed. "Is Alan hurt? Where have they taken him?"

"Can I have your name, please, Miss?" asked the officer, PC Clare Townsend.

"Madeleine Mills, Maddy. I'm Alan's partner. I've been

out searching for him. He went for his usual run but didn't come home at the normal time."

"This would be Alan Duncan. Is that correct?" asked PC Sam Hulbert.

Maddy nodded. She tried to see if there was anyone inside the police car. Where was he?

"Perhaps we can go inside, Miss Mills,"

Maddy opened the front door, and the two officers followed her inside.

"We received a phone call from a member of the public at seven fifty-three this evening," said the male police officer. "They reported seeing something suspicious in a field off Ham Lane. Do you know the area, Miss?"

"Of course I do," said Maddy. "We've lived in Bidde-stone for four years. Alan often runs along Challows Lane to Ham Lane. It's part of one of the regular routes he follows on Wednesday nights. He leaves here at half-past six and returns anything between eighty and ninety minutes later. What do you mean by suspicious?"

"Any problems in the relationship? Did you argue this evening before he left?"

"No, nothing like that. Everything's fine."

"No money problems?" asked PC Townsend.

"We both have decent jobs. There's not much left over for luxuries at the end of the month from time to time, but we manage fine. Look, what's going on?"

"I'm sorry to have to tell you, Miss Mills," said Sam Hulbert, "but we found the body of a man in the field off Ham Lane at eight thirteen this evening."

"It can't be Alan. There must be a mistake."

Clare Townsend described Alan's clothing when Maddy watched him leave the house earlier.

Maddy burst into tears.

"How could it have happened? He was as fit as a fiddle. Was it a heart attack?"

"We need to wait for the autopsy, Miss," said Sam Hulbert.

"Was it a hit and run? Boy racers often use the lanes during the summer months."

"The body bore no significant physical injuries, Miss."

"How long have you known one another?" asked Clare Townsend.

"Four years," said Maddy. "We met at a party. Alan came along with my best friend's husband. That's Wayne and Anna Phillips. They live in Chippenham. Wayne and Alan go cycling together every weekend."

"What did your partner do before you met him, do you know?" asked Sam.

"He joined the Royal Navy straight from school. When he'd seen enough of the world, he came home."

"Biddestone was his family home?" asked Clare.

"No, his parents live in Corsham. His father works at the same factory as Alan."

"Perhaps we could have those contact details, Miss. You're certain Alan wasn't depressed or had money concerns?"

"I don't know why you keep asking me that. Alan's the last person to feel depressed. He's quiet and conscientious. Nothing ever fazes him."

Maddy jotted the addresses and phone numbers on a scrap of paper and handed them to the female police officer.

"What happens now?" Maddy asked. "Can I see him?"

"Someone will be in touch about making an identification in the morning, Miss. We found Alan's mobile phone next to the body. There's no doubt, I'm afraid. It would be best if you weren't alone tonight. Do you want to call someone?"

"I can't call his parents," said Maddy, "This will crucify them. Alan's an only child."

"They need to know tonight," said Sam Hulbert. "We'll drive to Corsham from here."

"What about your friend?" asked Clare.

"Anna has a six-month-old baby. I can't ask her to leave him to keep me company. I promised I'd call back once I'd found where Alan was hiding. We thought he might have gone to the pub."

"You rang your friends earlier?" asked Clare.

"At half-past nine. I wondered whether Wayne knew where Alan was planning to run tonight."

"Did he?" asked Sam.

"Not a clue. Wayne offered to drive over to help me search. He reminded me of the phone. I hadn't thought to call Alan's mobile before. Alan always carried it with him when he went for his run."

"Was a pub somewhere he visited often? Which one was his local?" asked Sam.

"He didn't have a local. He rarely went into a pub without me. He was quiet. Alan was a friendly person but preferred small groups. He didn't enjoy going into crowded bars much."

"Will you be okay if we leave you now, Miss Mills?" asked Clare.

"I won't sleep, but it's only right that you tell Bob and Elizabeth tonight. If only we knew what happened."

"We'll know more by tomorrow, Miss," said Sam. "We're sorry for your loss."

Maddy saw the two police officers to the door and locked it behind them.

"What do you reckon, Sam?" asked Clare.

"My first thought was suicide, Clare," replied Sam Hulbert. "Now, I'm not so sure."

"You were right about one thing, Sam," said Clare Townsend. "We'll know more tomorrow."

Chapter Two

Monday, 30 July 2018

GUS STUDIED the heads of the team as they put the finishing touches to yet another case. What a start to a week. Little in the email that he'd received from Gareth Francis surprised him. For days Gus had prayed he was wrong. He hadn't even shared his thoughts with Suzie.

That a mother could be a party to the cold-blooded murder of her daughter was something he couldn't comprehend. Even after a lifetime of investigating crime, Gus felt sure he must have misinterpreted the evidence. Yet, last night on the canal banks, he'd come face-to-face with pure evil.

Debbie Read had shown no sign of regret, no protestation of innocence. Her partner-in-crime, Rod Maidment, had looked in her direction just once. That was enough for Gus to understand what lay ahead for the detectives at Gablecross. The couple's defence would be a wall of silence.

Blessing Umeh was the first to finish her contribution to

the Freeman Files. She looked up to see Gus looking towards the whiteboards.

"Would you like me to remove the Read case material, guv?" she asked.

Gus nodded.

Blessing could tell their boss was still reeling from the events of last night. After Gus spoke to them from the nature reserve, she had waited for Luke Sherman to call Mary Bennett. Lucy's grandmother had been going upstairs to bed. Luke told her to stay where she was; they would bring Lucy to Penhill to spend the night. Mary asked why, but Luke told her not to worry. He would explain when they arrived.

Blessing then got out of the car and rang the bell of Debbie Read's home in Gorse Hill. She rang and knocked without reply. Lucy didn't come to the door until Blessing called her through the letterbox.

Lucy had watched her mother leave. When she heard Blessing's voice, she answered the door. Lucy was confused. What had happened? Had her Mum had an accident? Did someone knock her off her bicycle? Blessing said it was nothing like that, which calmed the young girl, and Blessing told Lucy to gather her things and that they would explain once they reached her grandmother's house.

Luke had done the talking when they reached Penhill. Mary Bennett sat with her arms around her granddaughter. Blessing wasn't sure how much Mary took in of what Luke said. At that stage, and in front of Lucy, Luke couldn't give her the whole story.

Mary asked whether this was because they had left her granddaughter alone in the house.

"Since Stacey died," said Lucy, "Mum has slipped out of the house on her bicycle for an hour most Sunday evenings. I had to go to bed early when I was younger. Tonight, she just said she wouldn't be long and she'd see me in the morning."

"Where do you think she went?" asked Mary.

"She never told me," said Lucy.

"Perhaps it's something she started doing before Stacey died," said Luke.

"There was nothing to stop her if the girls were sleeping here or at Vanessa's place," said Mary. "Whoever it was, she was meeting. I told you; it was nobody else's business."

Luke told Mary that Lucy needed to stay with her because Debbie was helping them with their enquiries relating to Stacey's death. That halted the old lady in her tracks.

"You can't mean…" said Mary.

"Did you bring everything you needed, Lucy?" Blessing had asked.

Lucy nodded towards the bag she had brought with her.

"Why don't you show me your bedroom, Lucy? DS Sherman tells me you've got a choice of a bunk bed. I'm an only child, so I was never lucky enough to find out what it's like."

Blessing had gone upstairs with the young girl.

"This will be the first time I've slept here since Stacey died," said Lucy. "I can't sleep on the top bunk. It wouldn't feel right. What's going to happen tomorrow?"

"You'll stay here until everything gets sorted, Lucy," said Blessing. "Try not to worry."

"Will I see you again?" asked Lucy, who sat on the bottom bunk.

"I can't say," said Blessing. "Another police officer might call on you and your grandmother. My part, in this case, is done."

Lucy jumped up and ran into Blessing's arms. The young detective felt the hot tears through her blouse.

"Thank you," said Lucy. "You've always been nice to me."

"Try to get to sleep," said Blessing, feeling embarrassed. "Look after your grandmother. She'll need you."

Blessing left Lucy in the bedroom and returned downstairs. Luke was waiting in the hallway.

"All good?" he asked.

"If only," said Blessing. "Let's go home."

Luke had told her he'd answered as many of Mary's questions as possible.

"Do you think Debbie and this Maidment character have been meeting on Sundays for a while?" asked Blessing.

"From what we heard from the stakeout in the nature reserve, it was drugs," said Luke. "We had to deal with Lucy and Mary, so who knows?"

"Gus Freeman will know," laughed Blessing. "I hope he'll let us in on the secret in the morning."

Luke had driven to Worton to drop Blessing at the Ferris's farm and then headed home to Warminster. The alarm clock had woken him and his partner, Nicky, at half-past seven this morning. Luke hoped next weekend, Gus wouldn't find an urgent task that needed their attention. He and Nicky could benefit from a spot of free time.

Luke observed Blessing as she removed the street maps and crime scene photos. They had driven into the Old Police Station office separately this morning but arrived within seconds of one another. As they rode up in the lift, they wondered what had happened at the nature reserve after they switched off their comms devices.

Luke completed his contribution to the Read case's digital files and glanced through what Gus and the others had added. He realised that they now had every piece of the jigsaw. The evidence the team had gathered should allow the Gablecross detective team to construct a winning case for the Crown Prosecution Service.

"I can see a frown forming, Luke," said Gus.

"How did Debbie Read get in touch with Rod Maidment, guv?" Luke asked. "the number she gave us wasn't valid."

"Jake Chalmers found a number listed as RJNM Engineering in her contacts," said Gus. "That number never got deleted, whatever state of their relationship. The numbers that Debbie and Vanessa had in their phones were for old pay-as-you-go phones Maidment used. To have several burner phones at once isn't unusual for crooks like Maidment. Of course, he had to be careful not to get them mixed up."

"How much did Vanessa know about her sister and Maidment?" asked Luke.

"Based on what Gareth Francis has learned so far, not a lot," said Gus. "If Vanessa had known Maidment was Lucy's father, would she have allowed herself to get picked up at that nightclub by him?"

"With what we know of the family history now, guv, I wouldn't put it past her," said Blessing.

"Vanessa didn't know about her sister and Maidment," said Gus. "I'm also convinced Debbie didn't know that lover boy went straight to her sister when they split in October 2013. Gareth will seek to uncover the truth behind that split. Perhaps Debbie wanted a larger percentage of the profits from the drug side-line they set up in December 2012."

"Why didn't anyone realise James Neville and Rod Maidment were the same people, guv?" asked Neil Davis.

"Let me ask you this, Neil," said Gus. "How many people knew both men?"

"Karen Lock and her school friends knew Neville," said Neil, "but that was years ago. Karen hadn't seen him in person for years. His threats came through the post or by phone. When he approached his son, Ryan, he probably introduced himself as James Neville, but Ryan wouldn't have known how much his appearance had changed."

"Maidment had lost weight," said Gus, "and the full beard covered a scar by his lip that Karen mentioned. She told us he had no tattoos or piercings in 2001. They were a later addition. The hardcore sleeve was the most recent. That was a firm favourite in 2013."

"How come you know so much about tattoos, guv," asked Blessing.

"I don't," said Gus, "but after I met Kassie Trotter at London Road, I thought I'd try to understand what they meant and why anyone wanted to submit themselves to hours of torture. I'm still working on that."

"Debbie Read never met the James Neville persona, Neil," said Luke. "He used a variety of names for his relationships. It might seem odd that he stuck to Rod Maidment for the two sisters, but if he was ever going to bump into someone who would know him under another name, that was it."

"Pat Read and Rod Maidment worked different shifts at Honda," said Luke. "Even though Pat Read knew someone else fathered Lucy, he wasn't interested in finding out their name."

"Almost there, aren't they, Alex?" said Gus.

"Stacey Read was the only person to know a man with two names," said Alex. "She saw Maidment at her aunt's house one weekend and then on over one occasion when he spoke to Ryan Lock. Ryan referred to him as his Dad, and when they met up, Stacey pumped Ryan for more information. Stacey had learned that Ryan and Lucy had the same father, someone who called himself James Neville. So why did Auntie Vanessa call him Rod Maidment? Stacey was too young to remember Maidment if he'd been with her mother when she was a toddler. When he reappeared years later, Stacey and Lucy spent so much time away from home that it's not surprising Stacey didn't know the guy was seeing her mother. Debbie made sure the girls never learned of her affairs. Lucy didn't mention other men in any of the interviews."

"No wonder it came as a terrible shock that night when her mother cycled along the footpath," said Lydia.

"I think that's it," said Gus. "Can you collate everything for me to take to London Road, please, Alex? I'll ring them in a moment to get an audience with the ACC."

"On it, guv," said Alex.

"Another case done and dusted, guv," said Neil.

"Gone but not forgotten, Neil," said Gus.

He picked up the phone and called London Road.

Vera Butler answered.

"Kenneth Truelove's PA speaking. How may I help you?"

"It's Gus here, Vera. I was hoping to deliver our good news in person. Is Kenneth polishing the new crown on his insignia this morning?"

"I don't think the PCC has confirmed his appointment yet, Gus," said Vera, "although I can tell it's imminent. Have you been stirring things again?"

"I don't know what you mean, Vera," said Gus. "I'm a mere consultant. How could I possibly influence matters of such significance?"

"Mmm, Geoff Mercer is like a dog with two tails this morning. For the past month, he's kept everyone at arm's length. Kassie and I worried because Geoff wasn't eating as usual, no matter what she brought to tempt him."

Gus laughed.

"You don't need to worry on that score. Geoff ate extremely well at our expense on Saturday afternoon. Has he mentioned his new home in the country yet?"

"Not yet," said Vera. "In which part of the country is it? The Midlands, or closer to home?"

"That concerned me until Saturday afternoon, Vera," said Gus. "Christine wants to stay local and downsize, a great relief. Geoff told us they're moving to Clench Common. He's staying at London Road until they hand him his DCM."

"I heard nothing about a medal," said Vera.

"No, a DCM," said Gus. "Don't Come Monday."

"You are awful," said Vera. "I don't know where you get them. But, anyway, I wasn't far wrong, was I? You're moving the pieces around the board, with a nudge here and comment there. Did you convince Geoff to stay?"

"No, I can honestly say that was Christine. Geoff told us he had no intention of accepting the offer from West Mercia. It wouldn't surprise me if the PCC only had to walk along the corridor from Kenneth Truelove's office to find the next Assistant Chief Constable to fill the vacancy."

"That's what you've wanted since you returned to duty, Gus Freeman."

"It's for the best, Vera," said Gus. "I'm sure someone else would have realised it was the most sensible option in time."

"Kenneth has just returned from the Hub," said Vera. "I can hear him chatting to someone on the stairs. Ah, it's

Grace Packenham. They must have gone there together. Let's hope he's found another centre of operations at London Road for her to knock into shape. If she suggests one more penny-pinching, time-saving initiative, I'll tell her to stick it where the sun doesn't shine."

"Bite your tongue, Vera," said Gus. "Ms Packenham's a new broom. Give her a few weeks, and things will become calmer. I suppose I could give her a nudge, or pass a comment, to warn her you and Kassie are a protected species."

"As a mere consultant?" laughed Vera.

"Exactly," said Gus. "Geoff told me on Saturday afternoon that the CRT was not part of her remit. Has Kenneth escaped her clutches yet?"

"He's alone in his office. I'll buzz him, and you can fix your appointment. Maybe we'll see you later today?"

"I hope so. Did Kassie bake more of the bara brith yesterday?"

"Rock cakes, I think, Gus. By the way, Kassie has hot gossip about Rhys Evans."

"In that case, I'll be there later without fail," said Gus.

"I'm putting you through now. Bye," said Vera.

"Freeman?" asked the Acting Chief Constable.

"The new crown on your shoulder hasn't affected your memory, sir," said Gus. "We wrapped up the Read case last night with the help of Gablecross. I can deliver the files to you whenever you're free."

"Excellent news, Freeman," said ACC Truelove, "I have a sneaky feeling that you know this already, but Mercer isn't abandoning ship. He's remaining here at London Road. I misread the signs. Better not tell the PCC that, of course. I will drop another heavy hint that Mercer is the right man to sit in this chair. My wife is waiting, needle poised, to attach the new insignia."

"What time, sir?" asked Gus.

"No specific time yet, Freeman. Ah, you mean for our meeting. So get in that rust bucket of yours and be here as soon as possible. I can't sit around waiting all day. I'm a busy man."

"Be with you in thirty minutes, give or take, sir," said Gus.

Gus replaced the phone on its cradle before the ACC could comment. He collected the report file from Alex Hardy and made for the lift. Thirty minutes, what was he thinking?

The sun shines on the righteous, or so they said, thought Gus as he followed the tractor and trailer through Seend. He would struggle to be with Kenneth Truelove by lunchtime at this rate. When he turned off London Road into the visitor's car park, he could see the ACC staring out of his office window.

Gus paused in Reception to sign in.

"You *must* be Mr Freeman," said a female voice.

How she stressed the word 'must' suggested to Gus that he matched her expectations.

Gus turned around. He didn't need to ask the name that belonged to the unfamiliar face.

"Gus Freeman, yes, that's me. You *must* be DI Grace Packenham."

"I have it on good authority that you make a habit of being late for meetings, Mr Freeman. That is unacceptable. It does nothing to help deliver a first-class service to the residents of this county."

"I can see we're going to get along famously," said Gus,

taking the stairs two at a time. "Can't stop to chat. I don't want to have to tell Kenneth that you delayed me."

Vera Butler heard his comment and grinned at him as he moved across to the ACC's office.

"I warned you," she said.

Gus knocked and entered the office in one swift movement.

"Apologies for being late, sir. Our local farmers are making the most of the opportunity to make hay. I might have passed the tractor in Seend, but the trailer bobbing behind it proved too long an obstacle. So I'm here now, bearing gifts."

Gus handed Kenneth truelove the Read case file.

"You have your shortcomings, Freeman," said the ACC, "but you never cease to deliver the goods. A nasty business this one, I imagine?"

"One of the worst I've had to handle, sir," said Gus. "You're the second person this morning to mention my shortcomings. DI Packenham had a quiet word in Reception."

"I must get Mercer to rein in that woman, Freeman. He told Grace quite clearly that you were off-limits."

"It's water off a duck's back, sir. I've seen them come, and I've seen them go. Let's forget her for the present. Geoff Mercer's staying here, so everything is going to plan. As soon as the PCC announces your Coronation, you can nudge him into his next action. Onto the next matter. Gablecross will handle the Read case from here. What have got up your sleeve for the Crime Review Team next?"

"Do you remember the Alan Duncan case from 2008?" asked Kenneth.

"Was that the one the press dubbed the murder of the long-distance runner?"

"That's the fellow. Duncan lived in Biddestone, a picturesque village between Corsham and Chippenham."

"The village with the duck pond. I've driven through it but never stopped."

"Around five hundred inhabitants, but popular with tourists as it's on the edge of the Cotswolds and an Area of Outstanding Natural Beauty."

"No doubt you pay a hefty sum for a property around there," said Gus.

"Alan Duncan and his partner, Madeleine Mills, lived on Cuttle Lane in one of the more modestly priced cottages. They had lived there for less than four years. Duncan was thirty-six when he died, three years older than Madeleine. She had worked at a call centre in Chippenham for eleven years. Duncan worked as a draughtsman for a company based on the Leafield Industrial Estate in Corsham. Before he moved back to Corsham in 2004, he had served in the Royal Navy for over a decade."

"The press made a lot of the running and cycling this Duncan character enjoyed in his leisure time, didn't they?" asked Gus. "They were careful not to print any actual accusation that he was happier alone or with men than with his girlfriend. But that was the inference."

"I don't think the original investigation ever found anything to support that view," said Kenneth. "On Wednesday the twenty-eighth of May 2008, Alan Duncan left home at half-past six for a run. Madeleine Mills said these runs took several routes, but neither lasted longer than an hour and a half. Duncan was a familiar sight in the village, so we have eyewitnesses who saw him running on Cuttle Lane, by the Green and the duck pond, and on Challows Lane that evening. Those sightings ranged from six-thirty to a few minutes before seven. Challows Lane leads directly onto Ham Lane. As she rode past, a horse rider spotted a suspicious shape in one of her fields. Davinia Campbell-Drake phoned it in at once. I think she told the officer who took the call that her fields were not an area where fly-tipping would be tolerated. He recorded the details, plus her admission that the culprit would be horse-whipped if she caught him before the police did. Two uniformed officers went to investigate, and they found Alan Duncan's dead body at eight thirteen. His mobile phone lay on the grass beside him."

"Did the phone yield anything useful?" asked Gus.

"Nothing that led the investigating team to a potential suspect. DI Phil Banks was Senior Investigating Officer on the case, and his main partner was DS Connor Tallentire. They both worked out of Chippenham. They're at opposite ends of the country these days. Alan Duncan's contacts were what you might expect. His partner and parents, of course, plus a handful of close friends and work colleagues."

"Nothing relating to his naval career?" asked Gus. "I thought camaraderie was a strong point in the services. Friendships formed during training and on overseas operations can last a lifetime, so I've heard."

"They didn't make it onto his most recent phone, Freeman. That's all I can tell you. Madeleine Mills should be able to offer information on whether Duncan had an address book at home that contained names from the time before they met."

"Where is Miss Mills today?" asked Gus.

"Married with two children. One of each," said Kenneth. "The Telfer family live on the Cepen Park estate in Chippenham. Almost on the same street as Wayne and Anna Phillips."

"Why are they important?" asked Gus.

"Anna is Madeleine's best friend. They worked together for years. Wayne Phillips had met Alan Duncan through their mutual love of cycling. Wayne introduced Alan to Madeleine. In the first twenty-four hours after discovering the body, the only people Banks and Tallentire spoke with were his partner, parents, and those two. Until the coroner determined the cause of death, they followed the first instincts of one of the uniformed officers who found the body. He thought it was a suicide. Duncan appeared to lead a quiet, ordinary, mostly solitary life. His partner described him as Mr Dependable. When the cause of death turned out to be strangulation, it put a different slant on things. The murder occurred between seven and seven-thirty."

"A narrow window of opportunity. Who had a motive?" asked Gus. "What about Miss Mills, for instance?"

"She had no alibi until nine-thirty. Someone saw Duncan running alone thirty minutes after he left home. He was alive at seven o'clock. Anna Phillips received a call from Madeleine two and a half hours later because she was worried about Duncan not getting home at the usual time. Miss Mills said she was home alone throughout the evening doing housework."

"Madeleine might not have been at home when she made that call," said Gus, "but what was her motive?"

"The uniformed officers who notified Miss Mills asked if Alan was depressed, whether they had argued, but Madeleine Mills was adamant there were no financial worries and nothing was wrong with their relationship. Alan Duncan's parents said the same thing when the officers visited them later that evening."

"Women rarely strangle a male partner," said Gus. "What about Wayne Phillips? Where was he that evening?"

"He arrived home minutes before his wife received the

call from Madeleine. Wayne Phillips played five-a-side football every Wednesday evening. He had plenty of witnesses who confirmed he was kicking lumps out of them between seven and eight-thirty."

"So, where did Banks and his team turn to next?" asked Gus.

"I imagine they wondered whether they were dealing with the same case. Bob Duncan, Alan's father, had taken the rest of the week off work to stay home to comfort Elizabeth, his wife. Madeleine Mills spent much of the weekend with Wayne and Anna Phillips. All perfectly understandable; life was on hold as they came to terms with the devastating news. You don't need me to tell you what that period is like Freeman, between the end of life and the funeral. You exist and little more. Alan's father returned to work on Monday morning. His colleagues commiserated with him and offered their condolences, but he sensed they were holding back. Later in the day, he visited Alan's office, where he worked as a draughtsman."

"He worked at the same factory as his father?" asked Gus.

"He did, well, he had, until Monday the twenty-sixth of May. When Bob spoke to Alan's boss, he learned that Alan had walked into the office the previous Monday morning and quit. He left without notice or explanation. Bob phoned Madeleine Mills as soon as he returned home. She was as shocked as he had been. Alan had never mentioned being unhappy in his job. He had left for work and returned in the late afternoon at the same time as usual. Then she recalled her conversation with Wayne Phillips on the night Alan died."

"I thought Madeleine rang her friend, Anna," said Gus. "Was this part of the same conversation?"

"Yes," said Kenneth, "Madeleine thought Wayne was more likely to know Alan's plans for the evening. They spoke every weekend when they cycled together. Wayne didn't know which route his friend was taking for his run, but he offered to drive to Biddestone to help in the search. Madeleine said she would manage on her own and call back when Alan returned. The police were on her doorstep when Madeleine returned from a drive around the village lanes. When Bob Duncan told her Alan hadn't been at work that week, she remembered Wayne telling her he'd seen Alan in the centre of Corsham on Tuesday afternoon. He was on the pavement outside a bank. My wife and I didn't live together before we married Freeman, but we opened a joint account and closed our individual accounts as soon as possible. That was what one did back then. Although couples handle their financial affairs in various ways these days, Madeleine Mills and Alan Duncan had separate accounts in different banks. He transferred a monthly sum to her account by Direct Debit, and she paid the mortgage, utility bills, etc. When she contacted her bank, that month's amount had arrived as usual from Duncan's bank on the fifteenth of the month. Madeleine contacted the police to tell them of this latest development. When they checked with Alan's bank, they discovered that he'd closed his accounts and withdrawn the balance in cash."

"How much are we talking?" asked Gus.

"Eight and a half thousand pounds," said the ACC.

"The police found Duncan's mobile phone next to the body," said Gus. "Did any of the eyewitnesses report seeing him carrying a bag?"

"No, it wasn't a robbery, and blackmail didn't match what followed. When police visited the house in Biddestone, they conducted a thorough search. In the spare bedroom where the couple stored clothing and footwear, they found over two dozen pairs of Alan's trainers in shoeboxes. One box contained the eight and a half thousand pounds in fifty, twenty, and ten-pound notes."

"Hidden in plain sight," said Gus. "What was Madeleine's reaction?"

"Stunned," said Kenneth. "With every passing day, Madeleine was learning things about her late partner that made her question whether she ever really knew him. Alan's parents could not explain his movements. As someone once observed, the detectives had a puzzle wrapped in an enigma. Alan Duncan had no known enemies. He wasn't known to the police, and they could find nothing in his life to suggest he was in danger. So why did Alan quit his job and withdraw every penny he had in the world? Was he planning a midnight flit? If so, why not leave on Tuesday night once he had the money in his hands? Even at six-thirty on Wednesday evening, he followed his normal routine and went on a weekly run."

"There's no escaping that his behaviour was out of character," said Gus. "This could be our toughest assignment yet. Please tell me you have something more, sir?"

"Wayne Phillips recalled a second odd incident as they returned from a fifty-mile cycle ride on Saturday the twenty-fourth. They cycled along The Green, passing the Biddestone Arms and the duck pond before turning into Cuttle Lane. Phillips spotted a man standing by his car near the pond. He appeared to recognise Alan, who was leading and waved, but Alan ignored him and cycled faster. When Wayne asked who it was, Alan said he had seen no one."

"Could Phillips describe the man or identify the car?"

"Only a vague description," said the ACC. "Medium

height, medium build. Crewcut, fair-skinned, possibly late thirties or early forties. The car was a family saloon, but no make, model, or registration."

"It could have been anyone," said Gus. "Someone from work Alan Duncan didn't get on with, or he didn't recognise from a distance. Anything else?"

"A neighbour from Cuttle Lane reported seeing a Vauxhall Zafira pass her house on more than one occasion in the weeks before Alan Duncan's death. DI Banks appealed for the car owner to come forward, but he could not identify the car or the driver. It might have been the same car and driver that Wayne Phillips saw, but it could have been unrelated."

"Is that everything, sir?" asked Gus more in hope than expectation.

"I'm afraid so," said Kenneth.

Gus tucked the Alan Duncan murder file under his arm and left the room.

"Can't you spare time for a coffee, Mr Freeman?"

Kassie Trotter had just emerged from the dark recesses leading to Geoff Mercer's office. Ms Packenham hadn't curtailed Kassie's bun run as yet.

"I need to return to the office, Kassie," said Gus.

"My gossip will have to wait then," she sighed. "You're no fun anymore, Mr Freeman."

"Life's hard, and then you die, Kassie," said Gus. "Look, do you still catch the bus home to Worton after work?"

Kassie nodded.

"I'll pick you up this evening and drive you home. Save me any spare rock cakes, and you can chat while I carry out a taste test. I'll take a doggy bag home for Suzie."

"Thanks, Mr Freeman. See you later."

Kassie gave her trolley a shove and got moving again. Her next port of call was to the ACC.

Gus gave Vera a friendly wave and skipped downstairs. Anything for a quiet life.

Chapter Three

GUS GLANCED at the clock on the office wall as he exited the lift. The return journey hadn't improved his demeanour. Lunchtime had come and gone, and he could do with one of those rock cakes right now.

"Okay, listen up," he said. "I've got a murder file from a decade ago. Someone strangled Alan Duncan while running in the lanes around the village of Biddestone. So let's get started; you know the drill."

The team swung into action like a well-oiled machine.

"Where do you want to start, guv?" asked Luke.

"The victim's partner, Madeleine Telfer," said Gus. "That will be our first interview, but a visit to the village has to be top of my list. I need to get perspective. The murder file mentions lanes that run into lanes and past duck ponds. Villages vary considerably. Some are spread over a wide area; others are a single thoroughfare with several access points from surrounding towns and villages. Alex, perhaps you could accompany me?"

"Yes, guv," said Alex. "When do you want to leave?"

"A coffee first, and then we'll take advantage of this weather. It's a fine day for a walk in the country."

"I'll have a timetable for your appointments by the time you return, guv," said Luke.

"I can always rely on you, Luke," said Gus.

Gus checked his desk drawer to see whether the bara brith Kassie Trotter had entrusted him with last Tuesday was still edible. He needed something to say later this evening, good or bad.

Thirty minutes later, Gus and Alex were in the lift heading for the ground floor and the car park.

"Everything okay, guv?" asked Alex.

"One of Kassie Trotter's experiments is weighing heavy on my stomach, Alex," said Gus. "No worries. I'll walk it off as we stroll around Biddestone."

"Just as well that Biddestone is only a twenty-minute drive from here, guv," said Alex.

Gus sat back in the passenger seat and hoped Kassie's hot gossip occupied their conversation so much this evening that she forgot to ask if it was any good. The bara brith wasn't one of her triumphs.

"We're coming up to Chippenham Lane on our right, guv," said Alex. "That becomes Sheldon Corner in time, and then it joins the main A420 road by the Allington Farm Shop and café. The murder file showed that Alan Duncan used that as one of his runs: six miles door to door."

"Six miles?" asked Gus. "He was keen. I suppose it kept him fit for the weekend cycle tours of Wiltshire and Gloucestershire."

"We're on what they call The Green now, guv," said Alex, slowing to a crawl. "The actual green is on both sides of the road. If we turn left by the Pond bus stop ahead, that takes us to Church Road. Cuttle Lane is this road that veers off to the right. There aren't that many properties on the right before you enter the open country-side again. The cottage where Alan Duncan and Madeleine Mills lived is on our left, just before reaching the Wesleyan Chapel ahead. The village cricket club is on the opposite side of the road. Do you want to stop and walk from here?"

"Good idea, Alex," said Gus. "We'll walk back to The Green and the duck pond. I'd like to see where Wayne Phillips says he spotted this mystery car driver. What distance was that man from the two cyclists? Is it more likely that Alan Duncan recognised him and didn't want Wayne to know?"

Alex parked outside the Chapel, and the two detectives walked back along Cuttle Lane towards the centre of the village.

"That's the cottage where Alan Duncan and Madeleine Mills lived, guv," said Alex.

Gus paused and studied the tidy property. It was a typical two-bedroomed semi-detached cottage built in the 1930s with central heating and double glazing installed in the past thirty years. If it stood on a side street in a small town in the county, it might fetch two hundred thousand pounds. Here, in a well-to-do village on the edge of the Cotswolds, the asking price would be at least fifty percent higher.

Gus set off towards the duck pond. There was little point in looking inside the cottage. All traces of its inhabitants a decade ago had long disappeared. Gus stopped by the bus stop and took in the view.

"Picturesque, isn't it?" he said. "A sanctuary; rural life as it was a century ago."

"Have you ever watched 'Midsomer Murders', guv?"

asked Alex. "Somebody gets murdered in that village every week."

"I bet they're getting fed up with it, don't you," said Gus. "Stay here, Alex."

Gus looked both ways and crossed the road. He stood in front of the White Horse and waved at Alex.

"I'm standing roughly where our mystery man parked that Saturday afternoon," said Gus, raising his voice as a car drove past. "Phillips and Duncan cycled past him from my right and turned onto Cuttle Lane where you're standing, agreed?"

"Yes, guv," called Alex. "They were fifteen metres from him throughout, maximum."

"Or sixteen yards in English, Alex. It doesn't matter. Did either man wear glasses?"

"The murder file didn't mention whether Wayne Phillips wore glasses, but Alan Duncan's eyesight was 20:20."

"Phillips said that Duncan cycled faster as they passed this spot. A bit of a risk on a Saturday afternoon with more traffic on the roads. I reckon he knew the man. Phillips swore that he'd never seen him before. Why didn't Miss Mills or Duncan's parents offer a possible name? That man must have figured in Duncan's life somehow."

Gus rejoined Alex at the bus stop.

"Which way now, Alex?" he asked.

"Back to the car, guv. It's a tidy walk to the next junction with the A420. Duncan ran past the Chapel and stayed on the lane until the Crown pub at Giddeahall. Madeleine Mills told police that was the route Duncan took the Wednesday before he died."

Alex drove them to the pub car park and stopped.

"That wasn't three miles, Alex," said Gus. "More like

half that distance. I thought each of the routes Duncan took lasted eighty to ninety minutes?"

"You're right, guv. I suppose Duncan added a circuit of Church Road or elsewhere in the village to make up the difference. We can check with Mrs Telfer whether he came this way first or if he passed his house on the way back into the village."

"Drive back towards their cottage, Alex. There's nothing to help us here."

When they approached the cricket club, Alex slowed and turned sharply left.

"Another of his routes?" asked Gus.

"It's Yatton Road, guv. The village tennis club is on your right."

"Blimey, it's a well-appointed village, isn't it? The money in the area helps, I guess."

"Now, I know this will confuse you, guv, but this road crosses the A420, and then it becomes Biddestone Lane and leads straight into Yatton Keynell. It's twice the size of Biddestone. Duncan only came this way once, according to his partner. As you can tell, it's a busier road, and visibility isn't as good for pedestrians or runners."

Alex slowed once more and executed a perfect three-point turn before driving back into the village.

"The final route, in more ways than one, starts from his cottage and goes towards The Green. I'll turn right by the bus stops we were at earlier and travel along Church Road. Challows Lane is just ahead on the right, which is the route Duncan followed that evening. Alan left the cottage at half-past six and jogged along Challows Lane onto Ham Lane. At an even pace, matching what he achieved every Wednesday evening, Duncan should have reached the field where he died just before seven. That ties in with eyewitness accounts. And we're here, guv."

"A very windy lane, with no properties after it lost its Challows tag," said Gus. "Miles from anywhere and open fields on either side. I wonder in which direction the killer travelled. Did he follow Duncan from his home or meet him here? What's ahead of us, Alex?"

"A tributary of the River Avon called By Brook, guv," said Alex. "There's another of these long and windy lanes called Weavern Lane that leads back into Biddestone via The Butts and then Church Road."

"So, if our mystery man was our killer, he could have followed Duncan as far as Church Road. Then when Duncan jogged up Challows Lane, the killer headed down Weavern Lane and lay in wait around one of those many corners on Ham Lane."

"If he was the killer, guv, then it's a possibility," agreed Alex.

"Banks and Tallentire didn't place anyone else in the frame, did they?" said Gus.

"True, and they made zero headway trying to find anyone to provide an accurate description of that one man or his car."

"I wonder where the landowner lives. The lady who phoned in the initial report," said Gus. "I can see the attraction of an evening hack along the lanes, but I haven't seen a country pile worthy of the double-barrelled name yet."

"Davinia Campbell-Drake, known as Bunny to her friends, you mean, guv?"

"That will be milady to the likes of you and me, Alex. Remember to tug your forelock when we invite her for an interview."

"A proper invitation, guv?" grinned Alex. "You don't

plan on bombing up her driveway with lights and sirens blazing a la Gene Hunt, then?"

"Gene, who, Alex?"

"It doesn't matter, guv. Have you seen enough for today?"

"I think so, Alex. Let's get back and see what Luke has arranged for tomorrow."

Alex drove out of Biddestone and returned to the Old Police Station office.

The whiteboards were full of the usual maps, crime scene photos, and brief biographies of the victim and their known contacts.

Gus sighed as he noticed how sparse the room looked compared to several of their earlier cases. Kenneth Truelove hadn't given them much to work with, that was certain.

"I put the information you asked for on your desk, guv," said Luke.

"Thanks, Luke."

"Did the walking tour offer any hidden gems, guv?" asked Lydia Logan Barre.

"Not really, Lydia," said Gus. "I now know where the victim died. The killer chose a spot as far from civilisation as it was possible to get within the Biddestone parish boundaries. The odds against someone disturbing him were huge. If Davinia Campbell-Drake was a creature of habit, like Alan Duncan, the killer did their homework and knew when she was due to trot along the lane. The murder was well-planned and executed."

"Might that suggest we're dealing with a professional, guv?" asked Blessing Umeh.

"A hit, do you mean, Blessing?" asked Neil Davis. "That

came out of nowhere. Why would someone put out a contract on a man with no known enemies?"

"If it were a crime of passion, it wouldn't have been so efficient," said Blessing. "Maybe I'm wrong. Or maybe we're wrong. Alan Duncan had enemies, but the original investigation didn't find them."

"It doesn't feel like a crime of passion, Neil," said Luke. "Although strangulation isn't what I'd expect if it was a contract hit."

"Forensics didn't find any fingerprints on the victim," said Blessing, referring to the murder file. "That suggests they wore gloves. How often do you wear gloves in May, Neil?"

"Fair point, Blessing," said Neil.

"The eight and a half thousand pounds in cash," said Gus. "What was that about?"

"We need more information, guv," said Alex.

"Luke, can you check something for me, please? Did Wayne Phillips wear glasses?"

"I'll get right on it, guv?" said Luke.

Gus ran his finger down the page of names and potential interviews. Madeleine Telfer was available tomorrow morning from nine-thirty after she returned from the school run.

Bob and Elizabeth Duncan would be at home tomorrow and Thursday.

"Are the Duncan's out for the day on Wednesday, Luke?" asked Gus.

"No guv, Bob Duncan told me that Elizabeth struggles to get out of bed on a Wednesday. Even after ten years, the day is inextricably linked to the death of their only child. Since he retired, Alan's father has written Wednesdays off as far as doing anything other than comfort his wife."

"I'll drop over to see them tomorrow afternoon," said Gus.

"Wayne Phillips and his wife are free mid-morning on Wednesday, guv," said Luke. "He's got an appointment with his dental hygienist first thing. As for his eyesight, he wears contact lenses throughout the day, whatever he's doing. Wayne was adamant that he wore them that Saturday afternoon on the cycle run."

"Right, thanks, Luke. That clears that up," said Gus. "Lydia, I'd like you to come with me tomorrow morning when we speak to Madeleine Telfer in Chippenham. Then, Blessing, I want you with me when we visit Corsham and the victim's parents in the afternoon.

"Okay, guv," chorused Lydia and Blessing.

"Who do you want to handle the Phillips's, guv?" asked Luke.

"Alex and Lydia, I think. Lydia, you know what to do. Get the wife into the kitchen while Alex grills the husband in the living room. Don't worry, Luke, you and Neil haven't been put on the naughty step. You two can handle people at the firm where Alan Duncan worked. I don't know if it will help, but fix up a meeting with whoever's in charge of that call centre where Madeleine Mills worked for so long too."

"Got it, guv," came the reply.

"Anything else, guv," asked Neil.

"Kenneth Truelove glossed over what Phil Banks and Connor Tallentire are doing these days," said Gus. "Except to say they're working at different ends of the country. Chase them and get them to pass on any background they can remember that might have escaped the murder file we received. There's no need to visit them."

"That's plenty to be going on with, guv," said Neil. "Who's picking up the eyewitnesses?"

"Alex and Lydia can contact them by phone when they return to the office.. We're double-checking what they said they saw back in 2008. Ten years is a long time. We might have to remind them what we're asking about."

"What about the horse rider, guv?" asked Neil.

"If you've got five minutes, Neil, look her up in Burke's Peerage," said Alex.

"Posh, then, and having oodles of money," said Neil.

"The Campbell-Drakes could be as poor as church mice," said Gus. "Farmers always complain that the weather is too dry, or it's too wet, and they haven't got enough Eastern European labourers to guarantee the harvest will get finished on time. Unless you suddenly think she killed Alan Duncan, we'll keep our distance for now. I'll check with Vera Butler at London Road. Her family has connections among the landed gentry. They're bound to know how high the family has climbed the ladder. If I read the murder file correctly, the lady didn't even bother entering the field to see if Alan Duncan was still breathing. She quickly called the local constabulary as she trotted along the lane and went about her business."

It was twenty minutes past four. Gus thought he should be on his way. One thing to do before he left the office.

"Gus?" said Suzie, "is this a message to say you're going to be late?"

"I'm collecting Kassie Trotter from work at five o'clock and running her home to Worton. She's been itching to give me the inside track on Rhys Evans for days. At least, I think the gossip concerns him. What she's learned and why I need to hear it, I'm not sure yet, but Kassie needs someone to make her feel valued. That Grace Packenham has dented the poor girl's confidence."

"You fooled people for years into believing you were

thick-skinned and unemotional, Gus Freeman. Deep down, you're a pussy-cat, aren't you? Will you be long?"

"I don't plan to," said Gus. "Kassie will feed me a rock cake before we leave the car park, and I'll listen to her gossip while I try to eat it. Kassie will be out of the car like a shot once I pull up outside the old pub in Worton. She doesn't want the locals to get the wrong idea."

"You've done this trip before then?" asked Suzie.

"When Kassie was deeply involved in 'Game of Thrones', yes," said Gus. "She told me everything I needed to know about Monty Jennings."

"Say no more," said Suzie. "That meeting was a couple of days before we went for a Sunday afternoon stroll on the hillside, and you wooed me with your homemade soup."

"I did not know where that would lead," said Gus. "I have no regrets."

"I'll expect you around six o'clock then," said Suzie.

"Kassie promised me any baked goods that weren't snaffled by the senior staff today. I might have a doggy bag with me."

"Too many cakes will punish my waistline," said Suzie. "Look at what it's done to Geoff Mercer. I'll stick to the salad that I promised myself. You can self-cater."

"I have to dash," said Gus, "see you later."

Gus said goodbye to the team and left the building. As he turned into the visitor's car park at London Road, he passed Vera Butler walking home. They exchanged a friendly wave, as had become their custom. Kassie Trotter waited at the foot of the steps outside the main building with a large bag over her shoulder.

"Only two minutes late, Mr Freeman," said Kassie as she flopped her sizeable form in the passenger seat. "You're improving."

"Belt up, Kassie," said Gus.

"You're a laugh a minute," said Kassie, "unlike Miss Sourpuss there."

Gus looked up to see DI Grace Packenham staring at them. The new broom turned on her heel and headed for the Hub building with a look of disgust.

"Is Ms Packenham knocking the Hub whizz kids into shape this week, Kassie?" asked Gus.

"I agree with Vera, Mr Freeman," said Kassie. "As long as she's not bothering us, I don't care what she's doing. Shall I give you one now, Mr Freeman?"

"That's why I agreed to pick you up. Devizes to Worton, price—one rock cake."

"Did you throw my bara brith away, Mr Freeman? You can be honest. It wasn't my finest hour."

"I remember eating the large slice you gave me, Kassie. Perhaps, it was past its best when I got round to it. Don't despair. Practice makes perfect."

Kassie delved into her oversized bag and removed one rock cake. She handed it to Gus as they stopped for a red light.

"I don't get many complaints about my cakes, Mr Freeman," she said. "Mr Mercer always takes two."

"Well, he would, wouldn't he," said Gus, taking a bite.

Kassie was right. It was scrumptious. The lights turned green, and they were on their way to Worton.

"Hot gossip, Kassie," said Gus, brushing a wayward crumb from his lips. "That was the other part of the deal."

"Rhys Evans started work at London Road today, Mr Freeman," said Kassie. "He's in Peter Morgan's old office. I asked him which he preferred when I did the coffee and tea run this morning. He doesn't do hot drinks, Mr Freeman. My cakes are off the menu too. Mr Evans told me that his body is a temple. He drinks bottled water and practices yoga."

"The rumour mill was certain that Rhys was a Welshman who played rugby," said Gus. "I thought they played hard, drank hard, and existed on raw meat. Times have changed. Where does that leave you now, Kassie?"

"You were busy last week," said Kassie. "So, you didn't have time to chat with Vera and me. Do you even remember where he's living?"

"Monty Jennings found him a property," said Gus. "I remember now. It's just up the road from you."

"One hundred yards away, Mr Freeman. When Vera told me the news, I thought I'd died and gone to heaven. Thirty-two years old, single, and a rugby player. He sounded perfect. Monty handed Mr Evans the keys ten days ago. Our new police surgeon had a holiday owing, so he drove backwards and forwards in his car, transferring clothes and smaller items from his place in Bridgend. I persuaded Vera to drive to Worton on Saturday to keep me company while I did my morning baking."

Gus slowed to wait for a break in traffic. They were already in Potterne and leaving the A350. This story had better be brief.

"Mr Mercer reckoned the removal van with Mr Evans's furniture was arriving mid-morning," said Kassie. "We strolled up the lane at two o'clock with a few of my goodies and arrived just as the removal crew headed back to South Wales. Vera rang the doorbell and explained who we were. She said we were willing if he needed a hand getting things straight."

"What did Rhys Evans have to say?" asked Gus. He parked the car outside the pub.

"Mr Evans was very polite," said Kassie, "and invited us

in. That's when I noticed how short he was; he's fit, I admit that, but he's no man-mountain like you see on TV. Vera spotted a team photo on his Welsh dresser and asked what position he played. He said a scrum something, number nine."

"A scrum-half," said Gus, "traditionally, they were short, wiry, and nippy, with a good pair of hands."

"I wouldn't know about his hands, Mr Freeman, but short and wiry sums him up well."

"Did Rhys let you and Vera loose on his soft furnishings?" asked Gus.

"Unnecessary, Mr Freeman. Our police surgeon prefers the minimalist look. When Vera and I were on the doorstep five minutes later, Mr Evans told us that after another twenty minutes of tidying the place, everything would be where he wanted it to be. He planned to get his yoga mat out before driving into Devizes for a meal."

"What happened to your goodies?" asked Gus.

"I carried them back home," said Kassie. "You just polished off one of them earlier."

"Very nice, too," said Gus. "Ah, there you have it, Kassie. Rhys Evans doesn't cook for himself. Put the word out among your friends. Find out where he ate and what he ordered, and start planning a menu. Rhys may not enjoy cakes, but he has to eat. Perhaps you can find another way to his heart."

"No, it's time to move on, Mr Freeman," sighed Kassie. "For you and for me. Suzie will wonder what kept you. And the curtain twitched at number 73 just now. It wasn't to be."

"We'll find Mr Right for you in due course, Kassie," said Gus. "Well, now I'm up-to-date with your hot gossip. I'd better make tracks."

"That wasn't it, Mr Freeman," said Kassie, grabbing

Gus's arm. "I was catching up with the latest disappointment in my love life. No, I went into Devizes later that night and met friends for drinks. I was on a mission. When we left the last pub I remember going to; I saw your detective friend. He was working with you for a while."

"Rick Chalmers?" asked Gus. "He lives locally, I believe, and his marriage ended a while back. He's another one who doesn't cook for himself and exists on takeaways. Was he out with friends too?"

"One female friend, Mr Freeman," said Kassie. "That's why I was pleased to have this conversation alone. She hasn't breathed a word about a change in her relationship status and doesn't have a clue that I saw them together. My hot gossip concerned Rhys Yogi Evans as far as she knew."

"Amelia Cranston," said Gus. "She would be Rick's type. I'm not surprised. That young lady doesn't waste an opportunity to latch onto a detective that might further her prospects of joining the Crime Review Team."

"Amelia? No, it wasn't her, Mr Freeman. Vera Butler was all over Rick Chalmers like a rash."

"That's a turn-up for the books," said Gus.

"I had such high hopes, Mr Freeman," said Kassie, shaking her head. "Now, Vera's followed your lead and grabbed a younger model."

"Good for her," said Gus. "Right, time for me to get to Urchfont."

"Will you tell Suzie the news?" asked Kassie as she extricated herself from the car.

"You can't keep secrets for long in this town, Kassie; you know that. Suzie will hear soon enough. Vera and I are history; whoever your colleague sees is her business. How would Suzie react if Vera's love life were the first thing I mentioned when I got through the door?"

"I see what you mean, Mr Freeman. Least said, soonest mended. Do you ever listen to that radio?"

"Sorry? That was a sudden change of subject, Kassie. It works, but I don't enjoy their music in between the verbal diarrhoea."

"I love Ariana Grande," said Kassie. "What do you listen to at home then, Mr Freeman?"

"Sister Rosetta Tharpe would be my first choice," said Gus.

"What, a nun, the same as Mother Teresa?"

"Not a nun, Kassie," said Gus. "They both wanted to light the light on those in darkness on the earth. So, yes, I suppose they were similar souls," said Gus.

"You've lost me, Mr Freeman," said Kassie Trotter as she closed the door.

"Yes, I rather thought I had," said Gus as he started the car and headed home.

Chapter Four

GUS PARKED the Ford Focus next to Suzie's GTI and looked at the radio. Had he ever used it for anything other than a check on the weather or road conditions? If so, he couldn't recall when. His satnav was in the glove compartment to avoid getting nicked, and on the odd occasion he plugged it in, he muted the annoying voice.

How could anyone have a sensible conversation if the radio continually thumped away in the background? He preferred the quiet that enabled him to think without interference or the opportunity to exchange opinions with a colleague on a case. When he travelled with Suzie, they chatted whenever there was something to say, but they were equally happy to travel in silence.

Car designers had a lot of explaining to do. Music should be appreciated 'live', not alone in metal, plastic, and glass bubbles. Gus knew it drove people mad. He'd seen the evidence many times as they passed him on the road, singing to themselves at the top of their voice.

Someone banging on the car roof shattered the silence.

"Are you ever coming indoors?" asked Suzie.

"Sorry," said Gus, "Kassie had more stories to tell than I dreamed possible. She was so chatty that she forgot to give me that doggy bag she had promised. Have you eaten?"

"I ate that salad I mentioned on the phone," said Suzie. "It's too warm to sit indoors. I've got a glass of Chardonnay in the back garden with your name on it. We can chat while you decide what you want for dinner."

Gus trailed behind Suzie as she walked past Tess's climbing roses to the small patio at the rear of the bungalow. Suzie was right; this shady spot was ideal for the evening. Food could wait for an hour.

"How was your day?" asked Suzie.

Gus went through the Stacey Read case's final throes with her and the latest murder file the team had received from Kenneth Truelove. The Alan Duncan murder had occurred before Suzie's time with the detective squad at London Road. Death on the county's northern border made the local newspapers for a day or two, but the trail went cold quickly, and the world moved on.

"It sounds a tricky problem," she remarked. "What did Kassie Trotter have to say that was so urgent?"

"Kassie's hopes of a wedding to a hunky rugby player appear to have faded fast," said Gus. "Rhys Evans is more into yoga than sticky buns."

"Poor Kassie," said Suzie. "Have you decided what you're eating yet?"

Gus went into the kitchen to check the fridge and the freezer. He wasn't short of options, just time. While watching Suzie enjoying a second glass of white wine through the window, he spotted their list of essential telephone numbers next to the waffle maker. Gus ordered a pizza which the young girl assured would arrive in thirty-five minutes. If he couldn't eat the whole thing, he was sure Suzie would feel peckish later. Gus returned to the fridge and removed the second bottle of chilled Chardonnay, just in case.

Tuesday, 31 July 2018

WHEN GUS DROVE AWAY from the bungalow at eight-thirty, Suzie was behind him for a change. He was keen to get to the Old Police Station to start interviews on the Alan Duncan case. Suzie had lingered in the bathroom this morning. Gus had vague memories of days like that with Tess.

He had found it better not to pry. If there was anything to know, he heard about it when Tess was good and ready and not before. He assumed Suzie would be the same. As they reached the London Road HQ, Gus looked in his rear-view mirror and gave her a wave. Suzie flashed her head-lights before turning into the car park. Gus made a mental note to wait until Suzie spoke first tonight.

The Crime Review Team car park was busy. Blessing Umeh was reversing into a parking space under polite instruction from Neil Davis. Alex Hardy and Lydia were already upstairs because Lydia's red Mini sat safely in the extreme left-hand bay.

Luke Sherman drove up and waited while Neil and Blessing completed the manoeuvre without damage to Neil's car or Blessing's. Gus and Luke parked in the remaining bays and joined the others by the lift doors.

"Blessing's getting better, guv," said Neil.

"Thank you, Neil," said Blessing. "There's no need to highlight my shortcomings."

"Did you have any further thoughts on my last question yesterday, guys?" asked Gus as they travelled up in the lift.

"The money, guv?" said Neil. "I can't make head nor tail of it yet."

"Until we know more about Alan Duncan's life, we can't work it out, guv," said Luke.

"What do you think, Blessing?" asked Gus.

"It seemed an odd amount, guv," said the young Detective Constable.

"Exactly," said Gus.

Neil and Luke exchanged a glance as the lift doors opened. Another of their boss's cryptic remarks. What did it mean?

"We have thirty minutes before we're due at Madeleine Telfer's home," said Gus. "How long will that take us at this time of the morning, Alex?"

"Twenty minutes, guv," said Alex.

"Come on then, Lydia," said Gus. "We'll see whether your boyfriend is right. Let's not keep Mrs Telfer hanging around."

Gus and Lydia returned to the ground floor.

"Shall we take my car, guv?"

"Can you drive in those heels?"

"Fair comment. Alex drove us in from his house this morning."

"I would have suggested I collected you from your place in Chippenham," said Gus, "but I didn't want to ask if you'd be at home."

Lydia laughed.

"My place *is* on the Devizes side of Chippenham, guv. It would be perfect for you to have picked me up on the way to Cepen Park. I don't know why we don't just get rid of both places and find something big enough for both of us closer to the office."

"That feels like a commitment, doesn't it," said Gus.

"We're happy as we are, guv. I don't see that changing. I think Alex wanted to keep his options open when you suspended him. That's behind us now, and we're looking forward to a future together. As long as we're with the CRT, everything will be perfect."

"I can't control that one hundred percent, Lydia," said Gus. "As long as the senior team at London Road supports us, there shouldn't be an issue. A new person at the top might prefer to move one of you into a different role. There's still an old-fashioned view that couples can't work together successfully."

"Fingers crossed then, guv. I'm glad you had your satnav with you, guv," said Lydia, "I wouldn't have found Redwing Avenue so quickly. It's a rabbit warren around here, isn't it?"

"That must be Madeleine Telfer," said Gus, "just parking her new Ford Kuga on the driveway. She's moved upmarket since her days in that two-bedroomed semi in Biddestone village. I wonder what her husband does for a living."

The lady of the house stood on her doorstep with the key poised. Her hair and clothes looked immaculate, in keeping with her surroundings. Lydia had to remind herself that the woman was forty-three years old and had two young children.

"I'd better park on the road," said Gus. "My beaten-up Ford will get an inferiority complex."

"I don't think Mrs Telfer wants you to sully her pristine driveway with your motor, anyway, guv, based on that look she gave us," said Lydia.

Gus and Lydia walked up the short driveway to meet Madeleine Telfer.

"You're the detectives I'm expecting, I presume?"

"We are, Mrs Telfer," said Gus. "Perhaps we should continue this conversation indoors."

Madeleine Telfer opened her front door, and a Bichon Frise puppy came bounding along the hallway. Lydia prevented its escape, and once the door was closed behind them, Madeleine dragged the puppy into the kitchen.

"Monty will keep yapping and making a nuisance of himself," she said. "Please, come through to the lounge."

Lydia wasn't surprised at the layout of the main living room. It matched a high percentage of rooms they visited, focusing on a giant screen on the wall and plenty of comfortable seating.

Madeleine Telfer sat in a chair by the mock fireplace with her hands together in her lap. Lydia sensed a slight tension in her manner. Old memories, perhaps.

"My name is Freeman," said Gus. "My colleague, Ms Logan Barre, and I work with a Crime Review Team for Wiltshire Police. No unsolved murder case is ever closed. It's a decade since the original team failed to find out who murdered your partner, Alan Duncan. We hope to have more success."

"It's been so long," said Madeleine. "So much has changed. I'll never forget Alan or what happened to him, but surely, if there were leads to discover, they would have found them at the time. What can you do apart from using advances in DNA to re-analyse the evidence they gathered? Not that they had much of that in the first place."

"We ask questions that didn't get asked in the original investigation," said Lydia. "There's always something that comes to light."

Gus smiled to himself. In a few words, Lydia had achieved plenty. She had confirmed once more why he valued her contribution to the team so highly, and Madeleine Telfer's reaction proved that she had a secret. How important that would be in solving the ten-year-old mystery or not remained to be seen.

"Your accent suggests you weren't born in this part of the country, Mrs Telfer," said Gus.

"Call me Maddy, please; everybody does," she replied. "My family lived in a village outside Leeds. The Yorkshire accent has softened over twenty-five years, but I'll never lose it altogether, Mr Freeman."

"You moved to Chippenham when you were eighteen, is that right?" asked Lydia.

"I left school at sixteen and had three firms I worked for close on me in the next eighteen months. Finally, when the unemployment rate hit ten percent, I decided there was nothing for me up North. So I came here and was fortunate to get a job at the call centre."

"That was the company at Bumper's Farm?" asked Gus.

"That's right," said Maddy. "I loved it there, great colleagues, and although there was a high staff turnover, and pay wasn't much to write home about, a handful of us stuck it out because we became friends."

"Friends such as Anna Phillips," said Lydia.

"We're still mates today," said Maddy. "Anna and her husband, Wayne, live nearby."

"In Woodpecker Mews," said Lydia. "Yes, we're aware of where they live."

"Why did you choose Chippenham?" asked Gus. "Did you know someone here or have a relative living in the area, perhaps?"

"I didn't know anyone," said Maddy, looking at her hands in her lap. "My relatives lived in Yorkshire."

"A daunting prospect for a young woman to leave home and travel two hundred miles to a strange town. What was your family's reaction when you said you were leaving home? Did you apply for the call centre job before leaving Leeds, or was it necessary after you found yourself somewhere to stay? Talk us through that, if you will."

"I wanted my independence, Mr Freeman," said Maddy. "You must have met eighteen-year-olds who have left home searching for a new beginning. There doesn't have to be an ulterior motive."

"Did the detectives ask about your family ten years ago, Maddy?" asked Lydia.

"Why should they? It was Alan who died. I'm not close to my parents or my brother and sister. We don't live in each other's pockets like some families. We have our lives to lead."

"The grandchildren must have made a difference," said Gus.

"I send photos of Oliver and Emily to my parents with their Christmas cards. Chris is too busy with work to take time off to drive up there. They wouldn't expect it, anyway."

"What does your husband do for a living?" asked Gus.

"He's a successful property developer," replied Maddy. Lydia thought it was the most animated she'd been since they arrived.

"The file we received from the original investigation told us everything we needed to know about how you and Alan met," said Gus. "How long had you lived in Chippenham before you got together?"

"Three years," said Maddy.

"Did you meet anyone else in those three years?" asked Gus.

"No, I didn't," said Maddy.

Lydia noticed Maddy's hands clasped together tightly and her knuckles white. They should keep probing. There was something there.

"Did you have an unpleasant experience in Leeds?" she asked. "Was that what caused you to run away from home?"

"I didn't run away," said Maddy, her voice raised. "That's not what I said. I told you I decided to leave. I wanted to go it alone, and I did."

"There must have been a few disappointed young men here in town," said Gus. "You're an attractive woman, Maddy. Was there a particular reason you turned them down?"

"I don't remember," said Maddy.

Gus knew she was lying. He'd carried out a thousand interviews like this one.

Maddy Telfer didn't kill Alan Duncan. He was sure of that, and despite the passage of time, people remembered all manner of details. A good copper knows when they're telling the truth. A sure sign that they're lying is when they say they don't know or can't remember.

"We'll return to that, Maddy," said Gus. "What did you do when Alan went running on Wednesday evenings?"

"I did the housework and watched TV shows Alan didn't enjoy. But, of course, it was only for a couple of hours."

"You never left the house? Why not drive into Chippenham or Corsham?"

"Why? There was nothing I needed. My social life was with Alan."

"Was that the same on Saturdays when Wayne Phillips

came over to Biddestone to take Alan away for the afternoon? Did that not concern you?"

"Not you, too," said Maddy. "The papers hinted Alan was gay just because he used to be in the Navy. It's not compulsory, you know."

"I didn't give it a second thought, Maddy," said Gus. "I wondered whether you suspected Alan and Wayne were seeing other women."

"Anna would have known, so would I. Neither of them could cheat like that. It was the cycling they enjoyed. I was happy that they got on. Anna and I were already friends. It was a relief that our partners had become good mates."

"How long did Wayne and Alan know one another before you met?" asked Lydia.

"Several months, I believe. You would need to ask Wayne. Alan never told me a date. He just said they met through a love of cycling."

"Was Alan a local cycling club member?" asked Gus. "Perhaps that's where they met."

"Alan never mentioned it. Why?" asked Maddy.

"The detectives on the original investigation found no one who might have wanted to murder your partner," said Gus. "They questioned his parents, his workmates, and your neighbours. Nobody had an unkind word to say, yet someone followed Alan often enough to become familiar with the routes he took on his weekly runs."

"The police asked which routes he took," said Maddy, "and whether I ever noticed anyone outside in the lane when Alan left home. I didn't see a thing. It was a terrible shock to discover that someone wanted him dead. I could never understand it."

"Where was Alan living when you met?" asked Lydia.

"In Corsham," said Maddy. "When he left the Navy,

Alan came home and moved back in with his parents, Bob and Elizabeth."

"If Alan had known Wayne Phillips for several months before you met, it suggests that Alan was cycling almost as soon as he settled in," said Lydia. "What about the weekly runs? Were they something he started after you moved in, or was the Wednesday and Saturday exercise a pattern already established?"

"Alan told me he needed to maintain the high level of fitness he'd had while in the Navy. There wasn't a particular goal in sight. It was purely for his well-being."

"How did you feel about that?" asked Gus.

"If it made him happy, it was fine by me," said Maddy. "Why does it matter if he had already established a routine before we met?"

"We'll ask his parents this afternoon," said Gus, "but if Alan ran through several parts of Corsham every Wednesday evening, that provides occasions where he could come into contact with a person of interest. The murderer didn't appear out of thin air. They knew Alan's habits well enough to know where he would be at a specific time. They weren't waiting for him next to that remote field on Ham Lane by chance. They planned it to the minute."

"That's horrible," said Maddy.

"I agree," said Gus. "So, let's return to your lack of a relationship in the three years before you met Alan Duncan. This time, I want the truth. If there *was* someone, you remember their name *and* why you preferred not to disclose their details earlier. If there was no one in your life throughout that period, the answer lies in Leeds or the village you lived in before moving here. Which is it?"

"I left home because of a difficult relationship," said Maddy. "I started seeing a boy at school when I was fifteen.

Kyle was seventeen and had left school that summer. There weren't many jobs around, and he was on the dole. My parents wanted me to concentrate on my studies. According to my teachers, I was good enough to attend university, but Kyle had nothing to occupy his time. I thought I loved him, so I cut school to be with him. My exams the following summer were a disaster, and I left school with only a handful of average grades. I found work, but only for peanuts with start-up firms that didn't survive because of the recession. I argued with my parents because of how things had turned out. I argued with Kyle because he wasn't trying to find a job. We broke up after eighteen months. That's when it started. He wouldn't accept it was over. Kyle tormented me for the next two months. He'd wait for me outside work. I had to change my phone number so he couldn't text me a hundred times a day. Finally, I stopped going out in the evenings. Ultimately, I gave in and let him back into my life. He worked on a building site then and could afford to run an old car. We were okay for a while, and then he got fired for persistent timekeeping problems. I got the blame; that was the first time Kyle hit me."

"Did you end it after that," said Lydia.

"I tried," said Maddy, "but he apologised and bought me flowers. My parents were getting fed up with me making excuses for him. They saw the bruises when he'd lashed out again. My father and my brother wanted Kyle out of my life for good. My brother got arrested for assault after Kyle spent the night in the hospital. The police never listened to Darren's reasons for attacking Kyle. They had seen no proof I'd been in an abusive relationship. I lived at home, and although my brother accused Kyle of being responsible for my injuries, Kyle denied everything. I was too scared to report him myself. He knew that. My third job ended soon after Darren's case went to court, and then I was out of work and sat at home all day. I couldn't have a social life. Kyle knew better than to come near my home because of my family, but I knew I couldn't escape him as long as I remained in the village. That's why I came here."

"We need Kyle's full name and address, Maddy," said Gus.

"Kyle wouldn't have killed Alan," she replied.

"What makes you so certain?" asked Lydia.

"Kyle was a bully," said Maddy. "But he would never be smart enough to find me."

"Either you're naïve," said Gus, "or you did something to help you stay in hiding. What was it?"

"It will have to come out now," said Maddy. "I was never Maddy Mills in Yorkshire. I changed my name by deed poll once I reached Chippenham. Kyle was my boyfriend, and Darren really is my brother's name. If Kyle wanted me back after that time and devised an elaborate plan to kill Alan, surely Chris was in danger once I started seeing him? We've been happily married for seven years. Don't you think Kyle would have acted before now?"

"We still need to eliminate him from our enquiries," said Gus. "It would have been better if you had mentioned this to DI Banks and his colleagues ten years ago. Did it never occur to you that Kyle could have been the one person who might have wanted Alan dead?"

"I've tried to put that part of my life behind me," said Maddy. "The only contact I have with my family is those Christmas cards. I use my former name and post them from Swindon or Bristol when I do my Christmas shopping. They don't have my address. All they need to know is that I'm alive and well."

"You referred to Alan's parents as Bob and Elizabeth,"

said Gus. "Have you kept in contact since their son's murder?"

Madeleine Telfer shook her head.

"After the funeral, I found it difficult to carry on visiting them. I needed time to grieve alone. It affected his parents so much, especially Alan's mother, that I didn't think I would ever get over things if I spent too much time around them. I attempted to visit on the first anniversary of his death and spoke to Bob. He looked as if he'd aged ten years in twelve months. Elizabeth was still in bed. She refused to get up, even though Bob told her I was there. I think she blamed me for Alan's death."

"Why would she think that?" asked Lydia.

"I don't know. You would have to ask," said Maddy.

"When did you stop work?" asked Gus.

"A couple of months before I had Oliver. He's six, and Emily is four and a half. I plan to go back part-time when the children are older."

"Were you still at Bumper's Farm?" asked Lydia.

"Yes, I worked at the same firm throughout," said Maddy. "I started there in '93 and left on maternity leave in 2012."

"When did you meet Chris Telfer?" asked Gus.

"I didn't rely on Wayne and Anna this time," said Maddy. "I was in the deli aisle in Morrison's one Saturday morning, and he stopped to chat."

"Were you still living in Biddestone?" asked Lydia.

"No, I moved here, to this housing estate, six months after Alan died."

"Too many memories?" asked Gus.

"Exactly," sighed Maddy.

"When the police found Alan's cash, were you shocked by the amount?" asked Gus.

"It was one shock after another," said Maddy. "I knew something was wrong when he didn't get home by eight. When the police were outside the house after I returned from searching for him, I feared the worst. Even then, I thought it would be a heart attack, a hit-and-run, never a murder. The next four or five days are still a blur. When the police returned to search the house, I couldn't understand what they hoped to find. Then, that DI Banks you mentioned showed me one of Alan's trainer boxes and asked if I knew what was inside. I said a pair of white trainers, size ten, with a red flash. He opened the box, and I nearly died. I'd never seen that much cash."

"What did DI Banks ask you?" asked Gus.

"He asked me why my partner withdrew that much money and closed his current and savings accounts on Tuesday afternoon. I said I did not know. Alan hadn't said a word to me. Banks asked me the same questions as the uniformed officers had on Wednesday night. Did we argue? Were we in financial difficulties? I said no then, and I said the same thing to Banks. The other detective asked whether someone might have been blackmailing Alan. How much did I know of his past?"

"A fair question," said Gus. "You met at a party and moved in together after four months. You knew little or nothing of the first thirty years of his life."

"That's not fair," said Maddy. "We visited his parents often enough for me to learn about Alan from a baby to a teenager. They had loads of photos of Alan in his uniform, and from places he'd visited on various trips."

"Did he discuss his trips?" asked Lydia.

"He couldn't," said Maddy, "they were hush-hush."

"We'll ask Bob and Elizabeth later. Perhaps they knew what ships he served on," said Gus. "One last question for today, Mrs Telfer. Was there anyone you came into contact with after arriving here in Chippenham that could have had a reason to harm Alan Duncan?"

"No way," said Maddy. "Everything I did when I reached here kept me safe. No relationships meant no chance of getting hurt. I'd had more than enough trouble over the previous three years. When I met Alan, I believed I could love someone again. We were happy, and someone tore him away from me after four years. I was back where I started."

"You found love again, though, Maddy," said Lydia, pointing to a family photo of her with Chris and the two kids.

Maddy gave a wry smile.

"Chris adores the children and me. I gave him what he always wanted. He gave me financial security. Love didn't come into it."

"If you could supply my colleague with those details for Kyle, Mrs Telfer," said Gus. "We may need to speak with you again, but for now, thank you for your time."

Gus left Lydia in the lounge with Maddy Telfer and returned to the car. He checked his watch. They had time to return to the office for a debrief before heading to Corsham. His initial feeling had proved correct. However, this case had more twists than a corkscrew, and no doubt there were several more surprise revelations before they discovered the truth.

Chapter Five

LYDIA FOUND Gus standing on the pavement by his car.

"What do you reckon these homes fetch?" he asked.

"Four hundred thousand, minimum," said Lydia, "were you thinking of up sizing?"

"Heavens, no," said Gus. "Did you get the gentleman's details?"

Lydia waited until they were inside the Focus before speaking. A nosy neighbour was walking past with a puppy. Lydia thought she had bigger purses.

"Kyle Ellison, formerly from Marsden, West Yorkshire. The village is a forty-five-minute drive from Leeds and has around three-and-a-half-thousand inhabitants. However, the forty-five-year-old Kyle's current whereabouts are a mystery to Mrs Telfer."

"Check whether Ellison has a record when we get back to the office," said Gus. "Get Blessing to search for him on social media. I'm not happy that Mrs Telfer has yet told us the whole truth. Did she offer any additional names and addresses?"

"No, guv," said Lydia. "I guessed you left me alone with Maddy, hoping she might open up to me about her family. I pressed her for her birth name, but nothing doing. She wanted the past to stay in the past. What do you suggest?"

"We find Ellison, get proof of his whereabouts in the weeks leading up to the murder, and if he's clean, then we forget him. Do we need to contact her family?"

"Maddy sends Christmas cards with no return address," said Lydia. "That's sad, isn't it?"

"Her excuse was that it stops them worrying," said Gus. "They know she's alive and well. I assume her parents are still alive. If not, her brother can't write back to tell Maddy to save the stamp. Oh, I don't know. Maddy, or whoever she is, didn't kill Alan Duncan. Kyle Ellison may have had a motive, but how could he hope to locate the victim? As for the rest of her West Yorkshire family, there might have been the traditional teenage squabbles, but pursuing her half the length of the country to murder her partner seems unlikely."

Gus parked the Focus outside the Old Police station, and he and Lydia travelled up in the lift.

"What did you make of Maddy's last comment, guv?" asked Lydia.

"That she married for convenience rather than love? She wouldn't be the first, Lydia."

"That's cynical, guv," she replied.

"Perhaps, but there's more to come out yet. That woman has played a role since adopting the Maddy Mills persona. Unfortunately, I'm not sure she can distinguish fact from fiction after twenty-five years."

"You've got me there, guv. What did I miss?"

The lift doors opened.

"Let's tell the others what we learned," said Gus. "Get

those details checked out and update our copies of the digital files."

Twenty minutes later, Blessing Umeh was digging on Facebook, Twitter, and Instagram.

Luke Sherman asked the Hub if they had any information on Kyle Ellison.

Neil Davis searched census records for Marsden, West Yorkshire, for a family of two adults, with two children, where the eldest boy was called Darren. Neil knew he could search for some time. Somebody had to have the short straw.

"Let me in to the secret then, guv," said Lydia.

"What was your first impression of Madeleine Telfer?" said Gus.

"A beautiful, smartly dressed, confident woman who looked younger than her forty-three years, guv."

"When she was fifteen, her teachers said she could progress to university," said Gus.

"Yes, then the good-looking-but-thick-boyfriend, Kyle, put paid to that," said Lydia.

"Where did she work after she left school?" asked Gus.

"Three failed businesses, working for peanuts," said Lydia.

"No, she worked for three start-up firms that didn't make it. Maybe the right product at the wrong time. I wonder where those entrepreneurs are today. I wouldn't mind betting that at least one has retired with a bundle of money. Why did they give the young school leaver a job? Because they recognised potential, someone with a sharp mind. Maddy didn't say she did menial work, did she? I'd like to know more because when she arrived in Chippenham, part of her invisibility cloak involved wasting her talents at a call centre. A company she stayed with for nineteen years where she became an anonymous voice at the end of the line."

"What the heck does she have to hide, guv?" said Alex.

"And what does it have to do with Alan Duncan's death?" asked Luke.

"Don't look at me," said Gus. "I'm just starting this jigsaw. We haven't got half the pieces on the board yet. Perhaps we'll get more this afternoon."

An hour later, Gus was ready to drive to Corsham.

"Are you nearly ready, Blessing?" he asked.

"Give me two minutes, guv," she replied. "I'll explain to Lydia what I've done so far. Ten minutes, and Lydia should have a good idea of Kyle Ellison's digital footprint."

Blessing joined Gus in the lift, and they returned to the ground floor.

"The story so far, Blessing," said Gus.

"Ellison's Twitter posts were mostly about football, rugby league and the EDL, guv," said Blessing.

"I'm sorry you had to read that garbage, Blessing," said Gus.

"Kyle's not an active member of the extremist organisation, guv. The language isn't great, but he's careful not to post or retweet anything controversial. There's no sign they have removed him from the site at any time. I assess that he's an extremely low-volume user with less than thirty followers. Kyle follows several high-profile sports stars and female celebrities and goes weeks with no activity. His profile picture is the Leeds United badge. Everything else he posts is text only, no photographs."

"Never mind, Blessing. Perhaps he's more active on Facebook."

"It makes life easier for us when people live in a goldfish bowl," said Blessing.

"Odd isn't it?" said Gus. "If we encounter someone who doesn't have active accounts on these sites, we wonder what they've got to hide. Twenty years ago, it was possible to carry out clandestine affairs, commit bigamy, and get up to antisocial activities with no one being any the wiser. Or so they tell me."

"That's a good point, guv," said Blessing.

Gus drove them to Corsham. Bob and Elizabeth Duncan lived in a modest three-bedroomed semi-detached house on a small estate off Station Road. Gus thought the houses had stood there since the early 60s.

"What's my role this afternoon, guv?" asked Blessing as they walked to the front door.

"Listen to what they say; make a note of what they don't," said Gus.

The doorbell uttered a single harsh ring.

Bob Duncan answered the door and invited them inside. Gus understood what Madeleine Telfer meant. Bob Duncan was barely nine years older than he was, yet he could pass for an eighty-year-old. Bert Penman had more energy at eighty-five.

Alan's father didn't ask who they were or want to look at identification. He led them into a tired-looking front room, crying out for a lick of paint. The grey net curtains in the window had once been white, and the room felt dark and gloomy even in high summer.

"Elizabeth's in the kitchen," said Bob. "She thought you'd want a cuppa."

"Give Mrs Duncan a hand, Blessing," said Gus. "You know my poison."

"Only the dining room chairs for you to sit on, I'm afraid," said Bob. "We don't get many visitors."

"That's not a problem, Mr Duncan," said Gus. "You know why we're here?"

"Someone rang to say we were getting a visit from the police. You're raking over Alan's case again. That upset Elizabeth. She's not been the same since he died. Alan was our only child."

"We understand," said Gus. "My name's Freeman. My boss, who will soon be the county's next Chief Constable, asked my team to review Alan's case. We know it's been ten years, and talking about his death will still be painful for both of you, but we didn't find his killer. We must do everything in our power to correct that situation."

"Why?" asked Bob Duncan. "It won't bring Alan back. So why can't you leave things alone? We'll be dead and gone in a couple of years. I couldn't care less about what you do then."

Blessing returned to the room carrying a tray. Elizabeth Duncan shuffled in behind her and sat in a chair opposite her husband. Gus had already noticed the couple's wedding photograph and a casual shot of proud parents with their son in his naval uniform. It wasn't easy to accept that they were the same person. Elizabeth was a hunched, pale shadow of the woman in those photos. A decade of grief etched in every line.

"We have tea in the afternoon," she said.

Blessing handed the couple their cups of tea and raised an eyebrow as she passed Gus his black coffee.

"I was explaining to your husband, Mrs Duncan, that it's not our intention to cause you any distress by taking a fresh look into Alan's death in 2008. Someone went to a lot of trouble to plan and carry out that murder. What I want to do this afternoon is talk about Alan. Did he attend school here in Corsham?"

"Alan was top of the class, Mr Freeman," said Bob Duncan, "whether it was junior or secondary school. He got top grades in a dozen GCSEs and stayed on for the sixth form. He did well in his A levels, with A grades in Maths, Physics, and Chemistry."

"Did he want to attend university?" asked Gus.

"No, Alan always had his heart set on the Navy. I don't know why."

Blessing watched Elizabeth Duncan sipping her tea. She was miles away. Perhaps she remembered their son leaving home for the first time. Or maybe she'd forgotten they were even there.

"Where did he train?" asked Gus.

"At Dartmouth," said Bob. "He was there for seven months, training to become an Engineering Officer."

"I bet he couldn't wait to get to sea," said Gus.

"Alan served on several submarines, Mr Freeman. Nuclear-powered hunter-killer class. We were proud of the way he served this country."

"Rightly so," said Gus. He couldn't imagine what it was like to live for weeks at a time, many metres underwater.

"I know what you're wondering," said Bob. "Ninety days, if necessary, for a fully stocked craft carrying a full crew. We received holiday snaps from Alan when he got shore leave. He and his mates visited the Pyramids, temples in Thailand, Sydney Harbour Bridge, and Hong Kong. They had a great time relaxing after the pressures of the job."

"A necessary task in peacetime," said Gus, "despite the cost. We don't have the same capability as we did when Alan was a submariner. Did they ever have any incidents?"

"Did they bump into a Russian sub, do you mean? I think that would have made the headlines don't you? Alan couldn't discuss that with us, Mr Freeman. We didn't ask. It was enough for us that he came home safe when they returned to UK waters."

"What rank did he hold, Mr Duncan?" asked Gus.

"Alan was a Weapon Engineer Officer," said Bob.

"What made him decide to leave?"

"He said he'd had enough," said Bob. "We didn't press him. It disappointed me he didn't stay the full term, but Alan was adamant that he wanted out."

"How long was he at home before he started work?" asked Gus.

"Six weeks, maybe. We were happy to let our son stay as long as he liked. Elizabeth loved having him around. I spotted a vacancy for a draughtsman and mentioned it to Alan. I thought it would give him a modest income while he searched for a permanent position."

"Something more suited to the qualifications he'd earned with the Royal Navy?"

"The money a small firm like mine could offer was half what he got paid."

"Yet he stayed with the firm until a few days before he died. What do you think was the reason for that?"

"The firm offered Alan a three-month contract. I'd worked there for years, and the boss knew me well. He told me they were happy to give Alan work to tide him over until he found something better. The boss had lost a son during the Falklands War. Alan never complained about the work he did for the firm, but let's say it wasn't challenging for someone of his calibre. You could have knocked me down with a feather when he asked them if he could stay on permanently at the end of the three months. The next day Alan got up and said he'd met a girl at a party. We don't know what went on when Alan was overseas, it was none of our business, but he never had a girlfriend before he left home for Dartmouth. Elizabeth and I were happy for him, thirty years old, and the prospect of grandchildren on the horizon."

"Did you meet Madeleine soon after that?" asked Gus.

"Maddy? Oh yes, Alan brought her to meet us the next weekend. Before we could look round, they had moved out to Biddestone together."

"Did you approve?" asked Gus.

"Of Maddy? Or them living together before they got married? It's the way of the world these days, Mr Freeman. We didn't dislike Maddy. She was a pretty thing and bright."

"Did they visit you often?"

"Every other weekend, I suppose. Alan liked his mother's cooking."

"Did Alan ever explain why he stayed in the lower-paid job at your firm?"

"Not to my satisfaction. Alan just shrugged and said that they earned enough to survive. Their main ambition was to be happy."

"Were you a runner or a cyclist in your youth, Mr Duncan?"

"I ran at school, and I cycled to work for years, but I didn't take to it like Alan."

"Maddy told us Alan was determined to stay fit. That was why he went on a long run every week and did the cycle ride at the weekend. Where did Alan get that exercise while he still lived with you?"

"Alan ran by Corsham Court out to the Cross Keys. Another time he'd run out to Hawthorn or Pickwick. He preferred the countryside. His new mountain bike came from a shop in Chippenham. A darn sight different from my old bike, I can tell you. Alan met another chap that day keen on cycling. That perked him up no end. He had someone to chat to as they cycled."

"Wayne Phillips?" asked Gus.

"That's the chap," said Bob Duncan. "Funny thing that. Maddy worked with his wife. It's a small world, isn't it?"

"It can be Mr Duncan. So, once he had the new mountain bike, Alan and Wayne started meeting up every weekend, I presume?"

"On a Saturday, Alan kept Sundays free to visit us."

"Did Alan ever have any arguments with anyone while he was running or cycling while he lived here, Mr Duncan?"

"Nothing worth mentioning to me, Mr Freeman,"

"Was everything alright at work? Did he get on with his work colleagues?"

"Alan was a stickler for discipline in his life, Mr Freeman. It goes with the armed forces' territory, and he expected others to show a high level of discipline in their work. He wouldn't let a drawing leave the office unless it was accurate. Close enough, was sufficient for a few factory hands with their products, but not Alan. I heard a few words exchanged in the heat of the moment, but the bosses always backed Alan to the hilt. I told the detectives ten years ago that it had to be something more serious than that for someone to want to kill our boy. Nobody ever lost their job because Alan dug his heels in and insisted the job got done right."

"Have you seen Maddy lately?" Gus asked.

"Not for ages," said Bob. "She's married now, you know."

"Maddy would never have married Alan," said Elizabeth.

"Why did you say that?" asked Bob. "She was always good to us."

"Maddy told you what you wanted to hear; she was crafty. Alan couldn't see that she was hiding something."

Gus and Blessing shared a glance.

"Even you know what it was," said Elizabeth. "I saw you. She never shared that secret with Alan, but I knew there was something."

"Did Alan receive any money when he left the Navy, Mr Duncan?" asked Gus.

"They get a resettlement allowance," said Bob. "It was ten grand, or thereabouts. Why?"

"We've already established that Alan settled for a job that paid far less than he could expect to earn with his qualifications. Your wife suggested Maddy had something to hide. As you said, she's pretty and bright and more than capable of finding a well-paid job in the area. Yet she wasted her talents at a call centre, calling people who didn't want whatever she was selling. We heard a reason for that this morning. I'm still waiting to learn why Alan lost himself in a mediocre job. It appears they both had buried secrets. What do you have to say to that?"

"I told you Alan's explanation never satisfied me, Mr Freeman," said Bob. "We talked about it for hours, Elizabeth and me. It made no sense."

"Did any of his former shipmates attend Alan's funeral?" asked Gus.

"I wanted to contact his friends. The ones in the photos we have that Alan sent, but I couldn't find their details. Alan wrote names on the backs, like Andy, Smudger, and Taff. We thought Maddy had their details at the house in Biddestone. I rang her and asked her to search for his address book. He must have had one, but Maddy couldn't find it, so there wasn't a huge turnout. The boss sent a few representatives from the firm to the service at the crematorium. Wayne was there with his wife and several girls that worked alongside Maddy at Bumper's Farm. Other than that, half a dozen of their neighbours from the village attended the service."

"Were you working the day Alan quit his job?" asked Gus.

"It was a small factory, Mr Freeman. They've expanded into another unit since I retired, but I never heard a thing. A rumour passed from one end of the factory to another in minutes if there was a hint of redundancies. Alan worked in the offices, and I was in the Quality Control section on the shop floor. It was common for a week to pass without us bumping into one another. Alan must have asked his boss to keep it quiet. That's the only explanation."

"Alan never asked to borrow money?"

"We offered when Alan first came home, but he said he'd manage on the resettlement money. Then we offered again when they moved out to Biddestone. They could use the extra money for white goods, a new TV, or ready cash. Maddy assured us they were fine. When the police told me about the cash they discovered in that shoebox, I could see what they meant. We've never had eight hundred pounds lying around, let alone eight grand."

"The sum wasn't the important element, though, was it?" said Gus. "Why did Alan empty his bank accounts in the first place? Who, or what, was the money for, and why was it hidden in the house?"

"If Alan owed money to someone, he would have paid it," said Bob. "That's the way we raised him."

"When you returned to work on the Monday following

the murder," said Blessing Umeh. "That was when you learned Alan had quit, wasn't it?"

"That was when it came out. As soon as I heard Alan had quit work, I called Maddy. She phoned the police because Wayne had seen Alan outside the bank on Tuesday afternoon. That started the ball rolling. Within twenty-four hours, I knew Alan had closed his accounts, withdrawn the cash and hidden it at home."

"Maddy didn't know Alan had quit his job either, did she?" asked Blessing.

"Not a clue," said Bob Duncan.

"What did you do the day you retired, Mr Duncan?"

"Had a few beers with the lads."

"Were there any personal items you had in drawers or filing cabinets that you wanted to rescue?"

"The tools I bought myself to help me in my job. A few odds-and-ends, like a mug for my tea and a diary. Nothing that wouldn't fit in the bag in which I carried my lunchbox and thermos. The rest wasn't worth keeping and went in the bin."

"I imagine Alan collected bits-and-bobs that he wouldn't want to throw away," said Blessing. "I wonder what happened to them?"

"In a box under the stairs," said Elizabeth.

"When did that arrive?" asked Bob. "You never mentioned it."

"Maddy had another shoebox containing items Alan's boss brought to her from work. She dropped the box off the day before the funeral. You were at work. I chucked it in the cupboard under the stairs and forgot about it."

Bob went into the hallway and returned with the box.

"Do you want to open this, Mr Freeman?"

Blessing stood and walked across the room. She was already donning a pair of blue nitrile gloves.

"Better to have them and not need them, guv," she said.

Blessing removed the lid.

"A pocket diary, guv," she said, "pens, pencils, and a coffee mug, inscribed with, 'I might look like I'm listening to you, but in my head, I'm riding my bike.'"

"Is that it?" asked Gus.

"Other than a handful of coins in the mug, nothing."

"No photographs?" asked Bob Duncan.

"Why do you ask?" asked Gus.

"I'm positive we had a photo of Alan and his mates at Happy Valley Racecourse in Hong Kong," said Bob. "It stood on the dresser for several years. When Alan moved out, he left his photos behind. I thought he must have wanted a photo to brighten up his office and took it without mentioning it."

"The pocket diary could prove useful, guv," said Blessing. "We might have found those missing contact details. Alan Duncan filled in records for an Andy, a Smudger, a Taff, a Gooner and three or four more. Wayne Phillips is here too, plus several business contacts."

"What about the diary?" asked Gus.

"Alan logged times of meetings at work, dental appointments, and statistics for his Wednesday night run and Saturday afternoon cycle ride. Birthdays and anniversaries for Maddy and his parents. Nothing for Wayne. Perhaps Maddy handled them. It's still more comprehensive than any diary I've ever tried to keep."

"We'll take it with us, Mr Duncan," said Gus. "It could provide useful leads. Those ex-colleagues could be the key to solving this mystery."

"We should ask whether either of them was in that

Happy Valley photo, guv," said Blessing. "Maybe there's a name scribbled on the back of this diary. Maybe not. If that photo wasn't in his office or the house in Biddestone, then Alan removed it from the mantlepiece and got rid of it. Why?"

"Good thinking, Blessing," said Gus. "We'll ring Maddy Telfer when we get back to the office. I wonder if she can shed light on when it got moved and what happened to it. Also, we should check when this box got delivered to Biddestone."

"Is that it then?" asked Bob Duncan.

"I think we can let you get on with your day," said Gus. "Many thanks for your co-operation. This pocket diary somehow bypassed the detectives in the original investigation. Alan's boss wouldn't have known the possible importance of the addresses it holds. Maddy did what she thought was right and delivered the box to you. The police had finished their questioning. The names in the diary meant nothing to her. It was too easy to dismiss them as business contacts or acquaintances. Alan shared little detail of his Navy life with Maddy. We'll see where those names and addresses lead us, Mr and Mrs Duncan. Thank you for the coffee. Good afternoon."

Bob Duncan saw them to the front door. Elizabeth stayed in her seat, staring into space.

"You will let me know how you get on, won't you?" asked Bob.

"Of course, Mr Duncan," said Blessing. "We can't promise good news, but we'll do our best to find Alan's killer."

Bob closed the door when Gus and Blessing reached the car.

"What did you make of that, Blessing?" asked Gus.

"A step in the right direction, guv," she replied. "We'll understand more about what made Alan Duncan tick once we interview the people he served with."

"Let's hope they can explain why Alan left the Navy when he did and why he worked for a small company on an Industrial Estate in Corsham."

Gus drove them to the Old Police Station office and asked the rest of the team to update their progress.

"I scoured social media for more information on Kyle Ellison, guv," said Lydia. "As Blessing said, he doesn't give much away. No photographs, just the occasional post or a share of something topical."

"What does that suggest?" asked Gus.

"Why does it have to suggest anything, guv?" said Luke. "Ellison could work long hours, have a wife and family to support, and not have the slightest interest in joining in with the crowd."

"You don't have several social media accounts, guv," said Neil. "Ellison doesn't have a criminal record either. We checked."

"Nothing?" asked Gus. "Not even a speeding fine?"

"He's Mr Clean, guv," said Luke.

"Did you believe the story that Maddy Telfer told us, Lydia?"

"Yes, guv," said Lydia. "It sounded genuine to me."

"Me too," said Gus. "Which makes the fact that Ellison has stayed out of trouble for twenty-five years remarkable."

"Maybe the beating he got from Darren Forsyth showed Kyle Ellison the error of his ways, guv," said Neil.

"Darren Forsyth?"

"They were the only family on the census for Marsden matching the information Maddy Telfer gave, guv," said Neil. "David and Mary Forsyth, mother and father; Darren and Jennifer, their two children. Jenny Forsyth left Marsden at eighteen to move to Chippenham. Darren is still single and lives in Leeds. Dave and Mary haven't moved from the village. They're both retired now."

"Right, at least we know where to find them if we need them," said Gus. "Although I can't see they can offer us anything. Blessing, can you call Maddy Telfer, please?"

"I tried her number as soon as we got upstairs, guv," said Blessing, "but no reply. The school run is almost over. I can try again later, or do you want to speak to her?"

"Leave it to me, Blessing," said Gus. "those photographs have given me an idea."

Gus waited until after four o'clock, and then he made the call.

"Maddy, it's Gus Freeman from the Crime Review Team. Can you spare me two minutes?"

"I suppose so. What is it you need to know?"

"We visited Bob and Elizabeth Duncan this afternoon. Bob mentioned Alan's photograph with a group of his colleagues taken when they were in Hong Kong. Can you recall it?"

"Yes, they had several photos on display in various parts of the living room, dining room, and hallway. Why do you ask?"

"Bob hadn't seen that photo since before Alan died. He thought Alan might have taken it to work to put it on the office desk. I know it was long ago, but can you remember when you saw it last?"

"Now you're asking," Mr Freeman," said Maddy. "I've got photos in our home that I walk past a dozen times daily. I'd spot if someone moved them, but I can't swear that I'd notice if one disappeared. They become part of the furniture, well, you know what I mean."

"I do, Maddy," said Gus. "Can you at least recall who was in the photo?"

"The only one I knew was Alan," said Maddy. "The other four were on the same submarine. Bob said he'd written their names on the back, but I never took the photo out of the frame to check. Why would I? I didn't know them from Adam."

"I understand," said Gus. "What about a brief description?"

"Three of them were Alan's age. The man standing next to Alan was tall, well over six feet, with dark hair, possibly mid-forties. The next guy was the shortest, perhaps five feet six inches, with ginger hair and freckles. Then there was the heaviest one, blond hair cut short. He was five feet, nine inches. The last guy was closer to six feet, well-muscled, crewcut, dark hair."

"Any distinguishing marks?" asked Gus.

"Terrible Hawaiian shirts," said Maddy, "apart from that, nothing dramatic. No large tattoos that I could see. I'm sorry, I'm not much help, am I?"

"Never mind," said Gus. "I have another question. You dropped a box into Elizabeth on the Friday before Alan's funeral. Can you remember what it contained?"

"Oh, that was a box of rubbish from the factory. Alan's ex-boss drove out to Biddestone one evening and told me that Alan had collected his bits and pieces from the office, and in his hurry to leave, he must have forgotten it. The cleaner found it on a chair beside his desk."

"Can you remember when that was?" asked Gus.

"Friday, two days after Alan died. I was in no fit state to deal with it then. I spent the weekend with Anna and Wayne, and it went clean out of my head. A week later, I suddenly realised I still had it. I couldn't see any reason to keep it, so I put it into the boot of my car on Monday morning. In the end, it was Friday before I remembered to drive to Corsham and give it to his Mum. I thought it might have sentimental value."

"It wasn't all rubbish," said Gus. "We found the names and addresses of Alan's friends. Maybe the men in that Happy Valley photo."

"That's interesting," said Maddy. "I expect Bob will want to write to them. He didn't have the opportunity at the time. Do you know? Running through that photo's details just now, I remember commenting on those shirts when we were with Bob and Elizabeth the Sunday before Alan died. I glanced towards where it usually stood, and it had gone. Alan asked his Dad a question on a different subject, and I never got the chance to ask Elizabeth why she moved it."

"Now we're getting somewhere," said Gus. "What was it about Happy Valley that made it so important? Or was it one of the men in the photo? Could they have been the person Wayne said they saw by the pond on Saturday afternoon?"

"I do not know, Mr Freeman," said Maddy. "Was there anything else? I need to get the children's tea before Chris gets home."

"We won't keep you much longer, Maddy," said Gus. "It didn't take my team long to discover your true identity, Jenny. You changed your name from Jennifer Forsyth to Madeleine Mills when you escaped Marsden and Kyle Ellison. We established yesterday that Ellison had a motive to kill your partner. We haven't checked yet if he had the opportunity. I agree that your husband, Chris, would have been in danger if Ellison had been the aggressor. We'll move on to other potential leads once we've confirmed that Ellison had an alibi for the time of Alan's murder."

"I don't want my original name to come out, Mr Freeman," said Maddy.

"There's no reason for us to tell anybody that you changed your name, Maddy," said Gus. "I presume Chris does not know?"

"No, he doesn't," said Maddy. "Nor did Alan. Anna and Wayne only ever knew me as Maddy Mills. I told you I wanted to leave my old life behind me."

Maddy Telfer ended the call. Gus sat and thought for a while.

"That sounded useful, guv," said Blessing.

"What did I learn?" asked Gus. "The box with the pocket diary left the factory on Friday afternoon, and Alan's former boss took it to Biddestone. Maddy told us everything was a blur for the first four or five days after the murder. She spent the weekend with Anna, got home on Monday morning and thought she would let Alan's parents have the few personal items that were in that box. Maddy says she forgot about the box until Friday and delivered it to Elizabeth. Alan's mother was distraught at the loss of her only child, so she put the box in a cupboard under the stairs and forgot it."

"The timing is perfect, guv," said Blessing. "Bob Duncan went to work on Monday and learned that Alan had quit. He called Maddy on Monday evening, and she notified the police. DI Banks and DS Tallentire had already interviewed Maddy and Alan's parents on Thursday and Friday. When they discovered the money, the box was in Maddy's car. If they had talked with Bob and Elizabeth the same day or the day after, Elizabeth wouldn't have realised the pocket diary's possible significance. When Banks and Tallentire spoke to Alan's ex-boss and his work colleagues, why would anyone mention the box of miscellaneous items? It was like that trick that conjurers used to do on TV."

"Which cup is the ball under?" said Gus. "Yes, the trick is to move the ball without the audience seeing it. Each party involved acted in total innocence in this particular matter. I can't attach blame to anyone, certainly not Banks and Tallentire. It is what it is, but we can still take advantage of the diary and any secrets it contains."

"Did Blessing miss anything, guv?" asked Neil Davis.

"I wouldn't blame either of you for not picking it up, Neil," said Gus. "I summarised the conversation, which allowed Blessing to complete the timeline for the shoebox. However, I didn't include a sharp intake of breath in my summary."

"When you told her we'd found her family, guv," said Lydia.

"Exactly, Lydia. Mrs Telfer is anxious that her past doesn't get resurrected."

"That's only natural, isn't it, guv?" said Alex. "Kyle Ellison stalked Maddy and assaulted her."

"Do we have a current address for Kyle Ellison?" asked Gus. "Check whether he has an alibi for Wednesday the twenty-eighth of May 2008. If he has, we move on and let sleeping dogs lie."

Chapter Six

GUS ARRIVED BACK at the bungalow just before half-past five. He parked his Focus next to Suzie's Golf and went indoors.

"How did the interviews go?"

"Productive, for a change," said Gus. "We uncovered information that escaped the original investigation."

"Oh, that doesn't sound good," said Suzie. "Who dropped the ball?"

Gus explained why it wasn't anyone's fault. The box had moved just before the police arrived to carry out an interview or was in the boot of the victim's partner's car. Maddy Mills, as she was then, was never a suspect. She still wasn't.

"You can't say Madeleine is entirely unconnected to the murder, Gus," said Suzie. "She may not have murdered Duncan or arranged for someone to do it for her, but if Kyle Ellison acted in a jealous rage, their abusive relationship was the catalyst."

"I agree with Maddy's assessment," said Gus. "If Ellison still professed undying love for her, four years after she ran away from Marsden, then Chris Telfer would have become his next target."

"So, what do you think happened?"

"I haven't worked it out yet," said Gus. "From the outset, I've struggled to explain why a bright, intelligent girl went into hiding in Chippenham. We now know her true identity. I can travel to Leeds and interview four people. Her parents, Dave and Mary Forsyth, and her brother, Darren and Kyle Ellison. Perhaps that will provide the answer."

"How significant is that missing photograph?" asked Suzie.

"Alan removed it for a reason. I mulled that over in the car as I drove home. There were four men in the photo with Alan. If we can match names from the backs of the other photos in the Duncan home, then one of those four could have been the man Wayne Phillips saw waving at Alan by the pond in the village. Now that we have the pocket diary, we can contact Alan's friends and interview them. Do you know what struck me as I drove into Urchfont?"

"That low-hanging branch near the Lamb Inn?"

"No," said Gus, "If we can still identify everyone from the other photos in the house, then one person in the Happy Valley holiday snap is making his only appearance. Wayne was right. Alan recognised the man. Who knows, maybe the old friend had made an appearance in Biddestone earlier that same week. We'll never know. There's just one thing bothering me."

"Go on," said Suzie.

"Wayne Phillips described the man by the pond as medium height and medium build, with a crewcut. He was fair-skinned, in his late thirties or early forties. I must remember to ask Alex Hardy to check his hair colour with Wayne in the morning. It doesn't gel. Two guys in the picture who had crewcuts back then were six-footers and had dark hair. So we can rule out the redhead, one guy would be too old, and the blond fellow was heavily built and fair-haired."

"Perhaps it was the man holding the camera?" suggested Suzie.

"That could be a brilliant suggestion, Suzie," said Gus. "We need to match faces in the photos to names in the diary. Those ex-colleagues should be able to fill in the gaps. One of them will remember whether a gang member took that photo or if they grabbed a fellow tourist to take the picture."

"I aim to please," said Suzie.

"Those conversations could prove valuable in solving my other problem," said Gus. "Why did Alan Duncan follow a similar path to his partner and lie low in a small firm in Corsham when he was capable of much more."

"Love is blind?" suggested Suzie.

"Maddy Mills lived in Chippenham for ages before she met Alan Duncan," said Gus. "She was hiding from Kyle Ellison. Alan left the Navy in a hurry, came home, and took a nothing job that his father arranged for him. It was to fill in while his son searched for something better. Perhaps Alan Duncan had no intention of finding a better job. He was happy to remain anonymous, like Maddy. Remember how they met? They got introduced thanks to Maddy's friend, Anna Phillips. Without her intervention, would the pair have ever met? Maddy told us she had had no social life since heading south. Alan's parents couldn't recall their son having a girlfriend before leaving for his officer training stint in Dartmouth. No, when those two got together, there was an innate recognition of a kindred spirit."

"Does that even exist, Gus?" asked Suzie. "I thought opposites attract."

"When I read that book by Kierkegaard after Tess's death, it encouraged me to look for other authors who might explain my feelings. I hung onto the copy of Tess's old book and stored it in my shed at the allotment because it somehow kept my memory of her alive. In the spare bedroom, you might find several other books on similar philosophical subjects. Kindred spirits are like-minded people who experience an instant connection of love and understanding. People with common interests, values, or world views might be described as kindred spirits. From what I read in the murder file, Maddy said that as soon as Alan Duncan arrived at Anna's leaving party with Wayne Phillips, she was 'immediately drawn' to him. The couple rarely spent more than twenty-four hours apart over the next four years."

"I'm not sure that's healthy," said Suzie. "We need our space, don't we? I try to persuade you to ride with me, but I know it will not happen deep down. So I escape for half a day, even though I don't want to. Does that make sense?"

"Of course it does, darling," said Gus. "We have common interests because of our jobs. Most people who join the police have the same values and world views. We spend a large percentage of our time involved in our particular roles within policing. Still, when we come together at home, we have a wide range of topics of conversation where our opinions differ to fill our leisure time."

"So we're not kindred spirits then," said Suzie.

"When I'm around you, I feel calmer," said Gus. "Now, that could be because my spirit has realised that you know and understand me. I remember when we first met, on the day we arrested Leonard Pemberton-Smythe. You gave me a lift back to London Road."

"And I was rude about your Ford Focus," said Suzie. "I told you that my Dad used to have one years ago. Yet, you still asked Geoff Mercer to call me when you needed an extra pair of eyes to check on what was going on above Cambrai Terrace."

"You agreed to drive over," said Gus, "and accepted my invitation to lunch. Why did I ask? I felt as if I knew you right away. As if we'd always known one another. You sat here in this room flicking through my vinyl collection that same afternoon and didn't laugh out loud."

"I can see where this is heading," said Suzie. "I remember looking through those albums the other evening, and it surprised me that you hadn't separated them into 'yours' and 'mine'. The fact that the albums I brought with me from home were mixed with yours gave me a warm feeling. Do you think that was what it was like for Maddy Mills and Alan Duncan?"

"I don't know enough about the pair to comment on that yet," said Gus, "but one thing suggests they were experts at hiding their true selves. Maddy had already hidden her past by changing her name. Alan knew nothing of that. What did you make of the collection of shoeboxes in the spare bedroom?"

"Alan would have had several pairs of trainers. He was a runner, so that's only natural. As a cyclist, he probably had more than one pair of shoes for that pursuit, too. The boxes offered a convenient hiding place for the cash he'd withdrawn from the bank, but why do you think they were significant?"

"Maddy didn't run; neither did she cycle, yet she didn't complain about the clutter in that spare bedroom. When

Lydia and I visited Maddy's new home in Chippenham, it was spotless, despite their two young children."

"This suggests that Maddy was happy to ignore her partner's idiosyncrasies in a quest for maintaining her anonymity."

"I knew it. We *do* think alike," grinned Gus.

"Do you know what my Mum said to me?" asked Suzie. "She took me to one side the day we went to Worton to collect my things. She wished us every happiness and was glad I'd found my soul mate."

"Ah, now I'm on more familiar ground," said Gus, "because soul mates can differ. Kindred spirits are birds of a feather, while soul mates are more a case of opposites attract. You referred to that earlier. I think we're more soul mates than kindred spirits. One book I read described kindred spirits as co-conspirators. I didn't understand what that meant until I started working on this case. Maddy and Alan had secrets buried in their past that they would do anything to keep hidden. Something in their make-up drew them together. They interpreted the ease that existed between as love. Maybe they should have remained friends. We know part of Maddy's buried secret. I hope to discover Alan's secret in the days or weeks to come. We won't find Alan's killer until we dig up full details of both. I'm convinced of that."

"You do have a busy time ahead of you," said Suzie. "Why don't we walk to the Lamb and eat there tonight?"

"That sounds a plan, Suzie," said Gus. "If either of our friends is around, they'll steer the conversation onto more mundane topics. I've dragged you into enough philosophical analysis of relationships for one evening."

"We're good, though, aren't we?" asked Suzie. "Whether we're soul mates or kindred spirits?"

Gus could only think of one way to convince Suzie that everything was fine. They made it to the Lamb just before nine o'clock. Brett Penman met them by the door.

"I thought you two might have been at the allotment this evening," he said. "I dropped by to invite you here for a drink. I start work in Wootton Bassett tomorrow. The rest of the gang are here already; I popped home to change."

"We haven't eaten yet," said Suzie. "Things got away from us, and time has flown. We'll grab a bite and join you as soon as possible."

Brett led them inside. His grandfather wasn't in his usual seat at the bar, but Gus could hear his voice.

"You order, Suzie," said Gus, "my usual soul food. But, first, I'll say hello to Bert, Irene, and the Reverend."

"How can you be sure they're here?" asked Suzie.

"My copper's nose. It never fails."

Gus strolled through the crowded bar toward his friend's voice. He found Bert Penman, plus the usual suspects, in the far corner. Irene North sat next to Bert, hanging on his every word. At their time of life, did it matter whether they were soul mates or kindred spirits? Irene's late husband, Frank, had been a petty criminal all his life. Bert was as honest as the day was long. Somehow, those two found comfort in their companionship. Irene was ten years younger than the retired butcher. Funny how nobody seemed too concerned with an age gap when you were on the last leg of your journey. Of course, ten years differed from thirty. Next to Irene sat the Reverend Clemency Bentham. She had dispensed with the Laura Ashley tonight and wore a maroon blouse with her clerical collar over black trousers. Gus tried to recall a Saint's day at the end of July that might have caused Clemency to work a long shift.

"Gus, Brett tells us you're joining us later. We haven't seen you both for days,"

"My apologies, Reverend," said Gus. "Duty calls. I don't need to remind you of that. No sooner than we put one case to bed, my superiors have another emergency."

"Now you know what life is like when you're wearing this collar, Gus," said Clemency.

"I've kept an eye on your plants, Mr Freeman," said Bert. "They haven't run wild yet, but you can't leave them alone for too long. The land is very much like a woman, Mr Freeman."

That started a fit of giggles from Irene North. Brett returned from the bar with the party's next round of drinks. Gus thought that a soft drink was preferable for Irene.

"Suzie asked me to tell you a table will be free in five minutes," said Brett. "What's kept you away from here for so long?"

"Bert was just berating me for ignoring my plants," said Gus. "but my team and I had a tricky case to solve in Swindon. Suzie and I spent a pleasant afternoon on the allotment the Saturday before last. That must have been our last visit, I suppose. Time flies when you're having fun. I'll find Suzie, and we'll have our meal, then we'll join you."

Gus made his way to where he'd left Suzie, but he couldn't see her. He looked around the bar and spotted her returning from the loo.

"Where are we headed?" he asked. Suzie pointed behind him. A teenage girl was preparing the circular table for two more diners.

"I decided on a salad," said Suzie. "It's still too warm for anything heavy. I ordered a steak for you, with a side salad and a children's portion of chips. Was that okay?"

"You know me better than I know myself," said Gus.

"Now you're teasing me," said Suzie.

The food arrived and was delicious, as always.

"Do you want another glass of Chardonnay?" Gus asked after eating. He waved his empty glass of Merlot to show that he was ready for another.

"You carry on, Gus," said Suzie, "I'll have one of those soft drinks that the Reverend enjoys."

"Fair enough," said Gus. "The gang are seated in the far corner. You make your way there, and I'll fetch the drinks."

Five minutes later, the six friends gathered in the corner. Around them, the busy bar emptied.

"I think someone wants to make a speech," said Clemency.

Brett Penman stood and raised his pint glass.

"Thank you for making me so welcome since I arrived in this country. I knew my grandfather loved this part of the world. Until I saw things for myself, I imagined it was the countryside and the weird weather you guys get, but actually, it's the people. I moved into my new place yesterday, and my belongings from Canada will be here before I know it. Tomorrow, I start a fresh chapter in my life with my first day at the veterinary clinic in Wootton Bassett. I know what to expect. Lots of variety, dozens of anxious owners, and hundreds of temperamental pets. I can't wait to get stuck in. Starting a new job can be a traumatic experience, but I know I'll be coming home at the end of each day. That's how I think of Urchfont and Wiltshire now. It's my home."

"I'm sure we wish you the best in your new job, Brett," said Gus. "The place must seem quiet without him, Bert?"

"I spent many years alone after my Cora passed, Mr Freeman. I know what to do."

"I'm sure you do, Bert," said Suzie.

Gus spotted the Reverend watching Irene North.

Clemency was probably thinking the same as him. Bert wouldn't get much time alone now that Brett was out of the way.

The landlord politely reminded his last few customers that he'd called last orders ten minutes earlier. Clemency Bentham was the first to make a move.

"My trusty steed is outside," she said. "I'll walk home with you, Irene, if you wish?"

"That would be most welcome, my dear," said Irene.

"I'll drive Bert home," said Brett. "Are you two okay?"

"We walked along the lane to get here," said Gus, "it won't be a hardship to walk back."

Gus waited for Suzie to pay another visit and watched as Brett helped his grandfather into his car's passenger seat. Clemency Bentham pushed her bicycle towards the turning to the housing estate where Irene lived, and Irene trotted beside her, still talking nineteen to the dozen.

"Ready?" said Suzie.

"I wonder if we've missed something," said Gus.

"In what way?"

"The Reverend bringing her bicycle meant Brett couldn't offer to take her home."

"Where is this house he's renting from Monty Jennings?"

"I don't remember Brett telling us. Vera will know. I'll ask her the next time I'm at London Road."

"Perhaps it's close to the rectory, and Brett creeps across the back gardens late at night."

"I don't think Clemency would approve," said Gus, "let alone the Bishop of Salisbury."

They walked along the lane in silence. Gus opened the front door, and they went indoors.

"What now?" Gus asked.

"Tomorrow is another day," said Suzie.

Wednesday, 1 August 2018

"WILL YOU BE LATE TONIGHT?" asked Suzie.

"Not if I can help it," said Gus. "I plan to be in the office today. Alex and Lydia are interviewing Anna and Wayne Phillips this morning. Luke and Neil are in Corsham this morning and Chippenham this afternoon. I may need to send Blessing Umeh on the occasional short trip, but I should get home by half-past five with luck."

"I might pop over to see Mum and Dad after work," said Suzie. "I won't be later than seven. Do you want to cook tonight?"

"It would be my pleasure. Nothing too heavy, though, right?"

"I do love you, Gus Freeman."

"Glad to hear it," said Gus. "Now, I'm getting out of bed. We have thirty-eight minutes to shower, have breakfast, and get dressed for work."

As he stood in the shower, Gus tried to remember why thirty-eight minutes rang a bell.

Forty minutes later, he sat in the Focus and watched Suzie's GTI edge into the lane.

He prayed the Highways Department hadn't found another stretch of road between Urchfont and the Old Police Station that desperately needed resurfacing. He could still make the office by nine.

Suzie indicated right and turned into the London Road HQ with a brief wave.

Gus waved back and switched his thoughts to Alan

Duncan. Why had he worried? It was plain sailing into the town centre, and he parked the Focus next to Alex Hardy's car. Good, they were upstairs already. Alex and Lydia didn't need to leave for half an hour for their ten o'clock appointment with Wayne Phillips. As he got out of his car, Neil Davis edged into the bay on the other side of Alex.

"I'm so thoughtful, aren't I, guv?" he said.

"You've left Blessing with a choice of the vacant bays at either end, Neil. Very astute."

Neil and Gus travelled up in the lift. Alex and Lydia were hard at work.

"I have a question to add to your list this morning, Alex," said Gus. "Can you get Wayne Phillips to improve his description of the man he saw at the duck pond? What I'm after is his hair colour. Wayne said that the guy had a crewcut. Any extra hints he can add will be much appreciated."

"Got it, guv," said Alex.

"Anything new that Luke and I need to look for, guv?" asked Neil.

Gus shook his head.

Blessing and Luke emerged from the lift.

"Left or right, Blessing?" asked Neil.

"I reversed next to your car, Neil," said Blessing. "I didn't want to risk doing any more damage to the boss's car than a long life has accomplished."

"Are you ready to leave, Neil?" asked Luke. "We've got places to go, people to see."

"Sorry, Luke. Yes, I'm on my way."

Luke and Neil went downstairs and headed for the Corsham factory where Bob and Alan Duncan once worked.

"What should I focus on today, guv?" asked Blessing.

"You can follow those two to Leafield Industrial Estate, Blessing," said Gus. "I want you to revisit Bob Duncan."

"It's Wednesday, guv," said Blessing. "Elizabeth will be in bed all day."

"I'm aware of that, but we need to make progress on this case, Blessing. To do that, I need copies of every photograph Bob has of Alan and his fellow submariners. That's copies of the front and back, properly labelled so we can match them. If he knows the first name of someone who appears under a nickname, make a note of it. Every scrap of information will help when we analyse the pocket diary. Bob may not know the answer, but was it Alan's camera? Did he ask a passer-by to take a group snap, or was one of his colleagues behind the shot? Keep pressing him for as much detail as he can remember."

"I'll do my best," said Blessing. "What about Elizabeth?"

"If anyone could get something from her, it would be you, Blessing," said Gus, "Don't push Bob too hard on that subject. If she wants to speak, don't stop her, but I doubt she'll come down from her bedroom."

"Shall I call him first, guv?"

"No, Bob will want to delay matters until tomorrow. If you're on the doorstep, looking like you mean business, he'll be putty in your hands."

"Got it, guv," said Blessing. She was halfway to the lift.

"Blessing is a character, isn't she guv?" said Lydia.

"I imagine you've seen a significant improvement since you met her in Leamington?"

"It's you, guv. You bring out the best in people," said Alex.

"I demand nothing less, Alex," said Gus. "I find that works best."

"We'll get going, guv," said Lydia.

"Good hunting," said Gus.

With the place to himself, Gus opted for an early coffee. The quiet office would allow him to continue the musing he started on the road into town earlier. After half an hour, the only conclusion he had reached was that he was in trouble as he'd never mastered a 3-D jigsaw.

Gus stopped musing and flicked through the pages of the pocket diary. Finally, he produced a list of names from the address section at the back with postal and e-mail addresses, landlines, and mobile numbers. Plus, anything that Alan Duncan had recorded in the diary's daily area relating to a person on the list.

Gus skimmed the company's internal meetings and briefly considered whether the killer was someone Alan had argued with at work. When Luke and Neil returned later this afternoon, he would check whether the personnel they interviewed suggested a possible name. Gus checked Alan's meetings with visitors from other companies, some from the UK, others from overseas. Gus hunted for a name not included in the address section. He couldn't find one.

Where next? Gus wondered where DI Phil Banks was working these days. He remembered the two lead detectives in the original investigation were at opposite ends of the country but couldn't recall seeing details. So he called Geoff Mercer at London Road.

"Good morning, Gus," said Geoff. "How can I help?"

"Do you remember Phil Banks, Geoff? Did you two ever cross paths?"

"Gosh, yes, frequently. You know me, I trod on Phil's toes, trying to get my face in a more prominent spot in any photographs taken after a successful court case. He hasn't spoken to me in years."

"I'm not surprised," said Gus. "Perhaps you're not the right person to ask then. I wanted to know where to find him."

"Bradford," said Geoff. "West Yorkshire Police. He moved north around eight years ago. Phil Banks operates out of Trafalgar House. He worked on the Duncan case you've just started on, didn't he?"

"Yes, Geoff," said Gus, "I wanted to get any background on the main players that didn't make it into the murder file. They shouldn't have left it out if it was important, but I know there are many imponderables. Banks was there, talking to the victim's partner, his family, and his friends. We've ploughed through the paperwork and crime scene data and interviewed the people I've mentioned. However, I know that we're only scratching the surface at present. I want an insider's opinion of what one or more could be hiding."

"I've got the number for Trafalgar House here, Gus," said Geoff. "Banks was a Detective Inspector when he ran that investigation. He's moved up the ladder since then, so watch what you say. Phil was always a tad precious. He won't give you the time of day if he thinks you're dissing him."

"I'll be on my best behaviour, Geoff," said Gus, noting the number that Geoff gave him. "Shall I mention your name and say you suggested he was the best man for me to speak to?"

"Don't you dare; that's a sure-fire way to end any conversation before it begins."

Gus was still smiling when Geoff Mercer ended the call. It was too easy to wind him up; and too hard to resist an opportunity. An efficient-sounding officer responded at Trafalgar House on the second ring.

"Is it possible to speak to DCI Banks, please?" asked Gus.

"Who shall I say is calling, sir, and what does it concern?"

"I'm calling on behalf of Acting Chief Constable Truelove of Wiltshire Police. Freeman is the name. My team is reviewing a case from 2008 that DCI Banks handled when he worked at Chippenham."

"One moment, Mr Freeman,"

Gus recognised the piece of music that assaulted his ears at once. The Kaiser Chiefs were a local band, and for the West Yorkshire force to use them as background music when they put customers on hold was commendable. Gus wondered whether 'I Predict A Riot' sent the right message, though.

"Mr Freeman?"

"Is that DCI Phil Banks?"

"It is; what was it you were after?"

"Your impressions, sir," said Gus. "What did you make of Alan Duncan?"

"What's your background, Freeman?"

"Please call me Gus, sir. When I retired after forty years with Wiltshire Police, I was a DI in Salisbury. Kenneth Truelove rang me several months ago and asked me to lead a Crime Review Team. The Duncan case is our eleventh."

"Dear God, you're *that* Freeman. I kept hearing stories when I worked in Chippenham. Some of my superiors said you were a legend, and others reckoned you were lucky. How many cases did you say your team has handled?"

"Ten so far, sir," said Gus.

"Any joy?"

"Nine out of ten, sir," said Gus, "but we live in hope on the one that got away."

"Nobody's that lucky," said Phil Banks.

"Thank you, sir," said Gus.

"Well, I remember the Duncan case, of course, Gus," Banks continued. "When you asked what I made of him, I thought it was a daft question that must have come from a civilian. Duncan was lying dead in a field when I first saw him. I got the call from Sam Hulbert, the uniformed officer that found the body. The police surgeon arrived on the scene five minutes before DS Connor Tallentire and me. Our forensic people were on standby, but the night was falling fast. Preservation of the scene was paramount. Connor and I had to give SOCO the maximum opportunity for forensic recovery. The police surgeon was non-committal over the cause of death. Sam Hulbert had intimated suicide in his phone call to me. I decided we should establish a perimeter, close things down tight for the night once the body had left for the mortuary and get stuck in at first light. It would have taken hours to get proper equipment set up in a field miles from anywhere."

"I don't think I would have done any different, sir," said Gus. "Whoever strangled Alan Duncan wore gloves, and it wasn't until the surgeon examined the body more closely that he confirmed it was a homicide."

"When they returned at five in the morning, forensics discovered little evidence that might provide us with a magic bullet," continued DCI Banks. "They found no blood, no weapon of any kind. The ground was hard and dry. There were signs of small animals scuttling across the grass during the night, but the killer left nothing to lead us to them. We examined the ground from where the body had lain to the gateway twenty yards away. There were no fingerprints on the five-barred gate. The lane was dry and dusty. If the killer parked their car while they waited for Alan Duncan, they chose a spot where there was no risk of leaving incriminating tyre tracks."

"How did you determine that the murder occurred in the field?" asked Gus.

"The mobile phone found on the ground beside Alan Duncan was our only clue. Okay, the murder might have occurred in the lane, and the killer dragged or carried the body perhaps thirty or forty yards and dumped it out of sight. But we found no drag marks in the lane or the field. So if Duncan's phone fell from his hand or pocket during a struggle in the lane, we didn't think the killer would bother to pick it up and move it. If it had been a robbery, they would have taken it."

"What do you think were the sequence of events, sir?" asked Gus.

"The killer sat in his car until Alan Duncan came into view. DS Tallentire drove our car thirty yards further along Ham Lane and parked. I stood by the gateway and walked backwards until I saw him flash his headlights."

"How far were you from the gateway, sir?" asked Gus.

"Sixty yards. You've visited the crime scene, Gus. You know how that lane winds this way and that along its path. Connor signalled when I was perhaps two strides from disappearing from view. We calculated that the killer spotted Alan, got out of the car and walked along the lane on the left-hand side until he reached the apex of the bend."

"He assumed that Alan Duncan was running on the right-hand side facing any oncoming traffic," said Gus. "Then the killer switched sides at the apex, taking a calculated risk that Alan wouldn't look up as he approached the gateway."

"Exactly, Connor walked towards me, and I jogged along the lane. The next time I saw my DS, he was less than ten feet away. We were level with that gateway when we came face-to-face. I'd stopped jogging. We both agreed that Duncan didn't try to escape. He had little opportunity. Where was there to run? A jogger said he saw Duncan near the village's centre while heading in the opposite direction. That meant they met as close to seven o'clock as made no difference. You already know what time someone made the emergency number call. So, there was no protracted argument. The killer confronted Alan Duncan and attacked him at once. That was not a motiveless killing, Gus. I was sure Duncan knew who was facing him and why he was there."

"What about the money?" asked Gus.

"We didn't know about that then," said DCI Banks. "That only came out on Tuesday morning."

"I know that, but why did Duncan withdraw a relatively small sum, stash it in his spare bedroom, and then go out without it on a run that he knew might be his last? The money had to be for something or someone."

"We only concluded that he knew his killer after we found the hidden cash," said Banks. "If I put myself in Duncan's running shoes on Wednesday night, you're right. If the man Wayne Phillips saw the previous Saturday *was* the killer, he might have been stalking Duncan for days. Duncan had the cash; if that was what the man was after, why didn't he carry it with him?"

"I think we're back to my original question, sir," said Gus. "What did you make of Alan Duncan?"

"Every person we interviewed had the same opinion," said Banks. "Duncan was quiet, dependable, a good worker, a loving son and partner. Not one of them believed Duncan had an enemy in the world."

"Why do you think the press hinted that Duncan was gay, sir?"

"I believe a local rag adopted that line, Gus. I don't recall the nationals taking much notice of the murder. We spoke with everyone we could connect to Duncan in the area without finding a suspect with motive and opportunity. That you've called me suggests you aren't getting further than we did."

"Early days, sir," said Gus. He would not risk getting cut off by telling Banks they'd found the pocket diary. "Can I ask a big favour, sir?" said Gus, "Do you know a Kyle Ellison? He hails from Marsden and would be in his early forties now. He was the victim of an assault in 1993 by Darren Forsyth, who came from the same village. We would appreciate the chance to chat with Ellison."

"I've made a note of his details, Gus," said DCI Banks. "I'll get someone to look him up and tell them to call you back."

"Many thanks, sir," said Gus.

Gus made a mental note to tell Geoff Mercer that Phil Banks was a decent chap, provided you didn't tread on his toes.

Chapter Seven

GUS WONDERED how the rest of the team was doing this morning. But he didn't have long to wait. Minutes later, Blessing Umeh arrived back in the office.

"I've got everything we need, guv," she said.

"How were Bob and Elizabeth?" asked Gus.

"We got off to a sticky start," sighed Blessing. "I rang the bell, Mr Duncan answered. He wasn't keen on letting me indoors and gripped the door, blocking my entry. I followed your lead, guv. I told him we could do it the easy way or the hard way. He could let me in and help me find the photos we needed, or you would arrange for him to get taken to a police station for an interview under caution."

"That might have been extreme, Blessing," said Gus. "I'm not sure we have grounds."

"It worked, guv," said Blessing. "Mr Duncan said he couldn't leave his wife alone in the house for any length of time, so he relented and let me in."

"Well done, Blessing," said Gus. "Did you see Elizabeth?"

"Bob went upstairs while I waited in the living room. Our conversation at the front door must have woken her. He returned to tell me his wife was ready for breakfast and asked if I wanted a coffee. I carried on photographing the pictures we wanted, not forgetting those with writing on the back. When Bob returned with our coffees, he asked how it was going. I showed him what I'd done, and he pointed out two more photo frames in the hallway. While Bob took our empty cups to the kitchen, I asked to use the loo. Their bedroom is at the front of the house, so I knocked on the door and asked Elizabeth if she wanted me to take her breakfast things downstairs."

"Clever," said Gus. "Did she remember you?"

"Yes, guv," said Blessing. "Once seen, never forgotten, that's me. I could tell Elizabeth was depressed, but she was willing to talk. I told her why I'd come over today. She told me that what I'd copied were the ones they had framed. There were several additional loose photos in a drawer in what used to be Alan's bedroom at the back of the house. I asked if I could borrow them. She agreed. Most of them are photos that Alan took of places he visited, but a couple of them are of colleagues on their own."

"Even better, Blessing," said Gus. "Right, get everything on your phone downloaded. Let's see who we can match from the pocket diary. I'll scan in the loose snaps Elizabeth gave you. I wonder why Bob didn't remember they had them. Did he say anything when you returned downstairs?"

"Bob thanked me for collecting his wife's breakfast things, guv," said Blessing. "I didn't show him the photos I had in my handbag."

Blessing handed Gus the selection of loose snaps. He studied them and sorted them into three groups. Alan Duncan's casual shots of Sydney Harbour Bridge, the

Great Pyramid of Giza, and other famous landmarks he placed in a discard pile. The second group included pictures of one man standing alone, smiling at the camera. Never the same man. Some wore a naval uniform, which Gus took to be that of a fellow submariner. Others wore smart casual clothing. There wasn't a Hawaiian shirt in sight. That left just one photo. It was of Alan Duncan, in casual gear, smiling at the camera. Gus knew where someone had taken it. The buildings in the background were unmistakeably St Basil's Cathedral in Moscow.

"Are you ready to scan your snaps in, guv?" asked Blessing.

"Only half a dozen matter," said Gus. "Why, have you downloaded the others already?"

"That part was easy, guv," said Blessing. "I need to create a file to hold the data you collected from the pocket diary. First, I'll crop these images to give each individual's face. It will get easier after the first one because several of Alan's friends turn up repeatedly."

Gus looked at the clock on the wall. He would not be much use to Blessing on this job. Alex and Lydia would be back within the next thirty minutes.

"I can tell you need to concentrate, Blessing," said Gus. "I'll get out of your hair. Time to take a walk in the fresh air, get a sandwich from the deli in the Market Square, and make us both a drink when I get back."

"OK, guv," said Blessing. "I've got this."

When Gus returned thirty minutes later, Alex and Lydia were waiting for the lift.

"How was Woodpecker Mews?" he asked.

"Busy," said Lydia Logan Barre. "Most properties have more cars than they have driveways. Several have even converted their garages into extra rooms, so on-road parking appears to be the norm."

"Lydia's miffed because we had to park six doors away from the Phillips's place, guv," said Alex with a nod to her black trainers.

"I broke a heel on my shoes," Lydia wailed. "They were my favourite pair."

"Just as well you went prepared," said Gus as they entered the lift together.

"I learned early on that if you want to take me on a route march around a murder scene, I should carry an old pair of trainers and wellington boots."

"I promised Blessing I'd get her a coffee when I got back from my brief break," said Gus. "You two can get what you gathered this morning into the files while I'll do the honours. We'll debrief our efforts later."

"Okay, guv," said Alex.

Gus disappeared to the restroom to reacquaint himself with the Gaggia. The others were hard at work when he returned with four coffees in Alex's multiple mug holder. Gus placed their drinks on their desks and then sat at his desk. He wanted to hear what they had to say, but patience was a virtue.

"I've got the first part of the summary ready, guv," said Blessing a few minutes later. "The file is available for each of us to view within the Freeman Files."

"Good," said Gus as he swallowed the last dregs of his cup of coffee. "Let's stop what we're doing and switch our attention to that for a few minutes. I want to identify our next steps."

Gus, Alex, and Lydia brought up Blessing's work file on their screens.

"Lead on, Blessing," said Gus.

"For Alex and Lydia's benefit," said Blessing, "the photos held in picture frames brought from Bob Duncan's home, plus the pocket diary from Alan's office, allowed me to identify seven of his colleagues. I also found loose snaps that I've added at the foot of the page. I'll explain those in a minute. Taff, the ginger-headed man, featured in the photos most often, is Max Hughes from Swansea. Every man's record follows the same pattern. So, I've isolated the best headshot of Max Hughes for his profile picture. The columns include his home address, phone number, etcetera. The colleague's position reflects the frequency with which he appears in the photos. Keith Smith, Craig Anderson. Rico Menghini, Freddie Watts, Drew Taggart, and Bryan Tarbuck are fellow crew members that Alan Duncan went with on these shore leave trips. When he added their names to the back of the photos for his parents, they became Taff, of course, Smudger, Andy, Gooner, and Lofty. Chuff and Tarby."

"I can't think of why the Scots lad got called Chuff," said Lydia. "All the rest make sense."

"We're assuming that Alan Duncan wasn't keeping one or more of these colleagues' identities hidden from his parents by using nicknames," said Blessing.

"I hadn't given that a thought," said Alex.

"I think we should bear it in mind in the future," said Blessing. "Bob Duncan wasn't the only person to mention that Alan's underwater campaigns were top-secret. I believe it was Maddy who used the term hush-hush."

"Blessing's right to advise caution," said Gus, "Alan divulged little information about his naval career to anyone. Not to his family, his friends, or his work colleagues. Much like Maddy Telfer, he preferred to distance himself from his past. When we discover the reason for that, I hope we'll be closer to finding his killer."

"We've got interviews to schedule, guv," said Lydia. "How do we prioritise them?"

"I thought Blessing had done that for us already," said Alex, "but I suppose that's naïve. Bryan Tarbuck only appeared in one photo, the one taken in Cape Town. The others at the top of the list were Alan's best mates and could be shocked to learn of his murder ten years ago. Remember that Bob and Maddy didn't know this pocket diary was available to them to notify ex-colleagues of his death."

"Let me explain the photos underneath the main section," said Blessing. "Elizabeth Duncan allowed me to borrow these after I spoke with her this morning. Maybe Alan didn't send these to his parents. Perhaps he brought them home when he left the Navy, and Elizabeth discovered them one day when cleaning his old room. You can see that Keith Smith, Craig Anderson, and Freddie Watts appear to have gone on separate day trips with Alan. No helpful details are written on the backs, and the locations aren't immediately evident. You will recognise Alan Duncan in the photo taken in Moscow. Again, there's no sign of who took the picture. Perhaps it was one of the other three close friends, and the background in one of those snaps is a less popular part of Moscow. That leaves the last photograph."

"He's smartly dressed and in the mid to late twenties," said Gus. "What nationality would you say, Alex?"

"Our man looks European, guv, but how far East? I wouldn't hazard a guess. I reckon I know someone who could help, guv."

"Go on," said Gus, "we certainly need it."

"It will give you an extra gold star in the ACC's book," said Alex. "When I was working in the Hub on the Burnside saga, Divya, one of the techies at London Road, was a great help. So rather than tie up Blessing's time searching the metadata on these photographs, we should utilise the Hub's resources and get them doing the legwork. It could help fill in the gaps in our knowledge."

Gus recalled the ACC stressing the usefulness of the Hub to the Crime Review Team when he first approached him. But Gus preferred the traditional methods that had served him well in his career. He liked to think he wasn't too old to learn new tricks; it just took him longer than it used to, which meant he continued to do things his way. They might take longer, but he knew they worked.

"That's a great idea, Alex," said Gus. "Why don't you contact the Hub, speak to Divya to see if she's willing, and then ask her manager if we can utilise her skills on a quick project."

"Leave that with me, guv," said Alex. "Lydia can take you through her conversation with Anna Phillips while I'm doing that. Then, when you're free, I'll fill you in on her husband, Wayne."

"Fair enough," said Gus, "but before we move on, what does this second collection of photos suggest? I want to hear your opinion. Lydia?"

"Nice try, guv," said Lydia. "Before I started working with you, if I'd just read the murder file and these photos popped up, I'd wonder whether that local rag had a point and Alan Duncan was gay. We need to speak to Smudger, Andy, and Lofty to see whether they have a similar casual photo of Alan that they took simultaneously. Something to mark the occasion. We can ask about the nature of their relationship, but they can refuse to answer. It's none of our business. I won't pass an opinion until I've met the men involved or read their stories in the Freeman Files."

"What do you think, Blessing?" asked Gus.

"I'm with Lydia, guv," said Blessing. "We don't know when or where Alan and his pals took these snaps. We haven't even considered why. Lydia's right; until we get both sides of the story, we can't tell."

"That's the trouble, isn't it, guv?" asked Alex. "We're looking at a photograph that Alan Duncan valued enough to take and keep for years. I've got several similar photos at home. I have a photo of the guys I trained with on the motorcycle pursuit course with our bikes. I've kept a picture taken on the day I got discharged from the hospital, with the surgeon who operated on my legs and several nursing staff. You're questioning why Alan held onto photos of individuals. We're comfortable with the idea of his hanging onto the group images. As soon as everyone else goes away and it's one person, we join the dots. Would we have done that if the person in the photo was a young woman?"

The team mulled over Alex's words.

He picked up the phone and contacted the Hub.

"Maybe I'm overthinking things, guv," sighed Blessing. "Ever since you handed us the murder file, you've insisted that Maddy and Alan had secrets buried in their past. We have reviewed every scrap of evidence available to DCI Banks over a hundred times without producing a positive result. So, as these new pieces of information came through, I looked at them with suspicion."

"Why these men, and why that location?" said Gus.

"I even wondered if there was a significance to the nicknames and the position each man took in the photograph, guv," said Blessing. "I've watched too many spy movies."

"Your mind must have run riot when you found the loose photos this morning," laughed Lydia.

"I was creating scenarios that made sense of the

photographs, not sticking to the facts," said Blessing. "When I sit with Alex's computer expert to work through these images, no doubt the fog will clear, and I'll see them for what they are; simple snaps they took for fun. For example, two colleagues stopped for a second to create a memory on a rare day off. After all, they could have just spent ninety days trapped in a nuclear submarine under a polar ice-cap."

"Never stop thinking outside the box, Blessing," said Gus. "I've done it hundreds of times. If you can discard the more ridiculous notions before you convince yourself they're valid, you've got it made."

"Sorry, guv," said Blessing.

"Don't apologise," said Gus. "At least, not until Divya has exposed what lies beneath the surface of those photos."

"I see what you did there, guv," said Lydia.

"You've got a green light to join Divya in the Hub tomorrow morning, Blessing," said Alex. "She can make a start this afternoon. Send her the file with an outline of what you're looking for from her endeavours."

"Thanks, Alex," said Blessing. "I'll do it straight away. What's the parking like on London Road? I visited Reception in a taxi when I first arrived here. It's the only building I know."

"The main entrance is on your left when you drive from here," said Alex. "The Hub is in a new building to the left of the main block. Access is by a security card. Here's Divya's number. Call her when you've parked the car, and she'll come to let you in. So relax, don't worry about parking; you're fine."

Easy for you to say, thought Blessing. She could feel the tension building already. Tomorrow morning she was driving to an unfamiliar place and meeting new people. Blessing would be as nervous as her father.

Blessing accomplished the one thing she knew she was good at doing. The file was soon on its way to the Hub for Divya to analyse.

"Ready for me, guv," asked Lydia.

"Anna Phillips? Am I going to learn something new?"

"We did as you suggested, guv," said Lydia. "We arrived a few minutes before Wayne returned from the dentist. Anna wasn't keen on starting the interview without him. I suggested we go into the kitchen, leaving Alex to keep an eye out for her husband. Once I'd closed the door, I clarified that we would stay there until I was happy that she'd answered my questions satisfactorily. I stressed that anything she said to me wouldn't get shared with Wayne. Alex told Wayne the same thing when they talked. Anna wasn't thrilled, but to leave the kitchen, she had to get through me."

"I don't know where you two girls have picked up these strongarm tactics," said Gus. "Blessing threatened Bob Duncan, a senior citizen, with something similar this morning."

Lydia gave him one of her one-thousand-watt smiles and continued.

"Anna told me that her boss at the call centre had received a phone call in the autumn of '93 from a young girl desperate for a job. Anna was twenty at the time and hadn't met Wayne. The firm hadn't been open long, and there was barely enough work for their staff on the books."

"Was she already calling herself Maddy Mills?" asked Gus.

"Yes, guv," said Lydia. "I didn't tell Anna we knew her friend's actual name. I asked why they offered Maddy a job if things were that tight. She said her boss took pity on Maddy, and she didn't want to see her end up homeless, so she gambled that the firm's client list would improve."

"It must have done," said Gus, "both girls stayed there for years."

"Anna said she and Maddy got on well. They egged one another on to sign up more new clients. Their boss was pleased because they regularly performed up to twenty percent better than the other girls."

"If they got on well at work, did they socialise together?" asked Gus.

"Anna said Maddy was shy. Maddy drank and laughed with Anna's crowd, but she didn't get off with any of the lads. Several tried, but Maddy knocked them back. Anna said she got annoyed when someone she fancied got away a couple of times because of Maddy's reluctance to chat with his mate. That changed six months later when Wayne arrived on the scene."

"Didn't Wayne always live in Chippenham?" asked Gus.

"He moved there from Calne with his job, guv," said Lydia.

"Did that drive a wedge between Anna and Maddy?" asked Gus.

"They were still as thick as thieves at work, guv," said Lydia, "and they still socialised."

"When Wayne played five-a-side football, when he went cycling, and possibly while he played football on a Saturday afternoon," said Gus.

"There's no fooling you, guv," said Lydia. "Wayne cycled twice as much in the summers, but in the winter months, he played eleven-a-side football."

"Could Anna remember how Wayne met Alan Duncan?" asked Gus.

"Anna said the same as Bob Duncan, guv," said Lydia.

"Wayne was in Halford's one Saturday morning checking out yet another gadget for his racing bike, and they bumped into one another. Neither was keen on joining a local cycling club, but they agreed to cycle together at weekends after comparing their different level of ability. Anna stressed it was a fun way to exercise as far as both men were concerned, and having a companion was preferable to slogging it out on the roads on their own."

"Did they socialise on other occasions?" asked Gus.

"I don't think Alan was interested in football, guv," said Lydia. "No, the Saturday cycle ride was their only point of contact."

"So, they didn't meet as a foursome regularly?"

"That wasn't something either couple tried to pursue as far as I can tell, guv," said Lydia. "When Anna had the baby, it allowed Maddy to see her friend more often again. Alan and Maddy were her first choice as godparents. Wayne wasn't worried whether or not they had Joshua christened. He doesn't follow any religion. Maddy was happy to get asked. Because it wasn't likely to get arranged in a hurry, nobody appears to have asked Alan how he felt."

"I know I'm labouring the point, Lydia," said Gus, "but although these four connected through work, rest, and play, there was a distinct dividing line. Alan knew Maddy and Wayne; Maddy knew Anna and Alan."

"What does that mean, though, guv?" asked Lydia.

"It adds weight to the argument that Alan and Maddy didn't include many fresh faces in their life."

"The fewer contacts they had, the lower the risk their secrets came out," said Lydia. "It's something to consider."

"Did you run through the events leading up to the murder with Anna?" asked Gus.

"Anna told me Maddy visited her while Wayne and

Alan cycled the Saturday before Alan died. They chatted about Joseph and how things were going at the call centre, but nothing related to Alan. Maddy mentioned Alan tripping up the stairs after returning from his Wednesday night run. She thought it was funny. Then, after Wayne got home from the cycle ride on Saturday evening, he mentioned the incident at the pond in Biddestone. Anna told me she tuned his comments out because she didn't know the village well enough to know what Wayne was talking about."

"If I'm right, Anna and Alan weren't bosom buddies, so she wasn't interested."

"Right, guv," said Lydia. "The next Wednesday evening went as per the murder file. Maddy called at half-past nine. She wanted to ask Wayne if Alan had mentioned which route he was taking. Wayne offered to help in the search. The couple went to bed, hearing nothing further. The police called on the couple on Thursday evening. Anna told me they were both shocked to hear of Alan's death. She still considers Maddy her best friend to this day. Wayne lost a good cycling partner, and that hurt him."

"Maddy hadn't called Anna before then?" asked Gus.

"Anna said a DI Banks and a DS Tallentire called on them to make a statement. When she spoke to Maddy later that evening to send her condolences, she learned that the same detectives had been with Maddy and Alan's parents throughout the day."

"Final thoughts, Lydia?" asked Gus.

"Anna Phillips knows nothing of Maddy's past, guv. She had nothing to do with the murder, and neither did her husband. I can't see any point returning to Woodpecker Mews anytime soon."

"I agree," said Gus. "I could have saved you the cost of a new pair of shoes."

"Don't remind me. Do you want Alex to update you on Wayne Phillips now, guv?"

"Might as well get it out of the way."

Lydia returned to her desk, tapping Alex on the head as she passed.

"Lucky you," she grinned. "I reckon you'll get away with just the headlines."

Alex joined Gus and ran through his conversation with Wayne Phillips.

Gus listened intently but didn't hear a word that felt out of place or improve his opinion on who murdered Alan Duncan.

"Can we cross those two off our list now, guv?" asked Alex.

"Someone needs to go back to Woodpecker Mews first," said Gus.

"The latest photographs," said Alex, "of course. Wayne might recognise one submariner as the mystery man by the pond in Biddestone."

"We must take the same set of photographs to the Crown at Giddeahall," said Gus. "Maddy told Anna that Alan tripped as he was running upstairs when he got home on Wednesday before he died. Perhaps that was the first occasion when the mystery man showed his face. Maybe something spooked him. It's a stretch, but we've got to try anything at this stage,"

"Lydia and I could make those visits this evening if it helps, guv," said Alex.

"Good idea. Leave early," said Gus. "Visit the pub first, and then you'll reach Chippenham in time to catch Wayne before he goes to five-a-side football. That is, if he's still fit enough to run around. Did you ask whether he found a new cycling companion?"

"Wayne's a member of the local cycling club these days, guv," said Alex.

Gus glanced at the clock. There was no rush for him to get home tonight. Suzie was visiting her parents in Worton. Behind him, he heard the lift descend to the ground floor. Luke and Neil must be back.

It had already been a long day. Gus decided everyone deserved an early night.

"Welcome back, lads," said Gus. "How long does it take to update your files?"

"We won't get it done before five, guv," said Neil. "Not that we think we've brought back anything earth-shattering."

"Alex and Lydia are off to Chippenham in fifteen minutes. Blessing, you can gather the things you need for the morning in the Hub. We'll call it a day when Alex and Lydia leave. Tomorrow we'll start hunting those submariners, and let's hope one of them can put a name to the only unnamed man in that batch of photographs."

There were no complaints from the team. By a few minutes after half-past four, the office was empty.

Chapter Eight

"I DON'T THINK I've ever used this road before, Alex," said Lydia.

"It takes us to Corsham," said Alex. "I came this way with Gus when we did the tour of the village of Biddestone. We could use the same roads and lanes that Alan Duncan used to reach the Crown."

Lydia sat back and enjoyed the ride as Alex took them cross-country via Chapel Knapp and Gastard until they reached Corsham. Then, he threaded his way through town traffic towards Cross Keys and crossed the A4 London Road.

"I bet that road was busier before they built the M4 motorway," said Lydia.

"It was a major coaching route," said Alex. "Bath to London in two days. All that stopped in the middle of the nineteenth century when the railways took over. That was when Swindon stopped being a quiet market town. We might not have heard of it if Brunel had chosen a different route."

They were soon in the village of Biddestone, and Alex slowed as they passed the duck pond before turning onto Cuttle Lane.

"Maddy and Alan lived in that semi-detached house there," said Alex.

"How far is it to the Crown pub?" asked Lydia.

"A mile and a half," said Alex. "We'll stop in the car park behind the pub and have a nosey around before we go inside."

The car park only contained half a dozen vehicles. Five o'clock on a Wednesday evening marked a lull in trade for the pub that had stood beside the Chippenham to Bristol road for six hundred and fifty years.

Alex and Lydia strolled out onto Cuttle Lane to get their bearings.

"Duncan ran here from home," said Alex, "then he turned around and ran back past his house into the village. A quick circuit of the housing estate topped his mileage to six miles."

"Are you lost?"

Lydia turned towards the voice that had come from behind them. A tiny white-haired lady stood in the lane with a Jack Russell terrier straining at the leash.

"No, we're not lost," said Lydia. "Thank you for asking. Do you live close by?"

"My cottage is behind the hedge, dear. It's early for me to walk Nipper, but my sister's calling later."

"Have you lived in the village long?" Lydia asked.

"All my life, dear,"

Alex had kept his distance as Nipper seemed keen to live up to his name. He came closer when he heard the dog walker's reply.

"We're with Wiltshire Police," he said. "I'm DS Hardy."

"I'm Tilly Spiers," the lady replied. "It's ages since we saw police officers along this lane."

"Ten years ago, perhaps?" asked Lydia.

"I expect it would be, dear," said Tilly. "Time flies, doesn't it?"

"Did you know Alan Duncan, Mrs Spiers?" asked Alex. "He lived in a house further along the lane towards the village, just past the chapel."

"Oh, yes, dear, everyone remembers Mr Duncan. Officers in uniform, detectives, and Crime Scene Investigation vans were everywhere; it was an exciting time. My sister remembers when they used Castle Combe for a feature film. You couldn't move for theatrical types and tourists for months. Of course, this was different because it was a murder."

"Did you speak to the police at the time?" asked Alex.

"A young man dressed like yourself, not in uniform, called on me one afternoon."

"Was that a DS Tallentire?" asked Alex.

"Oh, I can't remember what he said his name was, dear. He was too young to be a detective, I thought. I usually walk my dog between half-past six and seven in the summer. I told the detective about the stranger."

"You had seen a stranger in the village, Mrs Spiers? When was this?" asked Alex.

"I left my cottage and walked the dog to the end of the road by the Crown. As I came back, I saw him sitting in the beer garden. The sun had been high in a cloudless sky since dawn. It was a scorcher, yet he didn't wear a hat or use the umbrellas they had sheltering the tables. Instead, he sat on a seat close to the wall and glanced along the lane as if he expected someone. I tried to place his face, but I couldn't. He wasn't a local."

"If I showed you several photographs," said Alex. "Do you think you could pick him out? What can you remember?"

Mrs Spiers looked across the lane into the field and thought for a while.

"He was seated, partly hidden by the wall," said Tilly. "I could only describe his head and shoulders to you confidently."

"That would be good enough," said Alex.

"His hair was cut short. I would guess he was around thirty-five years of age. He wore a white short-sleeved shirt, and I could see a tattoo high on his right arm, but I wasn't close enough to tell you what it said."

"The tattoo featured a word or words rather than pictures or symbols. Is that what you mean?" asked Lydia.

"Yes, dear," said Tilly. "It wasn't one of those complicated things they go for these days."

Alex took the profile photos that Blessing had produced and placed them in random order.

"Take your time, Mrs Spiers," he said. "Have a good long look at each photo and tell me if you recognise anyone."

Tilly Spiers studied the first submariner that Alex showed her. The old lady shook her head.

"Too old, dear," she said. Alex knew what to expect with the second photo.

"Not him," she said. "That stranger's hair was definitely not ginger."

Alex kept turning over photographs.

"That's Mr Duncan," cried Tilly Spiers. "That wasn't nice, DS Hardy. Alan was well-liked in the village. He always smiled when he ran by or cycled past with his friend."

"I'm sorry, Mrs Spiers. Just one more to look at."

"That's him," said Tilly. "As sure as I'm standing here. He's a few years younger in that picture, but that's the man who sat in the beer garden that evening."

Alex showed Lydia the photo, but she already knew it was the only one they hadn't identified.

"Did you see Alan Duncan later that evening?" asked Alex.

"He passed me as I reached the gateway into the cricket ground," said Tilly. "I used to let my previous dog have a good run there. She wasn't as boisterous as Nipper. Several minutes later, I saw Mr Duncan along the lane opposite his front door when I left the field to cross the road. He was running into the village as usual. I almost forgot to look right and left. A car drove past, and I had to step back into the gateway, dragging my dog with me."

"Did you see the driver?" asked Lydia.

"He passed me before I could catch my breath," said Tilly. "I saw the car earlier, though, in the pub car park. Close to where you parked when you arrived."

"Any idea of the make or model, Mrs Spiers?" asked Alex.

"I don't drive, dear," said Tilly. "My sister's got a Vauxhall. The stranger's car was a similar shape. That's all I can say."

Alex asked Tilly for a phone number in case they needed to get in touch again.

"You've been a big help, Mrs Spiers," he said. "I think it's time Nipper had his run."

"Whatever you say, dear. Where are you off to now?"

"We'll try the landlord of the Crown next," said Alex.

Tilly Spiers wrinkled her nose.

"He hasn't been there long, dear. A different company

runs it these days. It changes hands often. They don't get the passing trade they used to in the old days. Its most popular period was forty years ago. They encouraged a certain type of person back then. The place had a rather unsavoury name. But, of course, in this modern world we live in, we live and let live, don't we?"

Alex made a mental note to ask Neil Davis what Mrs Spier meant. His colleague knew the local dirt about a wide area of the county.

"Didn't you want to speak to Mrs Huggins, DS Hardy?" asked Tilly. Nipper knew where she was taking him next and was pulling her arm out of its socket.

"Mrs Huggins?"

"The caretaker for the Wesleyan Chapel. She lives next door. Val saw that car. I remember Val telling me she spoke to the older detective about it ten years ago."

"We'll pay her a visit on our way back into the village," said Alex.

Alex and Lydia headed back up the lane to the Crown.

"I didn't think we were ever going to get away," said Lydia.

"We learned something useful," said Alex. "Alan Duncan knew that man. Our return trip to Woodpecker Mews should be the clincher."

They spent less than ten minutes in the Crown. As Tilly Spiers had suggested, the landlord didn't have a clue. Alex asked whether any regulars were in who could have been in the Crown that Wednesday evening. The Portuguese landlord shrugged and said his clientele preferred fine wine and gourmet food rather than pints of cider and a burger and chips. So the first thing he'd done when he took the pub over was to encourage the locals to drink elsewhere.

Alex and Lydia returned to the car park.

"You didn't ask him about the old days that Tilly mentioned," said Lydia.

"I'd seen enough," said Alex. "Did you see the prices of their main course?"

"If you want the best, you have to pay for it," said Lydia.

Alex drove them along the lane, keeping a weather-eye open for Nipper jumping out from a gateway, but they reached the chapel unscathed.

Lydia knocked on the wooden door of the cottage next door. There was no knocker or bell.

"Are you the police officers?" said the plump, bespectacled lady who opened the door.

Lydia could tell that Mrs Spiers had popped in to warn Mrs Huggins that they were on their way. Alex reckoned that Tilly and Val attended the primary school in the village together shortly after WWII.

"We are, Mrs Huggins," said Alex. "I'm DS Hardy, and my colleague is Lydia Logan Barre."

"Tilly said you were after that car I saw," said Val Huggins, joining them outside on the front path. "I told Mr Banks at the time that I saw a Vauxhall Zafira several times a week in the weeks before poor Mr Duncan's murder."

"Was this in the village or just on Cuttle Lane?" asked Alex.

"It drove up and down this lane," said Val Huggins, waving her tea towel to demonstrate. "You didn't get many people using the lanes. You needed to be a local to know they were there. But, of course, more people have driven on them in the past couple of years since they started that satnav nonsense. When my Vic was alive, we never had cars using the lanes as a rat-run to reach the A420."

"If I showed you a photograph, would you recognise the driver?" asked Alex.

"It was a long time ago," said Val Huggins. "Go on; I'll give it a go."

Alex showed her the photo of Drew Taggart. She shook her head slowly.

"Don't think that was him," she said. "He had a different look. I'd better be careful what I say, but there's a place near the roundabout on Bath Road as you enter Chippenham. One of those car hand wash places where half a dozen lads jump on your car as soon as it comes to a halt."

"We know what you mean, Mrs Huggins," said Alex. "What about this chap?"

"That's the right look," said Val. "I couldn't swear to it in court, it was so long ago, but that could well be the driver. Was he something to do with what happened to Mr Duncan?"

"We don't know, Mrs Huggins," said Alex. "If we could identify and find him, we'd like to talk to him."

"Do you still get joggers on the lane, Mrs Huggins," said Lydia.

"The younger element loves that health kick stuff, don't they? My Vic played football in the winter and cricket in the summer. Add that to forty hours a week on shifts at Westinghouse in Chippenham, and he didn't have time or energy for much more exercise. What time is it?"

Alex realised it was much later than they had hoped.

"You'll catch Greg if you drive into the village later," said Val Huggins. "He used to run faster ten years ago, but Greg was running before Mr Duncan moved into the village."

"Does he live on Cuttle Lane, Mrs Huggins?" asked Lydia.

"No, Greg lives opposite the bus stop by the duck pond at number eighteen. You can't miss it."

Alex drove them into the village.

"Let's hope he's in," he moaned. "We'll miss Wayne Phillips at this rate, and I'm getting hungry."

A bald man in his late sixties opened the door to number eighteen.

"Greg?" asked Alex.

"Greg Meakin, that's me. What's this about?"

Alex explained who they were and why they had called on him.

"I saw Alan most Wednesday evenings," said Greg. "The police interviewed me at the time. I was running on Challows Lane when he passed me. Alan was alive and well at six-thirty eight, or thereabouts."

"Did you ever speak to one another?" asked Lydia.

"Nodded at one another," said Greg. "Alan wasn't much of a conversationalist."

Unlike Tilly Spiers and Val Huggins, thought Alex.

"Did the police ask whether you saw anyone else?" asked Lydia.

"What, someone running with Alan or after him, d'you mean? No, I saw no one else pounding the pavements that night. Alan was a loner. When he first moved into the village, I asked if he fancied company on his runs. He wasn't interested."

"Was there much traffic at that time?" asked Alex.

"One or two cars, I suppose," said Greg.

"You don't recall seeing anything or anyone unusual?"

Greg shook his head.

"Can't help you with that one, I'm afraid."

"Never mind, Mr Meakin," said Alex. "Thanks for your time."

Alex and Lydia walked away.

"Someone or something unusual," said Greg Meakin. "I can't remember anything that night, but I spotted an unfamiliar car over the road at the weekend. A bloke parked on the other side of the pond for four hours in the afternoon. Never saw the car before or since."

"When you say the weekend," said Alex, "you mean four days before Alan Duncan died."

"It must have been," said Greg. "I couldn't make the bloke out. He just sat in his car for hours on end and never moved. I went for a run later in the day, and he had gone when I got back."

"Did you see him outside the car at any point?" asked Alex.

"No," said Greg. Lydia sensed he was nervous.

"I noticed your Velux roof window, Mr Meakin. Do you have another hobby apart from jogging?"

"Astronomy," said Greg. "I have a telescope in the bedroom upstairs. I don't make a habit of using it for anything else. But that day, I ran upstairs to take a closer look. He drove a Vauxhall Zafira, and I got a good look at him through the windscreen."

Alex showed Greg Meakin three photos.

"Anyone you recognise here?" he asked.

Greg Meakin pointed at the mystery man.

"That's the feller," he said.

"Many thanks, Mr Meakin," said Alex, "we'll let you get on. Will you go for a run later?"

"Not tonight," said Greg. "I damaged my left ankle at the weekend."

"Bad luck," said Lydia.

"Not really," said Greg. "At my age, I should know better than to climb ladders to clean my windows."

Alex and Lydia returned to the car and left the picturesque village of Biddestone behind them.

"Meakin can't be short of money, Alex," said Lydia. "He owns a cottage in a prime spot, has a new car parked outside, and those high-powered telescopes don't come cheap. Why doesn't he pay for a window cleaner?"

"He seemed nervous, admitting that he used that telescope to check out our mystery man. It makes you wonder what else he can see from that window. I don't think Gus will want us to worry about that. Meakin had nothing to do with Duncan's murder."

"Funny, how things turn out, isn't it?" said Alex. "We're on our way to ask Wayne Phillips if he can identify someone from a handful of photos. That's redundant now. When we left the office, I thought the Crown would be our only chance of finding an eyewitness. Inside forty-five minutes, three villagers came out of the woodwork with useful information."

"To be fair to Banks and Tallentire," said Lydia, "they spoke to Tilly Spiers and Val Huggins. The murder file mentioned a woman who saw the Zafira several times in the weeks before the murder. A jogger confirmed Duncan was alive at around twenty to seven. As for the mystery man, the best description the police received was from Wayne Phillips. That was so bland that it could fit anyone."

"I hope Wayne Phillips is still home when we get there," said Alex. "It's twenty past six already."

Alex stopped outside the house on Woodpecker Mews for the second time that day

Wayne Phillips appeared in the doorway with a sports bag in his hand.

"Don't tell me you want to talk to me again," he groaned. "Can't Anna help you?"

"We'll only detain you for a minute, Mr Phillips," said Alex. "We have several photographs for you to view. Recognise anyone?"

Wayne dropped his sports bag on the driveway and looked over Alex's shoulder.

"That guy three from the end on the right," said Wayne. "He's the man who waved at Alan from the other side of the pond. No doubts. Who is he?"

"Not a clue," said Alex. "But you're the fourth person in the last hour to confirm they saw him in Biddestone in the weeks leading up to your friend's murder."

"Alan knew that bloke," said Wayne. "Why he denied it, I don't know."

"Did Alan ever talk about his career in the Navy?" Lydia asked.

"I told your colleague this morning that Alan loved the life but had had enough," said Wayne looking at his watch. "Don't you two talk to one another?"

"Things can move quickly in a case like this," said Alex. "We debriefed this morning's meetings with our boss, but there's been no time to update one another on the detail we got from you and Anna."

Lydia didn't quit. The five-a-side football could wait.

"Did Alan ever mention any of the places he visited when he was on leave?"

"I took Anna to Paris for a romantic weekend a year or two after I first met Alan. We visited the Eiffel Tower. Alan said he'd been to Paris with his mates, but they visited Longchamp to watch the Prix de L'Arc de Triomphe. Wherever we went, Alan could always go one better. He'd visited the Pyramids, Sydney Harbour, and Cape Town. You name it. Well, that's what the adverts said. Join the Navy to see the world."

"Did he never mention any of the mates he went with on these trips?" asked Lydia.

"Never," said Wayne. "Can I go now? It would pay you to put a name to that bloke in the photograph rather than waste your time pestering me. It strikes me he's your killer. He's had a ten-year head start."

Wayne Phillips grabbed his sports bag and threw it in the back of his car. Alex and Lydia stood by their car, watching him reverse off the driveway and speed away.

"He wasn't happy, was he?" said Alex.

"And he was breaking the speed limit," said Lydia.

"Let's get home, freshen up, and go out for something to eat. I've had enough for today."

IN URCHFONT, Gus had spent an hour at the allotment after driving home from the office. It was an excellent spot to sit and run through the day's events.

Gus hoped Alex and Lydia continued to make progress in Biddestone and Chippenham. He was confident that Blessing would offer more possibilities with the Hub's help in the morning.

Although he couldn't see a clear path to the killer, today's events raised his hopes of success.

"Evening, Mr Freeman," said Bert Penman. "It won't get done if you sit and look at it."

"Ah, Bert, good to see you," said Gus. "No, gardening and detecting follow a similar path. I've sat here, mulling over our latest case. Perhaps I need to stop thinking and do something. If only I knew what."

"I'm sure you'll find the right course of action, Mr Freeman," said Bert. "Where's Miss Ferris this evening?"

"Suzie wanted to visit her parents," said Gus. "I'm sure she'll be home if I wander up the lane in a few minutes."

"A fine young woman is Miss Ferris," said Bert.

"You'll get no arguments from me on that score, Bert," said Gus. "I don't suppose you've heard how Brett's first day went?"

"Not yet," said Bert, "He promised to ring me later. I suppose I'll see him at the weekend."

"What's the Reverend up to this evening? Will she join you in the Lamb later?"

"When Brett ran me home from the pub the other evening, he mentioned a trip to the cinema," said Bert.

"Brett and the Reverend? I'm pleased to hear it," said Gus. He made a note to tell Suzie that the budding romance hadn't crashed and burned.

"It's just as well. Irene has got no plans to go somewhere different," said Bert. "I could garden here on my own six months from now."

"I don't plan to move, Bert," said Gus. "I'll keep you company."

Bert shook his head.

"I'll lift a few potatoes and see what I can harvest for the weekend, Mr Freeman. Time to get off home for you, I reckon."

Gus left Bert grumbling in the background and returned to the bungalow.

Suzie was home.

"How were John and Jackie," said Gus.

"You had better come in and sit down," said Suzie.

Gus went into the lounge. Suzie was sitting on the settee with a box of tissues in her lap.

"What is it?" asked Gus. "Is it bad news?"

Suzie patted the seat beside her. Gus sat.

"Is it one of your horses, darling?"

"No, it's nothing like that," said Suzie. "I didn't go to see Mum and Dad this evening. I needed to confirm something. Since I was eighteen, I've used the birth control pill, so things don't always run like clockwork. I panicked the first time I missed a period, but it happened on odd occasions. I dismiss it as another hiccup and carry on. This time, things felt different. Tonight, I learned why. I'm around six weeks pregnant; I'm sorry, Gus."

"I wouldn't have thought it was a crying matter," said Gus wrapping his arms around her. "No method of contraception is foolproof, except celibacy, and that was never an option. What happened?"

"It wasn't deliberate," said Suzie. "You have to believe that. I learned this evening that the oral contraceptive has a failure rate of four percent. I'm certain I didn't forget to take one. It was just bad luck."

"There you go again," said Gus. "Why is it *bad* luck?"

"I don't know whether I'm ready to be a mother," said Suzie. "I asked you a fortnight ago whether you and Tess had wanted children. You can't possibly want one now."

"I want whatever you want, Suzie," said Gus kissing her on top of her head. He heard another tissue leave the box. "I love you. Nothing's going to alter that. I'll support your decision, whatever you decide."

"Why are you so understanding?"

"I don't know any other way to be, Suzie. This is as new to me as to you. It's exciting and frightening at the same time."

"I need time to think, Gus," said Suzie.

"Take all the time you need, darling," said Gus.

Thursday, 2 August 2018

GUS LEFT the bungalow at eight-twenty and drove to the Old Police Station office.

He had to get his head straight and concentrate on the Duncan case. When he arrived in the car park, he remembered Blessing was going from Worton to London Road. The others hadn't arrived yet, so he had the place to himself when he got upstairs.

Alex and Lydia arrived five minutes later. Alex gave Gus a summary of what had happened yesterday evening. At one minute to nine, Luke Sherman and Neil Davis exited the lift. Neil seemed pleased with himself.

"I can't wait to tell you the news," said Neil. "Melody's expecting. We waited until the twelve-week scan to get confirmation that everything was progressing as it should. The doctor told her last night that there was no reason to worry about a recurrence of our previous problems. Mother and baby are healthy."

"That's splendid news, Neil," said Lydia. "Give Melody our love. It is good news, isn't it, guv?"

"I told Gus when we were on the nature reserve two weeks ago that we were waiting until we were sure," said Neil. "It hasn't come as a surprise."

"When will you let Blessing know?" asked Luke.

"Blimey," said Neil. "She'll think I deliberately kept her out of the loop. I'll call her at London Road in a while."

"Back to business," said Gus. "Neil, you and Luke must update the Freeman files with what you learned from those meetings in Corsham and Chippenham yesterday. Alex and Lydia have some tidying up on yesterday evening's matters.

Can you give Luke and Neil the gist of what you told me earlier?"

"Yes, guv," said Alex. "We're no closer to identifying the Eastern European gentleman in the photograph that Blessing brought from the Duncan home. However, Wayne Phillips and two village folk are positive he's the man who stalked Alan Duncan in the weeks before he died. Tilly Spiers, a dog walker, placed him at the Crown on Wednesday, the twenty-first of May, 2008. Wayne Phillips and Greg Meakin saw him by the duck pond on Saturday the twenty-fourth. Greg was the jogger who told DI Banks that Duncan ran past him at twenty to seven on Wednesday the twenty-eighth. One more witness, Val Huggins, saw the Zafira on Cuttle Lane frequently, and that photograph was the only one that resembled the driver."

"What's our next move, guv?" asked Alex.

"Is there anyone we haven't spoken to that could add to our knowledge?" asked Gus.

"Connor Tallentire, guv," said Luke.

"Lady Davinia, guv," said Neil.

"I'd better handle her," said Gus. "Perhaps you could make the arrangements and accompany me, Luke."

"No problem, guv," said Luke.

Gus headed for the restroom. Alex remembered something from yesterday evening.

"What do you know about the Crown, Neil?" asked Alex.

"Now, or in the dim and distant past, Alex?"

"Way back, in the Seventies," said Alex.

"My Dad never drank there," said Neil. "He spent most of his time in pubs in Devizes and Swindon. Why do you ask?"

"Our dog walker hinted that the place had an unsavoury reputation," said Alex.

"Times have changed, Alex," said Neil. "A pub like that, in the middle of nowhere, on the main road, was probably a haunt for people looking for a certain type of company."

"That explains a lot," said Alex. "Gus always queried why the local rag hinted that Alan Duncan was gay. The less-enlightened older locals put two and two together and made five when Alan chose that running route. It was rubbish, but why let that spoil a salacious story?"

Gus had returned to his desk with a black coffee.

"We can leave as soon as you finish your cuppa, guv," said Luke. "Mrs Campbell-Drake granted us an audience at High Grove Farm."

"A tad pretentious," said Gus. "Does the Prince of Wales know?"

"I don't think milady will be too fussed, guv," said Neil. "A farmhouse has stood on the site for over four centuries."

"I'd better wear a jacket," said Gus. "I've got a tie in my glove compartment too."

"You look smart enough already, guv," said Lydia.

"I wasn't thinking about how I looked, Lydia. I bet an ancient building like that will be cold even in August. Farmers would have you believe they spend twenty hours a day outdoors. So why bother with installing central heating?"

Gus and Luke headed for the lift.

"Did you grab a copy of those photos, Luke?" asked Gus.

"Yes, guv," asked Luke. "Shall we take my car?"

"Daft question, Luke," said Gus.

Chapter Nine

"I ASKED Alex for the most convenient route to Biddestone, guv," said Luke. "It should take around twenty minutes to reach the village centre. I'm not sure where the farm is, though. Did you visit Slaughterford Road?"

"It's one of several that branch off from The Green in the middle of the village, Luke. It won't add five minutes to the trip. Are you worried we'll miss our slot?"

"She sounded brusque on the phone. I understand why the officer who took the original 999 call was flustered."

Luke found Slaughterford Road without incident and followed the meandering road until he saw High Grove Farm's sign. He drove into the farmyard and parked beside the main building. The farmhouse had a thatched roof, tiny windows, and wisteria blossom remains adorning three-quarters of the building's front. Everything looked to have been there for the entire four hundred years.

The front door wouldn't have looked out of place as the entrance to a castle. The dark-stained, formidable oak barrier was covered with metal studs and looked impenetrable. Cold callers, beware.

"You couldn't buy a door like that at B&Q," said Gus.

Gus heard the clip-clop of the horse's hooves behind him as he stepped from the car.

"I'll be with you in ten minutes. Alice will look after you until then."

The horse rider wheeled away, coming no closer and trotted to the far side of the yard. Gus presumed the large building on that side was the stables. He wondered how many horses one family needed.

Luke pointed to a wrought-iron attachment to the side of the door.

"Is that what they call a butler bell-pull, guv?" he asked.

"No good asking me, Luke," said Gus. "I've never had a butler. Especially not one called Alice."

Luke rang the bell.

Gus smiled at the comforting sound of a bolt getting drawn back and a well-oiled key turning in the lock. He was glad they were visiting this remote farmhouse in broad daylight. At night, in the depths of winter, that sound would evoke memories of every Hammer horror movie he'd ever watched.

The door opened, and Alice stepped forward into the sunlight.

"You rang?"

Gus resisted the temptation to ask whether Vincent Price was at home.

Alice qualified as an elderly retainer. Diminutive in stature, she had probably been living here since Davinia Campbell-Drake's husband was a child.

"We did," he replied. "Your employer told us you would

look after us while she stabled her horse. We're the police officers she's expecting."

"Follow me, please."

Alice was a lady of few words, it seemed. Luke and Gus followed her indoors.

The contrast between the bright sunlight outside and the low-ceilinged, dark interior caused Luke to stumble on the flagstone floor.

"Pick your feet up," said Alice. "You get used to it."

Gus hoped they were heading for a conservatory, or an orangery, at the rear of the house that offered light and warmth. A chill ran down his spine as a pair of brown eyes pierced the gloom. As he ducked his head to leave the hallway, Gus realised that one of Davinia's ancestors had employed a taxidermist on a fox's head and mounted it over the doorway.

They were in luck. Alice had brought them through to a sunny verandah that ran the width of the main building.

"I'll bring coffee," said Alice.

"Black without for me," said Gus.

"I'll bring coffee," repeated Alice, "with everything you'll need to suit your particular taste."

That's me put in my place, thought Gus. Luke was grinning at him over the top of Alice's head.

"It's as if the place is frozen in time, guv," said Luke when they were alone. "Can the whole farm be like this? How do they operate at a profit?"

Alice returned in less than a minute with a tray. Gus was disappointed she hadn't used the silver version. He had to accept that a copper tray was good enough for the lower classes.

Gus couldn't fault the tray's contents. Alice had even remembered the biscuits.

Gus heard boots on the stone floor outside the sunroom as he finished his second custard cream. It was the measured step of someone who wasn't in a hurry to reach them, despite having already delayed their meeting by ten minutes.

The door opened, and in swept the lady of the house. Davinia Campbell-Drake wasn't what Gus had expected. Nobody had described the farmer's wife to him. He had conjured an image in his head based on the report of her phone call to the police.

It showed once more that he shouldn't jump to conclusions. Davinia was tall and elegant, with a mane of blonde hair cascading over her shoulders. Gus reckoned she was in her mid-fifties, although the top-brand jacket, jodhpurs and boots helped to knock ten years off that, if not more. Davinia Campbell-Drake could pass for Suzie's elder sister.

Davinia sat on the opposite side of the room and poured herself a coffee.

"Call me Bunny," she said. "Everyone does. It made life easier when Mummy was alive. Mummy was Lavinia. Don't stand on ceremony; dig into the biscuits. I won't be joining you."

"I don't need to remind you why we're here, ma'am," said Gus.

Somehow, he couldn't bring himself to call her Bunny, and the meeting would stretch until lunchtime if he kept using her full name.

"You're taking another look into that dreadful business up at Fifty-Acre field," said Bunny.

"We are," said Gus, "and we'd appreciate it if you would describe the events of that evening."

"I ride out at various times of the day," said Bunny. "Ten years ago, I exercised our string of horses more often than I do today. We stable horses here for the hunt and for owners that send horses to point-to-point meetings, that sort of thing. It's a living in one sense, but retaining a way of life is important. I doubt you would understand. Sorry, I've forgotten your name."

"Freeman," said Gus, "my colleague is DS Sherman. Gus and Luke, to our friends. Which is the nearest Hunt to you?"

"People who ride with the Beaufort are our main source of income," said Bunny.

"Was a Wednesday evening ride a regular thing for you?" asked Luke.

"In the summer months, I rode at least four nights a week, so Wednesday was no different. I left here at six and used the fields and tracks to reach Challows Lane. Then I planned to stay on Ham Lane until By Brook. A combination of the Weavern Lane and more of our fields would have got me home by eight."

"Did you see any strangers around the farm in the weeks before the murder?" asked Gus.

"I would have reported them to the police if I had," said Bunny. "The animals in our charge can be valuable, of course, but they are worth more than money to their owners. Horse thieves are the scum of the earth. We've always had to watch any of our larger equipment closely. We've got security lights and CCTV for the main house and the yard. Foxes might get to the stables or the barn where we park our horseboxes, Land Rovers and quad bikes, but human vermin shouldn't get within one hundred paces."

"Did you see anyone after you set out from here that night?" asked Luke.

"Two dog-walkers from the village. Both of whom I've known for decades. They have permission to enter our fields. Other than that, I can't recall anyone except Mr Meakin. One tends to forget him. Meakin was forever running up and down the lanes."

"What about Alan Duncan?" asked Gus. "He ran every Wednesday evening during the four years he lived in the village. Surely, you must have noticed him?"

"I didn't know the man," said Bunny. "Four years in a village is but a blink of an eye. Someone told me later that Duncan had several routes he took for his weekly run. I might have seen him on Ham Lane once or twice, but I wouldn't have recognised him."

"What drew your attention to the body?" asked Gus.

"Let me correct you," said Bunny. "I did not know it was a body. I don't fall asleep in the saddle or stare at the tarmac; I keep my eyes peeled. To check the state of our fields as I ride, ensuring there are no open gates, broken fences, or unwanted litter. Townsfolk are prone to drive into our beautiful countryside to dump a piece of furniture or a freezer at any time of the day or night. As I passed the Fifty Acre field, I spotted something that shouldn't have been there. I grabbed my mobile phone from my jacket pocket and dialled 999. You must have that detail recorded somewhere."

"We do," said Gus. "The call came in at seven fifty-three. The desk sergeant sent two uniformed officers to the scene, and they arrived at around eight-fifteen."

"Well, there you are then," said Bunny Campbell-Drake. "Was there something else? I have a business to run."

"Not so fast, Bunny," said Gus. "You confirmed that you saw Greg Meakin that evening. Greg's important because he passed Mr Duncan and can verify Alan was still alive at twenty to seven. If you rode through the lanes and tracks from this farmhouse to Challows Lane and saw Mr Meakin, then you too were on Challows Lane well before seven o'clock. We've visited the Fifty Acre field and By Brook. So we know you could trot on horseback from the duck pond in the village's centre to the end of Ham Lane in twenty minutes. We believe that Alan Duncan died in that field between seven and seven-thirty. If you are telling us the truth about your route, you either saw the murder or were the killer. What do you have to say to that?"

"You can't possibly believe I killed that man," said Bunny.

"What I believe is solely influenced by the facts, nothing else," said Gus. "Until this evening, I didn't have a suspect that I could place in the field where the murder took place at the right time. You told us earlier that you never saw a stranger in the weeks leading up to the murder. We've been searching for a car and its driver who were seen on many occasions by villagers. We have sightings at the duck pond, out at Giddeahall, and on Cuttle Lane."

"I didn't kill Mr Duncan," said Bunny. "You must believe me."

"Did you leave this farm at six on the evening on the twenty-eighth of May, ma'am,"

"Yes,"

"Did you ride through the fields and on the tracks you described until you reached Challows Lane?"

"Yes,"

"Did you see Greg Meakin as he ran along Challows Lane towards The Green?"

"Yes,"

"Did you see Alan Duncan when you joined Challows Lane?"

"I didn't know who it was, but there was a person one hundred yards ahead of me."

"What were they wearing?"

"A dark singlet and shorts, navy blue, and orange trainers.

"What did you do next?"

"I stopped to let my horse rest for a while."

"Could you see the road junction from where you stopped?"

"To The Butts, d'you mean? Yes, I could."

"Did any cars pass you, or did you see anyone take the alternative road."

"I heard a car when I first stopped riding and dismounted. The driver must have taken a wrong turn, stopped, reversed, and followed The Butts road."

"This was around a quarter to seven, am I right?"

"About that, yes,"

"Did you see the make or model?"

"A Vauxhall, perhaps, but I couldn't be certain."

"When did you remount and ride on?"

"At ten to seven,"

"What did you see when you reached Fifty Acre field?" asked Gus. "The truth, please."

"Two men in the gateway, arguing. One was Mr Duncan. I didn't recognise the other man."

"What was the argument about; could you hear?"

"Worthless," said Bunny. "That was the only word I could make out. It was none of my business as long as they stayed off our land, so I rode past them and around the bend as quickly as I dared. That's when I saw the car. That was a Vauxhall too. Whether it was the same car, I don't know. The driver's door was open, and the motor was still running. It appeared to be a road rage incident where Mr

Duncan had strayed into the middle of the lane, nearly causing an accident. After reaching By Brook, I followed the lane for a while and cut through the trees and fields. I wasn't in Ham Lane when I saw the body. I was crossing the fields to bring me back to Slaughterford Road when I glanced to my right. It was Mr Duncan. I could see the orange trainers even from that distance. The other man had disappeared."

"Time?" asked Gus.

"Half-past seven."

"Carry on."

"I made my way onto the lane that leads to Slaughterford Road. As I rode into the farmyard, I heard a car. It was that Vauxhall driver. He must have driven to By Brook and taken the lane towards the White Hart at Ford. It's the only way he could have reached High Grove Farm from that direction. He slowed by the gateway and then sped off towards the village. I never saw him again."

"What did you do between then and seven fifty-three?"

"Wrestled with my conscience," said Bunny. "I had to tell someone what had happened, but I couldn't say how much I'd seen. So, I left it and then told the officer that someone had dumped rubbish in our field. That driver frightened me. I can see his face now, a sickly smile, and then he tapped his nose before driving away. As if to remind me, he knew where I lived."

"Is the man you saw arguing with Mr Duncan among these photos, ma'am?" asked Luke.

He showed Bunny an array of submariners plus the mystery man.

Bunny pointed out the same man as Greg Meakin and the others.

"That's him. Who is he?"

"We don't know yet," said Gus. "Our colleagues should

have had this information ten years ago, Mrs Campbell-Drake. I'm afraid this isn't the last you'll hear of this matter."

Gus and Luke left Bunny in the sunroom. Gus saw Alice appear out of the darkness as he closed the door.

"Lovely coffee, Alice. Thank you," said Gus.

Luke looked back when they reached the front door. Alice hadn't moved.

"You've upset her," she said.

"Your mistress might appreciate seeing a friendly face," said Gus.

"Where will I find one at such short notice?" said Alice.

Gus sat beside Luke and waited for him to drive them back to the office.

"What just happened?" asked Luke, sitting with his hands on the steering wheel.

"Three steps forward, two steps back, as usual," said Gus. "Lady Muck will have to face a charge. We can't let people decide how involved they wish to be in a murder enquiry. What that woman saw didn't change the time of death, but Banks would have had a decent description of the killer before the autopsy. Because someone whispered suicide in his ear early doors, he didn't pull the stops out until the autopsy revealed that Duncan died of strangulation."

"Banks and Tallentire didn't grill her in the way you did, guv," said Luke.

"Hang on," said Gus. "The times she stated in 2008 didn't gel with what she said this morning. I thought that something else had occupied her for an hour. Perhaps, a liaison kept her out of Ham Lane and Fifty Acre field until five to eight. Oh, Mr Meakin, what a large telescope you've got. These posh types often fancy a bit of rough from time to time. The last thing I expected was for her to admit that she'd seen the killer arguing with our victim."

"What did you make of the word that Bunny said she overheard, guv?"

"Worthless? The killer could have been commenting on Alan Duncan as a person or friend. We know they met when Duncan was on shore leave. Perhaps, Duncan sold the guy something that was supposed to be valuable, but it turned out to be a fake or a cheap knock-off. We must dig deeper, Luke. Let's get back to base. Why, what do you think?"

Luke started the car.

"From everything we know of Alan Duncan, I can't see anyone who would believe he'd get involved in anything shady, do you? He was Mr Dependable, one of the good guys. Neil and I spoke to several people at the factory yesterday. Duncan was a stickler for getting the job right. The company's clients knew they could rely on him to ensure the products they ordered met their specifications. The boss had a dozen pieces of correspondence he'd received after the news broke that showed how valuable Duncan was to the business."

"Whatever secret Duncan was hiding, he buried it deep," said Gus.

BLESSING UMEH HAD LEFT the Ferris's farm in Worton a few minutes early. The drive into Devizes and out to London Road was shorter than her daily drive to the Old Police Station office, but you could never rely on things being as you remembered them. Her father had drummed that into her often enough. Blessing didn't want to be late.

She turned into the London Road HQ and found the

Hub building exactly where her colleagues assured her it would be yesterday afternoon. After she took care parking in one of the many vacant bays, Blessing checked that she had everything she needed. It was still only a quarter to nine. Should she ring Divya to come to the main door? What if she wasn't in yet?

An Indian girl walked past her Nissan Micra and looked back. Was that Divya? Blessing waved a hand. The girl stepped back towards her.

"You must be Blessing Umeh," said Divya.

"Is it that obvious?" asked Blessing.

"Alex told me you were likely to be early. Come on. I'll show you around before the others pile in at nine o'clock."

Once they were inside the Hub offices, Blessing could see what Alex meant. The equipment was state-of-the-art and a priceless asset to the force. The pictures on the walls featured well-known beauty spots and historical interest places within the county boundaries.

"Have you worked here long, Divya?" asked Blessing.

"Ever since it opened," she replied. "I used to work at a computer bureau near Tottenham Court Road, but it proved too expensive to live in London. When an opportunity to get out came up, it was no contest. My husband and I moved to Marlborough. He's a junior doctor at the Great Western Hospital in Swindon. We have the same commute, twenty-five minutes. A quarter of the time it took in the city."

"I lived in Claverdon, a village five miles from Warwick," said Blessing. "I joined the police in 2015 and worked at Royal Leamington Spa. My team worked on a case that brought them to the Midlands in June. The next thing I knew, DS Mercer offered me a job. It was so lucky. My father got offered a new post at Bath University. My parents wanted to accept, but they were concerned about me living alone in Warwick or Leamington. Now they live just outside Bath, and I've got digs at a farm near Worton."

"So, you've only been in the county for a month? Have you made any new friends?"

Blessing laughed.

"My little car broke down when I moved here. A tall, handsome police officer from Malmesbury called Dave stopped to help. We've seen one another a handful of times. It's early days, but we get on well."

"They're a friendly bunch in Wiltshire," said Divya. "I've never felt threatened, not as I did in London. You couldn't move for people in the city. Out here in the countryside, you've got room to breathe. It must be great living on a farm."

"It can be quiet," said Blessing. "The work I do with the Crime Review Team keeps my mind occupied throughout the day. My oasis of calm in the orchard behind the farmhouse is the perfect spot to unwind."

The room soon filled with Divya's fellow computer geeks, and Blessing realised they weren't all as normal as her new companion. Several were eccentric, both in dress and behaviour. The room fell quiet again after several minutes.

"It's always like that," said Divya, "a mad five minutes, and then everyone gets switched onto their screens. The list of search routines never seems to get any smaller. Talking of which, shall we see what we can do to help your team with their latest case?"

"I wish I understood more about what you can do for us," said Blessing.

"I'll try to explain what I'm doing in layperson's terms, Blessing," said Divya. "Metadata in images and other files can give away more information than the average user thinks. For example, say I was a hacker and tricked you into sending a photo containing GPS coordinates; I could work out where you lived or worked simply by extracting the Exif data hidden inside the image file."

"You've lost me already," said Blessing.

"Exchangeable image file format data is information that accompanies image files," explained Divya. "Look at this example on my screen. Dozens of fields can be filled in or left blank."

"We know the photographs I sent you were taken while the victim, Alan Duncan, served in the Royal Navy. He joined in 1993 and left in 2004. However, looking at him in the photos we have, I don't believe he's left us anything earlier than the turn of the century. Alan was thirty when he moved back to Corsham. He's in his mid-twenties in what appears to be the earliest picture we have."

"That group shot taken in the Valley of the Kings, Luxor," said Divya. "Yes, I would agree. I've put your photos in date order based purely on how he and his colleagues aged. We can check that later."

"You mentioned hackers," said Blessing. "What they do is illegal. How can we access so much data from photos or files? Aren't we breaking the law?"

"There's a fine line, Blessing," said Divya, "but when people publish photos and images, then it's available for what they term open-source intelligence. I can use what's visible in the picture, plus the metadata about when the photo was taken. Sometimes the data includes the device used and the precise geolocation of the image."

"I thought I read somewhere that many social media platforms stripped out metadata from files," said Blessing. "I'm paranoid with what I post online."

"Me too," grinned Divya, "but then I know how

dangerous it is not to take advantage of every scrap of security available. If users don't know what data gets kept in a particular file format, they won't understand the risk they're exposed to by making a specific item public. We take advantage of that here in the Hub when pursuing a criminal case where suspects have left the data held on a file entirely intact."

"None of these photos has ever appeared online as far as we know," said Blessing. "Alan Duncan sent them home to his parents to show them what a great time he was having in the Royal Navy."

"They do look cheerful, don't they?" said Divya. "Right, let's make a start."

The time flew by, and Blessing realised it was lunchtime before she knew it. Several techies left the room, and a buzz of conversation made it difficult to concentrate.

"Do you want to take a break?" asked Divya.

"My landlady never lets me leave the farm without eating breakfast," said Blessing. "Every day, she hands me a lunchbox when I'm ready to leave for work. I left it in the car."

"Gosh," said Divya, "you're spoiled, aren't you? I grab a sandwich at the nearest deli if I'm lucky. Then, I'll take you to your car and walk into the town centre. I'll collect you on the way back. Shall we say thirty minutes?"

"That will be fine," said Blessing. "I've got a message from Luke on my phone. So I'd better get that."

"Luke? Is that another young man you've met since you moved here?"

"No, Luke's part of the team. He's gay and lives with his partner, Nicky, in Warminster."

"What's your boss like?" asked Divya as they returned to the ground floor and into the car park.

"Old-fashioned in some ways," said Blessing. "He's reluctant to use a facility such as this, but when interviewing a witness, he's got the knack of getting them to reveal something that progresses the case. The best thing is that he makes us feel like an equal part of the team. My old boss would tell me to listen and learn in interviews. I was very much a junior partner. Gus is happy for us to chip in if we spot a weakness in someone's replies and can help him prise out that nugget of information."

"I hope I've shown you this morning that the Hub can sift through far more sand for that gold nugget than is possible from a series of interviews."

"I understand what you're saying, Divya," said Blessing. "The search routines that are the Hub's bread-and-butter are more than helpful when trying to identify a burglar or a rapist who's in the system. Unless we're mistaken, these submariners won't have a criminal record. After we collate the data from those photos, I'll return to the office, and Gus Freeman will ask Luke to set up meetings. When he speaks to someone like Keith Smith, Gus will know his friends call him Smudger. He'll know that Smudger was in the Valley of the Kings on December the sixteenth, 1999. If you were Keith Smith, would you try to hide anything from someone who seems to know everything?"

"Maybe you're right," said Divya. "I'll see you in half an hour, Blessing. Enjoy your lunch."

Blessing sat in her Micra and opened her lunchbox. How would she ever lose weight if Jackie Ferris gave her such delicious food? Blessing grabbed her phone and checked the message from Luke.

Blessing learned that Gus and Luke had returned from meeting with Davinia Campbell-Drake. That sounded like a fun discussion. The farmer's wife lied about where she was and what she saw on the night of the murder. Yesterday, they highlighted the mystery man, who may or may not have come from Eastern Europe, as a person of interest. Today, he had moved to the top of the list. When Divya returned, they should prioritise the search for this man. The submariners could wait.

Chapter Ten

BLESSING CALLED Dave Smith to catch up. His shift pattern didn't make life easy organising their next date. Dave's phone went to voicemail, and Blessing had to leave a message.

"Only me. Are you free this weekend? Miss you. Bye."

Blessing looked at the only item remaining in her lunchbox—the chunky orange Kit-Kat. There was something all kinds of wrong about that bar of chocolate. It was as wrong as someone deciding a blue banana was a great idea.

Divya tapped on the window. Time to return to the fray.

"Did you enjoy your sandwich?" asked Blessing as they headed up the steps to the door.

"I try to eat healthily," said Divya. "It might do me good, but I never feel full."

"Are you allowed chocolate?" asked Blessing.

"It's a sin," wailed Divya.

Blessing retrieved the Kit-Kat from her bag. She'd brought it with her to throw in the bin.

"If you're desperate for a chocolate fix," she said.

"Wow! Are you sure?" said Divya.

"Positive," said Blessing.

Seconds later, at least the wrapper ended up where Blessing had intended.

"By the way," said Blessing. "Luke wants us to concentrate on identifying the mystery man in the ninth photo. Gus needs to know where and when our victim took that photo and the identity of that man."

The two women spent the rest of the afternoon analysing the nine photographs. When Blessing left the Hub at five o'clock, she hoped she had everything Gus needed.

"Thanks for your help," said Blessing hugging Divya.

"We aim to please," said Divya. "Try to convince your boss that we're a force for good. His superiors keep telling him we're here for his benefit."

"I'll try," said Blessing. "Can you remind me; do I turn right when I leave the car park?"

Divya studied her phone.

"Take the A361 and A360 to Court Hill in Potterne," she said.

"Thanks, Divya. I know my way from there."

Divya walked to her car and watched Blessing edge her Nissan Micra into the heavy traffic.

Whatever this case that Blessing's team was working on, it had just taken a strange turn. Divya wondered how far they could pursue it.

GUS FREEMAN DIDN'T PASS Blessing Umeh on London Road as they both made their way home after a busy day. He'd spent the afternoon trying to fathom why Bunny Campbell-Drake had felt it necessary to lie to the police. He and Luke had updated their versions of the Freeman Files and updated the others with the morning's events.

"How does this case feel to you, guv?" asked Neil.

"If you're asking that question, you must have an opinion you want to share, Neil," said Gus. "Don't let me stop you."

"We have learned nothing in the past forty-eight hours that has brought us closer to identifying the killer, guv," said Neil. "Despite conducting dozens of interviews, we've turned up the same scrap of information from several sources."

"If we used your jigsaw analogy, guv," said Alex, "we've found half a dozen pieces that fit together to complete a tiny portion of the entire picture."

"When you finish the jigsaw, you realise how insignificant the section you took hours to puzzle out proved," said Lydia.

"You think I wasted time this morning interviewing Davinia Campbell-Drake?" Gus asked. "She lied to the police. Phil Banks could have sewn this case up within a week if he had known what she witnessed."

"I can't argue with that, guv," said Neil, "but Tilly Spiers, Val Huggins, and Greg Meakin had already confirmed that the man in Biddestone in the days before the murder, and the mystery man in that photo, were the same."

"Blessing could have concentrated on that photo from first thing this morning," said Lydia. "It's the only one that matters. The others are just holiday snaps, aren't they?"

Gus wondered whether Suzie's announcement last night had prevented him from giving the case his full attention. He'd always found a way to park any personal problems during his marriage. They had been few, thank goodness, and he couldn't recall when he felt his performance fell short of his self-imposed high standards.

"Sorry, guv," said Luke. "We're struggling with this case. I don't think this morning was a complete waste. We have to stick to the methods you insisted the team adopt from the beginning. The only way we'll succeed is through solid and meticulous detective work. If it means going over the same ground, checking and re-checking witness statements, then so be it. When we left High Ridge Farm this morning, you said that Alan Duncan's secret was well hidden. He did that for a reason, and the holiday snaps might hold the key. All the photographs, not just the one of the mystery man who scared Bunny Campbell-Drake to death."

"Thanks, Luke," said Gus. "We'll catch a break in the end. If only we knew why that particular photograph went missing."

"The one from Happy Valley with five guys in Hawaiian shirts, guv?" asked Neil.

"It had to mean something," said Gus.

Gus didn't believe the others agreed. He recognised Luke had his back, but Alex, Neil, and Lydia thought the case was floating towards the rocks. He would drive home, talk with Suzie, and return to the office in the morning with a clear view of how to solve this case.

As he turned into the gateway of the bungalow, Gus saw they had company. The Reverend's bicycle was leaning against the fence on the right-hand side of the driveway. Gus parked alongside Suzie's Golf and got out of the car. He heard voices in the back garden.

"Hello, Reverend," he said as he turned the corner, "what a pleasant surprise."

"We're enjoying a cool lemonade," said Suzie, "shall I fetch you a glass?"

"I'll get it," said Gus, "you two carry on chatting."

"Oh, we've only just started," said Clemency. "Suzie passed me on her way home. I'd visited a few sick parishioners and needed my spirits lifted. Suzie waited in the gateway for me and then invited me in to cool off."

Gus fetched a glass from the kitchen and poured a measure of lemonade.

"I think a Chardonnay would have hit the spot after the day I've had," he groaned.

"A tough day?" asked Clemency.

"Several team members aren't convinced we're taking the right approach on the case we're working on. I've told them that the original detective team would have solved it if it were easy. Here, if certain people had told the whole truth from the beginning, it's true; we wouldn't have needed to take this second look."

"People don't tell the whole truth for various reasons," said Suzie.

"It's not as simple as them having something to hide, d'you mean?" asked the Reverend.

"It's always that they have something to hide," said Gus. "No matter how they dress it up and justify what they left out. There's no excuse."

"I didn't expect you to see everything as being so black and white, Gus," said Clemency.

"Perhaps we should change our topic of conversation," said Gus. "How did Brett fare on his first day at the clinic?"

"Have you spoken to Bert?" asked Clemency. "The old rogue probably suggested I was monopolising his grandson's spare time."

"Bert mentioned a trip to the cinema," said Gus.

"We watched 'Life of the Party', where a middle-aged mother returns to college," said Clemency. "It was a comedy. As for his work at the clinic, it's fair to say it was busier and more varied than expected."

"Will you and Brett be around at the weekend?" asked Suzie.

"I don't see why not," said Clemency. "Are you two free?"

"I have no plans to work this weekend whether or not the case is falling apart," said Gus.

The Reverend finished her lemonade and got to her feet.

"I'd better get on my bike, as they say. I'm keeping you two lovebirds from your evening meal. It's time to cycle to the rectory and pray for those poor souls I visited this afternoon. They won't be with us much longer, I fear. Still, neither of them will see eighty again. They've had a good life."

Gus and Suzie followed Clemency to the driveway and watched her cycle through the gateway and along the lane.

"How are you?" asked Gus.

"No change," said Suzie. "Still weighing the pros and cons."

"Sit yourself back on the patio," said Gus. "I'll get dinner and bring it out when it's ready."

"That case must be getting to you," said Suzie. "You *were* a tad brusque with the Reverend. Everything isn't black and white in your world, is it?"

"Of course not, darling," said Gus. "Luke made a valid point today when he suggested that solid, old-fashioned police work would uncover the evidence we need to find our killer. Since the ACC handed me the murder file for Alan Duncan, I've had this awful feeling that there's more behind it than meets the eye. Tomorrow, we could find a clue that will have the same effect as dropping a heavy pebble in the middle of a pond. The ripples will go on for ages."

Gus went inside and started cooking from scratch. A takeaway wouldn't cut the mustard tonight, and Suzie didn't need a crowd of people around her while she made her deliberations. His role was to support her and avoid putting his size ten feet in his mouth. Least said, soonest mended.

Friday, 3 August 2018

GUS AND SUZIE left the bungalow together at half-past eight. As she opened her car door, she turned back.

"I love you, you know," she said. "It helped last night, just the two of us. I'd like to do the same tonight. This time, I'll cook."

"That's fine by me," said Gus. "All things being equal, I'll arrive home by half-past five. If something crops up to change that, I'll call you."

Suzie blew Gus a kiss and got in her car. He followed her Golf through the gateway, and they travelled into Devizes in convoy. When Suzie turned into the London Road HQ, Gus spotted Vera Butler walking to work from her cottage. He waved, but Vera was studying the pavement.

Thirty minutes later, Gus eased the Focus between Blessing Umeh's Micra and Luke Sherman's motor. He was the last to arrive.

When Gus entered the office, Blessing stood up and brought a folder to his desk.

"I imagine this is the fruit of your labours, Blessing," said Gus.

"It's the fruit of Divya's labours with a little help from me," said Blessing.

"Okay, everyone," said Gus. "Blessing's ready to give her report."

"Me, guv?" asked Blessing.

"DC Umeh, if you wish to become a DS one day, you need to be prepared to present your work in front of senior officers and convince them you are ready for promotion. Practice makes perfect, DC Umeh. Carry on."

Blessing posted copies of the nine photographs they were interested in on a whiteboard.

"The same device took these photographs," said Blessing. "A Nikon D1; the first fully integrated digital SLR camera. It had a 2.7-megapixel sensor and provided 4.5 frames per second shooting—a respectable speed even today. These photos haven't changed since the day they got taken. Nobody Photoshopped them."

"When did that camera come on the market?" asked Neil.

"Six months before that first photograph in Egypt," said Blessing.

"How can you be certain they came from the same device?" asked Lydia.

"A small chip within all digital cameras tracks the metadata of that device," said Blessing. "They're known as Charge-Coupled Device chips. CCD chips are light-sensitive circuits with minor factory flaws unique to the individual CCD chip."

"What did Divya include in your report?" asked Alex.

"There should be plenty to satisfy what we need in this case review," said Blessing. "If we find our killer and need additional detail when the case gets to court, we only have to shout. Divya's given us camera settings: ISO speed, shutter speed, focal length, aperture, white balance, and lens type. We know the make and model of the camera. We now have the date and time relevant for each photograph. In eight out of nine cases, the location was obvious. The last photo was the one that could prove to be the most significant. We've identified the location. Alan Duncan took this photograph at the Moscow Zoo in the Presnensky District on Saturday the eleventh of May 2004."

"Do we know the exact date that Alan Duncan left the Royal Navy?" asked Gus.

"The thirtieth of June, guv," said Alex.

"Duncan must have known he was leaving the service in seven weeks," said Alex. "How much notice do you have to give?"

"Twelve months," said Luke. "I checked last night. The Navy can make you stay the full term if they wish. We need to check whether they let Alan Duncan go earlier."

"It's safe to assume that Alan Duncan took that picture," said Blessing. "The time in the Exif file recorded it at two-fifteen in the afternoon, which gels with the St Basil's picture of Alan Duncan himself. The camera settings were the same, and the time recorded that photograph at eleven forty-five in the morning that day."

"Duncan and our mystery man visited several typical tourist attractions in the Russian capital," said Gus. "Where were his submariner friends?"

"Could Divya identify Alan Duncan's companion?" asked Lydia.

"Yuri Kovalev," said Blessing. "He was twenty-seven at the time of that photo. Divya found his profile on the usual social media sites, but it proved impossible to discover his current or past occupations. He was born in Moscow in 1977 and left University in 1998. Yuri is an only child whose parents died in a car crash in 2007. His hobbies are learning foreign languages and running."

"That sounds manufactured," said Neil.

"Like ninety percent of social media profiles," said Lydia.

"How did they meet?" asked Gus. "Don't bother, Blessing. We can't expect you to know."

"I don't think Bob and Elizabeth Duncan will know either, guv," said Alex. "The running could be a clue. Perhaps they bumped into one another."

"That's not as daft as it sounds," said Luke. "The district where the Zoo is based straddles the Moskva river. According to Trip Advisor, there are several great runs on both sides of the river. As Gus said, where were Smudger, Taff and the others? Did Alan Duncan visit Moscow alone? If so, why? We need to talk to the submariners in these photographs."

"Can Bob Duncan tell us which of Alan's mates were in that missing photograph from Happy Valley?" asked Lydia. "We need to get him to pick them out from the photos we have."

"That might be a stretch," said Gus. "Let's try something else first. Blessing, take us through the photographs in date order, please?"

"The first one was from December 1999 in the Valley of the Kings," she said. "The men present with Alan Duncan were Taff, Smudger, Andy, and Gooner."

"Taff, or Max Hughes, should be our first contact, Luke. I think he appeared in every photo," said Gus. "If Bob can't help with the names from Happy Valley, then Max Hughes will."

"Max should be able to tell us who took the photo, too," said Alex.

"Got it," said Luke.

"The gang visited Sydney in August of the following year," said Blessing. "This picture under the Harbour Bridge got taken on the ninth. The only change is that Lofty replaced Gooner."

"Perhaps they took it in turns to take the photos," said Lydia.

"It could be as simple as that, guv," said Neil.

"Taff should confirm that, Neil," said Gus.

"There was an eight-month gap to the next trip, guv," said Blessing. "The picture of the gang with Table Mountain in the background is dated the twentieth of April. Chuff, this time joined Taff, Smudger, and Lofty. No sign of Andy or Gooner, but one could have been behind the camera."

"We can't emphasise the time gaps, Blessing," said Gus, "not at this stage. They could be significant, but Alan would have had two or three holidays yearly and only sent his parents a small selection."

"True, guv," said Blessing, "and Alan might not have been the only man with a camera. His friends could have dozens of photos available."

"Good point," said Gus. "Luke, forewarn each submariner when you contact them. They need to rescue their photograph albums from the loft."

"The fourth photo was from Paris, guv," said Blessing. "Taff was there as usual, with Smudger, Andy, Gooner and Lofty. The photo Alan sent to his parents featured the Eiffel Tower."

"Remember what Wayne Phillips said, guv?" asked Alex. "Wayne and Anna went to Paris for a romantic weekend. Alan told him he wasn't interested in the Eiffel Tower;

Wayne thought the gang had gone to Paris for the racing out at Longchamps."

"It dates the photo to the twenty-fifth of October 2001," said Blessing.

Luke checked on Google.

"That's around the date when they run the Prix de L'Arc de Triomphe, guv," he said. "The racecourse is a ten-minute taxi ride from the Eiffel Tower."

"Where in the world do we go next, Blessing?" asked Gus.

"Waikato, New Zealand, guv," she replied, "in early February 2003. Taff, Smudger, Lofty, Chuff, and Tarby accompanied Duncan on that trip, plus the photographer."

"Waikato's a famous heritage site, guv," said Lydia. "They're noted for the volcanic black sand beaches and fine surfing conditions."

"Everyone deserves a holiday, Lydia," said Gus. "I'm interested in the gap this time, Blessing. Could the missing Happy Valley photo come somewhere between Paris and Waikato?"

"We don't know that before talking to Max Hughes and the others. So the gang ended up in Tokyo in September that year, guv," said Blessing. "Taff, Smudge, Andy, and Chuff joined Alan in the city's heart. That's the Shibuya Crossing."

"I hate crowds," said Gus. "You wouldn't catch me there in a month of Sundays."

"The last one comes from Dubai on the twenty-seventh of March in 2004," said Blessing. "Taff, Smudger, Andy and Lofty appear in front of the camera with Alan. Divya reckoned they were on loungers at a hotel in the Al Jaber complex. It's probably the Shangri La."

"Well done, Blessing," said Gus. "Where do we go from here?"

"Scotland, guv," said Blessing. "HM Naval Base Clyde —commonly known throughout the Navy as Faslane—it's the Royal Navy's major presence in Scotland. The base is home to the Submarine Service's core, including the nation's nuclear deterrent and the new generation of hunter-killer submarines. The Royal Naval Armaments Depot at Coulport, eight miles from Faslane, handles the storage, processing, maintenance, and issue of key elements of the UK's Trident Deterrent Missile System. Faslane is the base for three thousand service personnel, eight hundred of their family members and four thousand civilian workers. Freddie Watts, to give him his actual name, would be in his late fifties now. He retired after twenty-eight years of service. If we wish to speak to him, it will require a trip to the Isle of Man. Freddie Watts runs a pub in Douglas."

"Are the others still in the Royal Navy?" asked Neil.

"How old are they, anyway?" asked Lydia.

"They're between forty-seven and fifty years old," said Blessing. "Four still serve at sea. They are Craig Anderson, Bryan Tarbuck, Rico Menghini and Drew Taggart. Max Hughes and Keith Smith work at Faslane in a training capacity."

"Well, that's the first stroke of luck we've had on this case," said Gus. "The two guys who appeared in every photograph are virtually on our doorstep. Supposing the others are still at sea, how would we get hold of them?"

"We can't call them on the numbers we have from Alan Duncan's pocket diary, guv," said Blessing. "No cell phones allowed on submarines."

"Right, Luke," said Gus. "How far have you got with fixing a meeting with Max Hughes?"

"Waiting for a callback, guv. The same goes for Smudger Smith. Do you want me to try the innkeeper on the Isle of Man?"

"Do you honestly think Geoff Mercer will let us go on a day trip in the Irish Sea?" asked Neil.

"Either the ACC wants this case wrapped up, or he doesn't," said Gus. "I'll ask nicely and see what he says. I don't suppose we can just wander onto the Faslane base. We may need to arrange video calls with the first two men. No doubt they'll have Naval legal representation present. It could get messy. That Moscow trip concerns me. If Alan Duncan and his pals had a holiday in Dubai at the end of March, how did he wangle a weekend break to Moscow in the second week in May? I thought these submarines stayed deep underwater for up to ninety days."

"As my mother says, that will come out in the wash, guv," said Neil. "Alan Duncan's crewmates will know the full story. Just because they aren't in those two photos that Blessing has, it doesn't rule out them being there. We're looking at a series of snapshots of our victim's life, not a joined-up feature film."

"Neil's right, guv," said Lydia. "It's so easy to fabricate a story around the images we have on the whiteboard, but his friends will add context and perhaps provide extra photographs that blow any conclusions we might draw out of the water."

"Right," said Gus. "I'll contact London Road for permission to speak with the three most significant submariners, Hughes, Smith, and Watts. Blessing, you must return the originals of those loose photos Elizabeth Duncan steered you towards. Ask Bob Duncan what he remembers of that Hong Kong photograph. There might still be a missing name."

"Will do, guv," said Blessing. "I'll also ask Bob what he knows of the final few months of his son's naval career. Unfortunately, we didn't have the dates for those photos when we interviewed him. Perhaps he can explain the brief gap between holidays."

"Alan couldn't say much about what they did on those operations, guv," said Neil. "It's a long shot to expect him to have had a heart-to-heart with his parents. Everything we've learned about Alan since he died suggests that he had closed that chapter in his life and moved on."

"He didn't spend his Saturday afternoons regaling Wayne Phillips with stories of life at sea either, guv," said Alex.

"It won't hurt to ask, Blessing," said Gus. "There's something else you can ask them while you're there. Were there occasions when Alan came home during his periods of shore leave? Surely, he didn't go to Dartmouth at eighteen and not return until he was thirty, or did he?"

"I'll call Bob before I drive to Corsham," said Blessing. "I'll try to get as much as possible out of both of them; Elizabeth won't stay in her bed today."

"Do your best, Blessing," said Gus. He phoned London Road, and Vera answered.

"Vera, Gus here. Is Kenneth free?"

"Good morning, Gus. Yes, he is. Just a minute."

"What is it now, Freeman?" asked the ACC.

"Sorry, sir," said Gus. "Have I called at an awkward time? You know I only bother you when I've wrapped up a case or need your much-valued advice."

"I doubt you've solved the Duncan case so soon, Freeman, and when you throw compliments around, I know you want something. What is it this time?"

Gus saw the opportunity to turn this conversation in his favour.

"One of my team spent the day in the Hub yesterday," said Gus. "What a valuable tool the place proved to be in this case. We've made great strides thanks to the service the technical staff could provide. Your people helped identify several witnesses we now urgently need to interview. One is a retired naval officer who lives on the Isle of Man. Two others are now at Faslane on the Clyde. Could you liaise with your counterpart with the Ministry of Defence Police so we can talk to these serving officers without treading on anyone's toes?"

"Consider it done, Freeman," said the ACC. "It's taken you long enough to wake up to my championing of the Hub and what it offers the modern police officer. What would you intend to do, drop into the Isle of Man as part of the round trip?"

"That's a good idea, sir," said Gus. "If we get it done in one go, it will reduce the costs."

"Who will you take with you?" asked the ACC.

"One of the lads, sir," said Gus, "we must book a room. We can't get it done in a day."

"I'll get Vera to phone you back once we've made the arrangements with Faslane," said Kenneth Truelove. "I presume you plan to travel to Scotland on Monday morning?"

"Yes, sir," said Gus.

"Carry on, Freeman."

Gus ended the call and congratulated himself on a job well done.

"How long will it take us to get to Faslane?"

"It's an eight-hour drive via the M6, guv," said Alex.

"You would need to change trains more than once, guv,"

said Neil. "I don't reckon you would get there any quicker, just less knackered."

"Did the ACC sanction the trip to Douglas, guv?" asked Luke.

"He did, Luke. If we leave here at eight in the morning, we can interview Hughes and Smith, then drive to Liverpool for an overnight stay in a budget hotel. Get us on the first available ferry in the morning. If memory serves, it's a three-hour trip, give or take. We can talk to Freddie Watts at lunchtime, catch a ferry back to Liverpool mid-afternoon, and be back by ten at the latest. Don't worry, whoever gets the short straw to accompany me; I'll not expect you in the office until noon on Wednesday."

"Will those of us who stay here get to set up video calls with the remaining submariners, guv?" asked Neil.

"I'll reserve judgement on that, Neil, until I see what we learn from the first three interviews. We'll follow up if they point us toward a particular crew member. It could be a logistical nightmare to arrange meaningful calls with Taggart and the others, thousands of metres under the sea's surface in four corners of the world."

"Fair enough, guv," said Neil.

"Have you decided who you want with you, guv?" Lydia asked.

"Alex," said Gus.

Blessing was ready to leave for Corsham.

"I'll be off then, guv," she said. "I'll see you later."

Gus gave her a nod as she passed his desk. He was about to speak when his phone rang.

"Freeman speaking. How can I help?"

"It's Phil Banks. I decided I ought to call you back in person. There's something odd that I can't explain."

The case had moved in several directions since he'd

spoken to Phil Banks. It took a moment for Gus to remember what Phil had agreed to look into for him.

"Kyle Ellison," said Gus when the fog cleared.

"I asked someone to find him," said Phil. "They got back to me this morning with the news that they can't find a trace of him."

"One of my team found him easily enough on social media, Phil," said Gus.

"Well, my officer verified Ellison's date of birth. He checked where Ellison went to school and his few qualifications when he left. He spoke to the building firms that employed him. We've tracked the driving school that got him through his test and the lady who sold him the one car he's ever owned and got insured. His name appeared as the victim of an assault charge brought against Darren Forsyth. That was in 1993. After that, my officer couldn't confirm his sighting in Marsden or anywhere in the Leeds area. Kyle Ellison appears to have disappeared off the face of the earth."

Chapter Eleven

"THAT'S A TOUCH DRAMATIC, PHIL," said Gus. "How far have you gone? Is this now an official missing person investigation?"

"You know the score, Gus," said Phil. "We need to gather sufficient information on the missing person to enable an effective and thorough investigation; the depth of that information varies according to the risk."

"Do we believe that Kyle Ellison was at risk twenty-five years ago," said Gus. "Well, we know that Darren Forsyth wanted to separate Kyle's head from his body, but young Darren felt justified because Ellison was using his sister, Jennifer, as a punchbag."

"Allegedly," said Phil Banks.

"Do you know something I don't?" asked Gus.

"Not at all. You've interviewed the girl; I haven't. Were you convinced by her version of events?"

"I'm long enough in the tooth to realise that until I speak to Kyle Ellison, I won't appreciate whether there were discrepancies between their stories. My gut feeling was that the young girl was terrified of Ellison and got as far from him as possible. She hid her tracks well and hasn't been bothered by him since. That doesn't mean he's missing."

"We now have detailed information for Kyle and a life-style profile," said Phil. "My officer is taking a full statement from the last person to see him. That's the guy who owned the flat in Leeds where Kyle rented a room. The place is an HMO and the passage of time rules out forensics. We can't consider seizing any electronic devices or computers or getting details of usernames and passwords. I'm uncertain we can unearth a photo of Ellison. At least, not one more recent than one he had taken at secondary school. Kyle had a mobile phone, but we don't know if he had it when last seen."

"I assume that if he still had the phone from 1993, we could send him a message asking him to let someone know he's safe," said Gus. "But what about that car of his?"

"I suggested to my officer that he placed markers on the PNC without delay, but the flat owner remembered Ellison scrapped the vehicle a few weeks before he went missing. It was a banger back then. Fat chance it was still on the road today."

"Did Kyle have a passport?" asked Gus.

"No," replied Phil Banks. "Before you ask, we don't have DNA samples or fingerprints either."

"So, Kyle's still in this country, posting on social media via an electronic device. Can we trace him via that route?"

"A computer-based enquiry is an important aspect of a missing person investigation, Gus, as you know. Online activity may provide crucial clues, but we don't always have the legal right to access that information. Individuals have the right to privacy and don't have to inform their families and friends about their whereabouts. An investigation into personal data is intrusive by nature. We may justify access to such data to determine if a crime has occurred. We would need more than what we have to get a warrant."

"What do Kyle's family know of his whereabouts?" asked Gus.

"No living relatives, as far as we can discern," said Phil.

"Your people should be able to find when the deaths got registered," said Gus. "Even if it was only a few months after Kyle was last seen in Leeds, it suggests there was no love lost between him and his parents. I should get your guy to double-check there were no siblings while he's at it. We can't just sweep this under the carpet. Look, Phil, with what we know so far, are we concerned for Kyle's welfare?"

"I'm concerned that you want to speak with him in connection with your case, and we can't locate him," said Phil Banks. "I intend to upgrade the search to include the various government and private organisations which may hold relevant information. The Department for Work and Pensions, the DVLA, his GP if he had one, and maybe even car rental companies."

"That check should establish if Kyle has chosen to disappear or if harm has come to him," said Gus.

"What if Ellison became homeless?" asked Phil. "If he's registered with a GP, perhaps we'll find evidence of a drug habit."

"If it weren't for one thing, I'd say that could be the answer," said Gus. "Let's say that Kyle suffered a slow descent into addiction, fell through the cracks in society, existed on the streets for several years and eventually died from an overdose. We don't have dental records or DNA. There would have been nothing to prove his identity. It's a daily occurrence."

"Except for the social media accounts," said Phil Banks.

"Quite, after you've exhausted your enquiries to establish whether Kyle is alive and well and using a different name wherever he's living, you need to speak to members of the Forsyth family," said Gus. "Dave and Mary from Marsden, Darren from Leeds, and Jennifer. She's called Madeleine Telfer now, and I can pass you her contact details in Chippenham."

"We'll cross that bridge when we come to it, Gus," said Phil. "I didn't imagine this turn of events when you called the other day."

"Nor did I, Phil," said Gus, "but something had to explain why Jennifer Forsyth hid away in a dead-end job two hundred miles from home."

BLESSING UMEH DROVE into Corsham with more confidence today. It helped to have made the trip before. But her time working with Divya had provided so much more than the data they extracted from the photographs. Gus had encouraged her to stand in front of the whole team to take them through the details. Six months ago, that would have frightened her so much that she wouldn't have been able to speak.

Bob Duncan answered the front door as she walked up the path from her car.

"Hello, Mr Duncan,"

"You're back again," said Bob. "How much more can there be to say."

"Let the girl get inside the door, Bob," said Elizabeth. "How are you, Blessing?"

"Very well, thanks, Mrs Duncan," said Blessing. "I'm returning the originals of the photographs we borrowed. Shall I help Bob put them back into the frames?"

"Does that mean you're staying long enough for a cup of tea?" asked Elizabeth.

"I don't see why not," smiled Blessing. Elizabeth headed for the kitchen.

"What did you learn from the photographs, anyway," said Bob.

"We know the names of everyone that Alan recorded on the backs of the photos," said Blessing. "I can let you have Alan's pocket diary back too. We're talking to several of his colleagues early next week, and we're conscious that they're unlikely to have learned that Alan died in 2008. So I thought if you wanted to call them over the weekend, it might soften the blow. They were good friends of Alan's and thought a lot of him."

"That's a nice thought, Blessing," said Elizabeth as she returned with three cups of tea on a tray.

"Gus Freeman would like to know what you remember of the missing photo, Mr Duncan," said Blessing. "The one from Hong Kong taken at the Happy Valley racecourse."

"Alan and the others wore those horrid shirts," said Elizabeth, screwing up her face. "I think they had been drinking."

"I must have looked at that photo a hundred times over the years," said Bob. "Whether I remember who was in it, I don't know."

"Alan was on the left," said Elizabeth, "next to the man with ginger hair."

"Taff," said Blessing. "His name is Max Hughes, and he comes from Swansea."

"We never knew that did we, Bob?" said Elizabeth, "He was just Taff to us."

"If I show you the other photos, do you think you

remember seeing any of them in one of those horrid shirts?"

Bob and Elizabeth studied the photos, and Bob pointed at Keith Smith.

"He was there, Smudger. He was in most of Alan's pictures."

"Keith Smith," said Blessing. "Well done, we're almost there. Who were the other two?"

"This chap looks familiar," said Elizabeth. She pointed at Craig Anderson.

"Yes, Andy," said Bob. "That's right; he was on the opposite end to Alan with his arm around the shoulder of...."

"Go on, Mr Duncan," said Blessing.

"He's not here," said Bob, checking the photos.

"Are you sure?" asked Blessing.

Elizabeth flicked through the photographs. She shook her head.

"No, my memory isn't what it was, but surely he was shorter and carried more weight."

"Fatter in the face and around the middle," said Bob. "I remember that now; his shirt buttons were doing a grand job holding it together,"

Bob and Elizabeth laughed at the memory.

"Did Alan write names on the back of that photo?" asked Blessing.

"I can't remember, I'm afraid," said Bob.

"I remember when we got that photo," said Elizabeth, "Alan sent it to us with my birthday card in August."

"Which year was that?" asked Blessing.

"Perhaps two years before he came home for good," said Elizabeth.

"August 2002 then," said Blessing.

179

"Does it matter, dear?" said Elizabeth.

"It could do," said Blessing. "You mentioned when Alan came home for good. Sometimes he came home to visit, I suppose, when his submarine returned to Faslane at other times?"

"Not often," said Bob. "Alan rang us from Faslane to check that we were both well. He spent a weekend here every year, no more than that."

"Was there a particular reason for that, Mr Duncan?" asked Blessing.

"Alan and his father didn't always see eye to eye," said Elizabeth.

"Alan kept telling us he was working on things he couldn't talk about," said Bob. "I thought he had something to hide. I couldn't work out what it was, but it bothered him. On those odd occasions when he slept here, especially in the last couple of years in the Navy, Alan was always on edge."

"Did Alan learn any foreign languages?" asked Blessing.

"French and Spanish at school," said Elizabeth, "but he dropped those subjects when he did his A-levels."

"What about Russian?" asked Blessing.

"Why would he need that?" asked Elizabeth.

"Even though the Cold War was over, the Russians still pose a significant threat," said Bob. "It's possible Alan, and his crewmates picked up more than a few phrases. Everyone monitors everyone else when they're patrolling or carrying out manoeuvres under the ocean. That's common knowledge, whether or not Alan spoke to us about what he did."

"What about this photograph?" asked Blessing, showing the couple the photo taken in Moscow...

"What about it?" said Bob.

"Surely you know where Alan is?"

"I can't say I do," said Bob, "did Alan write on the back?"

"You've probably never seen it before, Bob," said Elizabeth. "Alan kept several photos in a drawer in his bedroom. He left them behind when he moved out to live with Maddy. They couldn't have been important."

"That's St Basil's Cathedral in the background," said Blessing.

"What, in Moscow?" said Bob.

"Yes," said Blessing, "and this man took the photo." She showed Bob and Elizabeth the photo of Yuri Kovalev. "Alan returned the favour at Moscow Zoo in the afternoon. Alan was in Moscow less than two months before he left the Navy."

"I don't recognise that chap as one of Alan's crewmates," said Bob.

"Yuri Kovalev wasn't a crewmate," said Blessing. "We don't know what he does. Their meeting could be innocent. Kovalev was a keen runner. Perhaps they just met while running, and the young Russian offered to show Alan around his home city. One thing that bothers us is what brought Alan to Moscow in the first place. This photograph from the poolside of a hotel in Dubai is from the end of March. If Alan and his colleagues were on leave in March, how did he get more shore leave in early May?"

"The submarine needed repairs," said Bob, "there was a collision with a trawler. Everyone got stuck at Faslane. Because Alan had opted to leave, his commanding officer didn't want him hanging around waiting for the next voyage. It was uncertain when that might be. They could have forced Alan to stay until his twelve months' notice was up, but rather than have a Weapon Engineer Officer on a tour of duty who didn't want to be there, they cut him loose early."

"Did Alan have a change of duties after returning to Faslane from Dubai?" asked Blessing.

"They weren't best pleased with having invested so much time and money in training him to find that he wanted to throw it away," said Bob. "They found him a desk job."

"Alan wasn't happy, Bob," said Elizabeth. "What's the point of life if you're not happy?"

"Why didn't you mention this earlier, Mr Duncan?" asked Blessing.

"Bob was ashamed," said Elizabeth. "For years, we'd been so proud of Alan serving his country with distinction. Then within two years, Alan changed. He wasn't the happy-go-lucky person he'd once been. When he finally came home, we could tell that a great weight had lifted. Whatever had troubled him was in the past. Alan settled into his job at the factory, found a girlfriend, and although Bob never understood why Alan quit when he did, he accepted things had improved. Then someone murdered Alan, and the doubts came crashing back. What caused that black period in his life? How did he recover from it? Did someone from his past kill him, and why?"

"As soon as you started looking into the murder again, I knew something dreadful would come out," said Bob. "If he was meeting with the Russians, it can only mean one thing."

"One of my colleagues made a good point about these photographs," said Blessing. "We can only see the events that Alan posted to you. His crewmates will have others from the same time or dates in between. So it would be best if you didn't jump to conclusions, Mr Duncan. We'll talk to Taff, Smudger, and Lofty next week. Then, maybe, we'll get the opportunity to talk to Yuri Kovalev or at least discover who he is and where he works."

Blessing knew she needed to return to the office to update Gus, but she was concerned for Bob and Elizabeth Duncan. They had done nothing wrong. They didn't deserve this. But it must come out if there was more to get uncovered from their son's past. Gus wanted to find Alan's killer, and no matter what other secrets he had to dig up to find that killer, he would keep digging.

"I'm sorry if going over these photographs again has upset you," she said. "I'll get back to the office. Please remember, none of this is your fault."

"We know, Blessing," said Elizabeth. "Bob and I will get through it together, somehow. We must."

Bob Duncan saw Blessing to the door. When she reached her car, she turned back to wave, but Bob had gone back indoors already. Blessing sat for a while to gather her thoughts. Could Alan Duncan have sold secrets to the Russians? Was that where that eight and a half thousand pounds came into the case? Blessing didn't know the sums that might change hands for details of a submarine's weapon systems, but surely it had to be worth more than that?

Her phone rang. It was Dave Smith calling.

"Hi, Dave," she said. "You got my message then?"

"Things have been hectic,"

"Are you free this weekend?"

"I'm sorry, Blessing,"

"You don't want to see me again, is that it?"

"It's been fun, but I'm not ready to settle down yet. I'm off to Jersey for a week's holiday with a few mates next weekend."

"Oh, okay," said Blessing. "Well, have a great time.

You've got my number. I'm sorry too, Dave. I like you a lot. Bye."

Blessing started the car and drove back to the Old Police Station office.

Blessing told herself that she could wait until she reached the farm and the safety of her bedroom before she allowed herself to cry.

Gus and the others were winding down towards the end of another busy week. Vera Butler had called to confirm that their visit to Faslane had received a green light. Luke had finalised the details of the ferry journeys and the stopover in Liverpool.

Blessing exited the lift. Gus wasn't in his usual seat.

Neil nodded towards the restroom.

"Gus is getting a coffee, Blessing," he said. "You missed all the fun. The case took another corkscrew twist."

"Another one? I thought I was going to give him a surprise. What now?"

Gus opened the restroom door and returned with his drink.

"What news from Corsham, Blessing?" he asked.

"Bob Duncan gave me a part-explanation of how Alan ended up in Moscow, guv," she replied. "His submarine needed repairs, and as Alan was serving out his notice, his superiors kept him on a desk job at Faslane rather than send him to sea. I've got names for everyone except one person in the Happy Valley photo. Taff, Smudger, and Andy were there with Alan, but a shorter, fatter man joined them in that one photo. They didn't know his name, I'm afraid. We must rely on one of the other crewmates to identify him."

"Did you show them the photo of Kovalev?" asked Gus.

"Yes, guv," said Blessing. "I don't think Bob had seen the Moscow photos before, only Elizabeth when she discovered them in the drawer. Because Alan left them behind when he moved to Biddestone, she didn't think they were important, so she didn't show them to Bob. It stunned Bob that Alan had met Yuri Kovalev. His immediate thought was that Alan was meeting with a Russian spy."

"Right, get what you learned this afternoon into the Freeman Files. You'll see there's something for you to digest regarding Maddy Telfer. DCI Banks contacted me just as you left the office. So when you think you have heard everything, someone proves you wrong. At least I was proved right by assuming that both Alan and Maddy had buried secrets."

"About that, guv," said Blessing. "Something else cropped up during my conversation with Bob and Elizabeth. She mentioned that Alan's personality changed two years before he left the Navy. His mother said he was in a dark place. When he was out of the Navy and settling into his new life in Corsham, it was as if a weight had lifted from his shoulders. He was happy again, something missing during those two years."

"So, we're talking the middle of 2002 through to the middle of 2004," said Gus. "Interesting."

"Is there anything you want us to concentrate on while you're away, guv?" asked Lydia.

"Luke and Neil need to be on standby," said Gus. "If Phil Banks and his team don't find Kyle Ellison, I want them in Bradford sitting in on the interviews with the Forsyth family. When those get completed, they can accompany the West Yorkshire detectives to London Road. One of you should go with them to Redwing Avenue when they collect Jennifer Forsyth."

Blessing was lost. She must have missed more than she

thought. It was time to update her files and catch up with what Gus and the others had added.

"As for you and Blessing, Lydia," Gus continued. "I need you to trace Yuri Kovalev. We suspect that he's our killer. When did he arrive in the UK, and when did he leave? If he's still here, where is he? Most important, who are his employers? As soon as you hit a closed door, call DS Mercer. He'll persuade the ACC to apply pressure in the relevant quarters."

"Yuri Kovalev will claim diplomatic immunity, guv," said Lydia.

"As I say, if you find you can't pursue an enquiry because of our suspect's nationality, don't hesitate. Fire it upstairs. Let someone on a higher paygrade earn their money. Sometimes you have to accept that you've taken a case as far as possible. Can we prove Kovalev is our killer beyond a reasonable doubt? We have an eyewitness who saw Kovalev and Duncan arguing in a gateway to a field. Thirty minutes later, Duncan was dead. What's Kovalev's defence? The lady was mistaken. We Eastern Europeans look alike. So, if you accept it, your task is to confirm he was here, searching for evidence that he was in Biddestone. Did he sit in the Crown's beer garden at Giddeahall without going inside to order a cold drink? Did he pay by card? If he was in and around the village for two to three weeks, where did he stay? Where did he hire that Vauxhall Zafira? Or did he rock up to second-hand car dealers in Chippenham and pay cash? Think outside the box, Lydia. Keep sticking pins in Kovalev until that field traps him on Ham Lane with no escape."

"Got it, guv," said Lydia.

Blessing caught Lydia's eye. They both smiled. One thing was sure; although Gus and Alex would be hundreds of miles away from here on Monday and Tuesday, there would still be plenty to keep them occupied.

"I'll collect you from home on Monday morning, guv," said Alex. "Shall we say six o'clock?"

"I'll cope," said Gus. "Don't forget your toothbrush."

After the office emptied at five o'clock, Gus knew he shouldn't hang around. There was plenty to consider about the case, but matters at home had to take precedent.

The weekend lay ahead, and six o'clock on Monday morning would arrive in the blink of an eye. As he followed Blessing Umeh to the lift, he thought her shoulders looked lower than usual.

"Congratulations, Blessing," he said. "You performed well this week. I thought that would have put a spring in your step. Why so glum?"

When the lift reached the ground floor, Gus held the door for a while as Blessing dug a tissue from her bag and blew her nose. If this was what lay ahead this weekend, perhaps he should stop on the way home to buy a man-size box.

"Man trouble, guv," said Blessing. "PC Smith dumped me this afternoon. I didn't see that coming. I was hoping to see him this weekend. I'll probably drive over to visit my parents on Sunday instead. I need TLC from my mother."

"These things are sent to try us," said Gus. "Jackie Ferris will offer a comforting shoulder, I'm sure. What I can say is that it's Dave Smith's loss. I'll see you on Wednesday morning. Take care."

"Thanks, guv," said Blessing. "I'll keep busy and think pleasant thoughts. Good hunting next week."

Gus drove back to Urchfont and considered the highs and lows affecting his team members. Alex and Lydia's relationship was as solid as a rock. Neil and Melody had bounced back from a heart-breaking disappointment and now had something positive to look forward to at the end of the year. Luke and Nicky never seemed one hundred percent in sync but somehow ironed out their differences.

As for Blessing, well, she was only twenty-one. Had he known what he wanted from life at that age? Dave Smith obviously thought of his early twenties as the time to play the field, not get tied down until he found the right person. Gus wondered whether he was looking back with rose-coloured spectacles as he swung the car into the bungalow's gateway. He and Tess had met, courted, and married before he was much over twenty-three. They enjoyed thirty-five years together. Did Blessing think she'd already missed the love boat?

Gus heard music coming from the lounge as he walked into the house. Suzie was home and singing along to one of her favourite records. Gus put his car keys in the tray on the hall table. He looked at himself in the mirror. Why worry if you haven't found love at twenty-one? How had he been so lucky to find someone at his time of life? He hoped he and Suzie would weather the storms like Luke and Nicky. Nothing was impossible for two people who loved one another.

"Gus, is that you?" said Suzie.

"Just got in," he replied. "I was enjoying the sound of your voice."

"Dinner's in the oven," said Suzie as she came from the lounge. "I hope you're going to freshen up and change your clothes before we eat?"

"Yes, dear," said Gus. "Are we dining alfresco this evening?"

"On the patio, as we did last night," said Suzie.

"Although our meal owes more to French cuisine than Italian."

"You spoil me," said Gus, gathering her into his arms and kissing her.

"Bathroom, now," said Suzie. "It's been a long, hot day. I guess you were busy?"

"Alex and I are off to Scotland and the Isle of Man for two days next week," said Gus. "Luke and Neil will drive to Bradford to sit in on interviews unless I'm very much mistaken. Things have moved quickly today, not necessarily in the direction I would like or expected, but that's life."

"Shower and change," said Suzie, "then tell me more while we enjoy our food."

Gus did as he was told, and the couple spent the next three hours outside chatting, eating, and enjoying just being alone. Finally, they returned indoors as dusk fell, and Suzie topped up Gus's glass.

"I've weighed the pros and cons," she said as she sat beside him and laid her head on his shoulder. "I'm ready to share my decision with you. I want this baby. Assistant Chief Constables around the country have taken time out from their careers to have children. It's possible they won't make the next step up because of that decision, but I've decided I can live with that if it proves to be the case."

"I told you I would support any decision you made, Suzie," said Gus. "What else have you considered over the past couple of days?"

"When Clemency was here last night, I didn't mention a thing. I haven't told my parents yet. Only you, me, and the doctor know I'm pregnant. When I asked Clemency how things were going with Brett, she admitted she was considering the possibility of marriage for the first time since she became a vicar. Clemency asked whether I had ever considered getting married. I laughed and said that someone would have to ask me first. The way I see it. We're happy as we are, Gus. Getting married couldn't make it any better."

"I'm happy if you're happy," said Gus. "Will you tell John and Jackie this weekend, or do you want to wait?"

"We might as well get it over with," said Suzie. "I'll call Mum in the morning and invite them to Sunday lunch."

"I'll book a table at the Waggon & Horses," said Gus.

"Not so fast, Gus Freeman," said Suzie. "While I've been deliberating whether I want to be a mother, haven't you ever had doubts?"

"What? About wanting to be a father at my age? It will take getting used to; that goes without saying, but it will be an unfamiliar experience. We'll adjust together. Geoff Mercer won't be happy with us taking time off simultaneously, but he'll cope. If it's a girl, can we call her Rosetta?"

"I'm not sure you're taking this situation seriously," said Suzie. "If you've finished nursing that glass of wine, come to bed and convince me I've made the right decision."

Chapter Twelve

Saturday, 4 August 2018

AFTER A LATE BREAKFAST, Suzie drove to Worton to ride her horse. She had already decided that after her twelve-week scan, she would stop. It was going to be a wrench. In the future, there was the prospect of having a son or daughter to introduce to the joys of Pony Club. It had provided her with a lot of enjoyment and a lifelong love of horses.

Her father was at the other end of the farm, hard at work, when she collected her horse from the stables. Suzie wandered over to the farmhouse and called out for her mother. Jackie was in the kitchen with Blessing Umeh.

"We'd love it if you and Dad could come to dinner with us tomorrow, Mum," she said. "Will you be able to manage, Blessing?"

"I'm visiting my parents," said Blessing. "So, you don't need to worry about me.".

"What are we celebrating?" asked Jackie.

"Why does it have to be something special?" asked Suzie. "We just thought it was time we treated you. Gus is booking a table at the Waggon & Horses. I'll call you later to confirm the time."

Suzie left before her mother grilled her further.

"Right, Blessing," said Jackie. "What have you heard?"

"Nothing," said Blessing. "Honestly, the only news I heard this week was that Neil Davis and his wife are expecting a baby."

"That's wonderful news," said Jackie. "Let's hope everything runs smoothly this time. I often wonder whether I'll ever be a grandmother. My sons seem happy to remain single, and Suzie is a career girl. Now, what's been happening in your life this week?"

"I'm not seeing Dave anymore," sighed Blessing.

"Oh, dear," said Jackie. "Which is it to be, chocolate cake and a cup of coffee? Or a tub of ice cream and a glass of wine? You need a shoulder to cry on and comfort food."

Monday, 6 August 2018

GUS HEARD the alarm at half-past five and rolled out of bed. He had showered and dressed in time to get two slices of toast and a cup of coffee inside him before Alex arrived outside.

"Tell Alex to drive safely," called Suzie.

"I'll call you tonight from Liverpool," said Gus.

He grabbed his bag and headed for the front door.

"Morning, guv," said Alex. "Early starts don't suit Lydia. I guess Suzie didn't get up with you either?"

"Six o'clock is halfway through the night in her eyes," said Gus.

It was too early to tell Alex that Suzie was suffering from morning sickness. She had followed him into the bathroom half an hour ago, feeling wretched. Although they had shared the news of Suzie's pregnancy with John and Jackie Ferris yesterday afternoon, Gus didn't want any distractions on this trip. Perhaps, if they brought the case to a successful conclusion, he could arrange a team get-together next Friday night to make the announcement.

As weekends went, the one just behind them had been memorable. After Suzie returned from her morning ride on Saturday morning, they spent the afternoon in the spare bedroom making plans. They walked to the Lamb for a snack in the evening. Bert Penman had a few words of advice for Gus about the state of his allotment. Gus promised to tackle the growing pile of tasks as soon as they had put his latest case to bed. Irene North dragged Bert away to talk about something other than gardening, and he and Suzie enjoyed a conversation with Brett and the Reverend, which topped off a quiet but satisfying Saturday.

It surprised Alex at how quiet his boss was today. Perhaps it was the early start. He wanted to go over several points concerning the interviews that lay ahead, but Gus was deep in thought. Alex took the shortest route to the M4. The sooner they were on the motorway network, the better. It was never easy to make progress on country roads first thing on a Monday.

"When do you plan to stop?" asked Gus, emerging from his reverie.

"Every couple of hours, guv, depending on our progress."

"If you need me to take a spell at driving, I'm ready, Alex," said Gus.

"I'll shout if my leg plays up, guv, but if we take regular breaks, I should be okay."

Alex approached the checkpoint at HM Naval Base Clyde at three forty-five. The security staff were expecting them. They impressed Gus with how smoothly they got them from outside the gates to the office where the interviews would take place.

"These guys could teach London Road Reception a thing or two," he grumbled.

"It was a long trip, guv," said Alex. "I asked whether they could fix us up with coffee. Finger's crossed."

"A tot of rum in it wouldn't go amiss," said Gus.

"They've stopped the daily ration, guv. Our first interview is with Chief Warrant Officer Max Hughes, guv," said Alex. "He knew Alan Duncan for the longest period. They were at Dartmouth together."

There was a sharp knock at the door, and Max Hughes entered the room.

"I'm Max Hughes, Taff to my mates. If there's anything I can do to help, just ask. The news of Alan's murder came as a shock, I can tell you. His father, Bob, rang me out of the blue on Saturday morning. Ten years, not a whisper. We knew one another from training, you know. A lovely bloke, Alan; we always got on well. Hark at me, rambling on. What did you want to ask?"

Max Hughes took a seat. Gus recognised Taff from the photographs. The ginger hair had a tinge of grey these days, but he hadn't altered much apart from a few extra pounds around the waist.

"We're interested in the photos Alan sent his parents," said Gus. "You can add context and detail that weren't forthcoming when our colleagues investigated the murder ten years ago."

"I see," said Max. "I hope I can remember where and when they occurred."

"No need to worry," said Gus. "Our computer whiz kids have dealt with that."

"Of course," said Max.

"What was Alan Duncan's role as Weapon Engineer Officer?" asked Gus.

"He led and managed a team of up to sixty technicians," said Max. "they included specialists in IT and communications and people with a unique knowledge of explosives and electronic sensor systems."

"Alan kept the craft fully operational and ready for action, I presume?" said Alex.

"The Vanguard is a state-of-the-art fighting machine," said Max. "Alan had to guarantee the performance of our weapons and sensor systems. So that we could always fire quickly and with accuracy, he worked with the world's most advanced defence systems."

"Did you ever hear from him after he left the Navy?" asked Gus.

"A Christmas card for the first two years," said Max. "An occasional text asking how things were going. Of course, I could only respond in general terms."

"You appeared to be great friends, based on the photographs we found at his parent's home," said Alex. He spread the photos on the desk in front of the Welshman.

"We were," said Max, "but Alan knew the score. When you're in, you're in."

"As soon as Alan was no longer a serving officer, everything you had in common disappeared," said Alex.

"Exactly," said Max. "I would have looked him up when

I retired, phoned him, to see if he wanted to come out for a beer. That won't happen now."

"Bob Duncan called you at the weekend, you said," asked Gus.

"Right out of the blue," said Max. "It shocked me. A car crash, or cancer, would have been bad enough. But murdered, that stunned me."

"Did Bob tell you what Alan did after he left Faslane?" asked Gus.

"He mentioned a small engineering factory," said Max. "It sounded odd."

"For someone whose engineering knowledge allowed him to work in such a challenging environment," said Gus. "Yes, that seemed odd to me too. Where did you think he would be employed?"

"His qualifications marked him out for a role as a Chartered Engineer," said Max. "He could have worked on Guided Weapons Systems, Cyber Defence, Explosive Ordnance Engineering, or Project Management. The sky was the limit."

"When did you first notice the change in his personality?" asked Alex.

"I'm not sure I understand the question," said Max.

"Who arranged the trips in these photographs that Alan sent his parents?" asked Gus.

"I sorted out the visits to Egypt and Sydney," said Max. "A gang of us joined at the same time and found ourselves on the same submarine. We always got on well."

"Who decided on Table Mountain?" asked Alex.

"I think it was one of the others. We flew to Cape Town and spent several days on the beach at Plettenberg Bay and Port Elizabeth. Smudger wanted to see Table Mountain. There was a race meeting at Kenilworth, although not everyone was keen to go. Alan went with Freddie, Chuff and Oddjob in the end."

"Oddjob?" asked Gus. "His name didn't get mentioned by Alan's parents."

"He was usually tied up with something else. Lenny Lambert was his name. I haven't seen him in ages. He was older than us, even Lofty, so he would have retired soon after Alan quit."

"He wasn't in the photo, which suggests he was behind the camera," said Alex.

"Lenny wasn't keen on having his photo taken," said Max. "He was a bit of a porker."

"Did Alan organise the trips after that?" asked Gus.

"He did, yeah," said Max. "Odd because he was happy to go along with the crowd. Alan never pushed himself forward to organise anything or get involved in any committees or societies onshore at Faslane or when we were at sea. So if that's what you meant about a personality change, I guess it was a departure from how he usually behaved."

"The next trip was in the autumn of 2001 to Paris, when they stage the big race out at Longchamp," said Gus. "Did Lenny Lambert travel with you on that trip?"

"He backed the winner, Sakhee, ridden by Frankie Dettori. The rest of us came nowhere."

"Was horse racing something of a passion for several of you?" asked Gus.

"Not really," said Max. "It was a passion for Lenny Lambert, of course. That's how he got his nickname. Lenny was the go-to man for the odds on any big races. He'd been following the horses since he left school. Lenny knew what was going to shorten on the day and vice versa. Spending weeks at sea it brightens your day if you can get a bet on the Grand National or the Derby. I could take it or leave it."

"What about Alan Duncan?" asked Gus.

"Hard to tell with Alan," said Max. "He gave little away about anything."

"We've heard that from almost everyone who knew him from 2004 onwards," said Gus.

"There's a pattern developing here, guv," said Alex. "Cape Town and Paris sound innocent enough tourist spots, but the visits coincided with race meetings. Some were internationally famous, and others that were run-of-the-mill. In June 2002, the gang visited Hong Kong."

"Lots of interesting places to visit there, Max," said Gus. "Bob Duncan remembers a photo with several of you wearing gaudy Hawaiian shirts. Alan removed that photo from the house for a reason. Someone took a photo of you out at Happy Valley."

"Blimey, that was a laugh. I can't remember who decided on fancy dress. I'm glad I never kept a copy. Embarrassing."

"Lenny Lambert was in that photo," said Gus.

"He was; Lenny was next to me," said Max.

"Who went behind the camera?" asked Alex.

"Drew Taggart. It had to be. He was wearing one of those shirts that day too."

"Out of interest, why did you call him Chuff?" asked Alex.

"He was a trainspotter when he was a kid."

"There's no point telling Lydia and the other young-sters," Gus told Alex.

Max laughed. He knew what Gus meant.

"I used to go to Barry Island when I was a boy. There was a steam train graveyard there. Hundreds of engines are all waiting to get scrapped. You have to be a certain age to remember the engine sound before everything went to diesel and electric. No magic in them these days, is there?"

"That's progress for you," said Gus. "Alex is right. After Alan assumed responsibility for your trips, a racetrack was always close to the principal centre you visited. The Te Rapa course is near Hamilton in New Zealand, which you visited in February 2003."

"I went surfing with Chuff and Lofty the day the others went to the races," said Max. "That was one of the few trips where Bryan Tarbuck joined us."

"We're speaking to Keith Smith later, as I'm sure you're aware," said Gus. "Tomorrow, we'll catch up with Freddie Watts on the Isle of Man. Have you kept in touch with the others?"

"After we stopped working together on Gold Watch, we went our separate ways. Lofty retired; Smudger stayed here with me, winding down to retirement. Contact has been less and less with people like Tarby, Taggart and the rest."

"Did Alan Duncan fall out with any of the men who went on these trips?" asked Gus.

"Never," said Max shaking his head. "If our skipper thought there was friction between anyone in his crew, their feet wouldn't have touched. You can't take deep-seated grievances underwater for seventy to ninety days. I guarantee there was no animosity between anyone that went away for a holiday that I went on. I would have reported it as soon as I returned to base. We all would."

"Did you visit Moscow when Alan was still serving in the Navy?" asked Gus.

"You are joking," said Max. "Never in a million years."

"Alan went there in May 2004, a few weeks before he left the service. Do you remember what you were doing then?"

"I was in Cancun, enjoying a boozy holiday with Lofty, Smudger and Rico Menghini. We got an extra spot of leave after colliding with a trawler in the Irish Sea. Who went with Alan? I heard nothing about that trip."

"We believe he travelled alone," said Alex.

"I don't like the sound of that," said Max.

"There's nothing to suggest Alan might have sold secrets to the Russians," said Gus. "What else could have encouraged him to travel alone to Moscow?"

"I've no idea," said Max. "Alan wasn't capable of doing something like that, anyway. That's ridiculous."

"Perhaps," said Gus, "but if you consider the personality change and the trips to tourist cities where a racecourse was close by, what might that suggest, do you think?"

"You're assuming Alan was gambling heavier than we knew and got in trouble."

"Is that possible?" asked Alex.

"Who might know the answer?" asked Gus.

"Lenny Lambert would know," said Max. "There are dodgy people on the fringes of that racing world, Mr Freeman. If Alan owed money to a bookie on the High Street, that's one thing, but if he was borrowing from a shady bloke Lenny knew, that could explain why he got killed."

"I would agree with you if we hadn't identified a suspect," said Gus. "Several people in the village where Alan lived saw a man called Yuri Kovalev. One person saw Kovalev arguing with Alan less than thirty minutes before he died. The Russian connection is the sticking point. We believe the man Alan met in Moscow is the man who strangled him four years later."

Gus slid the two photos in front of Max Hughes.

"Alan Duncan, you know, and the other man is Kovalev. Have you seen him before?"

"I haven't, Mr Freeman. But, look, if you think Alan's relationship with this man is linked to spying, I need to report it at once, despite the time that's passed."

"If Alan had gambling debts and wanted to get himself out of trouble, what did he have access to that was worth a considerable sum?"

"We all had access to valuable information, but that didn't mean we ever thought about acting on it," said Max. "Smudger would know more about this than me. We've moved on since 2004, Mr Freeman. So it would be difficult to know whether the Russians learned something from Alan that we didn't want them to know."

"I imagine the undersea manoeuvres are a game of cat-and-mouse similar to what's occurring with cybersecurity personnel of both sides on the surface or in space?" said Alex.

"That's all above my pay grade," said Max.

"Thanks for your help, Max," said Gus shaking the officer's hand. "We'll let you get back to your trainees. Get the security people to send in Chief Petty Officer Smith if he's ready."

"I wish I could be more help," said Max. "None of this sounds like the Alan Duncan that I knew for twelve years. It's a mystery."

Max Hughes left the room, and minutes later, they were joined by CPO Keith Smith.

"Hello there," said Smith. "What's all this nonsense about Alan Duncan? I spoke to Bob on the phone yesterday afternoon. Alan was a mate. Max Hughes felt it necessary to flag a potential security breach the second he left this room. That's part of my role here. We're talking about something that may or may not have happened fourteen years ago. We always detect Russian vessels, including subs, near the base.

They lurk in UK waters hoping they'll identify the acoustic signature of our nuclear-armed submarines. They could track and potentially sink them before they launched their missiles if they succeeded. The cheeky beggars had a submarine that stood off Faslane in 2010, waiting for one of our Vanguards to leave port for its three-month patrol. Recorded incidents are increasing, but the idea Alan could have offered the Russians something valuable takes some swallowing."

"Why?" asked Gus.

"If the Russians knew everything they wanted to know, they wouldn't need to keep hanging around outside our front door, would they?"

"Fair point," said Gus.

Gus and Alex took Keith Smith through the same procedure as Max Hughes. Smudger confirmed the initial trips had been Max's idea.

"Was there ever a trip you didn't attend?" Gus asked.

"You make it sound like I was always on holiday," laughed Keith. "We grabbed every opportunity for an experience light years away from our life at sea. Marriage never appealed to me. I enjoyed the sightseeing and the camaraderie. It will leave a massive hole in my life when I reach fifty-five, and I have to retire."

"I know how that feels," said Gus. "I was fortunate that there was still a role I could fill that kept me in touch with everything familiar. I guess that will be more difficult for a submariner. What about the choice that Freddie Watts, Lofty, made? Could you see yourself as mine host in a pub somewhere?"

"Lofty enjoyed a drink," said Keith. "I can't see him making much money at that game. The temptation to consume the profits would be too great. I could always take it or leave it. A pub that concentrated on good grub might be more up my street if I was that way inclined. But, no, I'll probably move abroad and play golf somewhere warm. A lot of open countryside around, that's what attracts me. I've had my fill of confined spaces."

"When you had a day at the races, did you sense Alan was betting more heavily than the rest?" asked Alex.

"Not at first," said Keith. "You know what it's like, all mates together. We bet five or ten quid on every race in whatever currency we had in our pockets. Some of us won a few quid, and most of us lost. But we drank a few beers, found a restaurant for a late meal, then went to a club to make a night of it."

"Max said Alan took over organising your getaways," said Gus. "More emphasis went on visiting a racecourse as part of the trip. Was it possible he got into financial trouble, which prompted the desperate move Max suggested to you just before you came to see us?"

"Alan wasn't any better or worse at picking winners than the rest of us. Lenny Lambert got in his ear about certain sure-fire winners out at Longchamp, and Alan laid big bets. I believe he won big on the Prix de Diane; the French Oaks, they call it. We heard all about the money Alan won that day. Whether he kept betting larger sums and hit a losing streak, I don't know. He wasn't a moody beggar; that's definite. Alan never let on that things were getting away from him. Alan was a patriot through and through. He would never have sold secrets to the enemy. If he needed ten, or even twenty grand, to get out of a hole, he could have talked to the gang. We might not have been able to rustle up the full amount, but we would have helped out enough to stop a thug from knocking seven bells out of him. So there has to be another explanation."

"Max told you about the Russian connection," said Gus.

"Max is a straight arrow. He knows how serious an accusation like that could be. You might not have wanted him to mention what you discussed between these four walls, but national security is paramount."

Gus showed Keith Smith the photo of Yuri Kovalev.

"Where was this taken?" Smith asked.

"Moscow Zoo on the afternoon of the eleventh of May in 2004. Kovalev took a photo of Alan outside St Basil's cathedral earlier that day."

"I was in Cancun around that time," said Keith. "I saw Alan in the week before we flew out of Glasgow. I asked him why he wasn't coming with us. He shrugged and said he had loose ends to tie up before he left Faslane for good."

"How did you react when he told you he was leaving?" asked Alex.

"We were all surprised," said Keith. "It takes a special person to become a submariner and stick at it for the full term. Alan had what it takes, but something convinced him he should call it quits. As far as we know, the gambling question you've raised was never an issue. His mental health was still good. We all underwent checks regularly. You don't want someone to have an episode halfway through a ninety-day trip. Alan was as level-headed the last time I saw him as he was the day we met. I don't think we understood his reasons for leaving, but we were back at sea within a couple of weeks. When we got home three months later, Alan was gone."

"As Max Hughes told us - when you're in…" said Gus.

"Too right," said Keith Smith. "The next patrol could be your last. You needed to trust the crew around you inside that ship, not reminisce about an old mate on civvy street."

Gus wondered whether there was anything more CPO

Smith could add. But, unfortunately, the only person who could confirm beyond all reasonable doubt that Alan Duncan had a damaging gambling addiction was Lenny Lambert, whereabouts unknown.

Gus doubted Freddie Watts would offer much more than an extra dose of disbelief that Alan Duncan could have sold secrets to settle a gambling debt. Was that worth the ferry trip to Douglas?

Keith Smith hurried away to follow up on the possible security issue Max Hughes had handed him.

"We have another long drive ahead of us, guv," said Alex. "Shall we delay the debrief until we've reached the hotel?"

"A good idea, Alex. Why don't you let me drive on this leg of the journey?"

"Okay, guv," said Alex. "You can have fun operating the windows. They don't stick halfway on my car."

Tuesday, 7 August 2018

"I SUPPOSE that eight-hour ferry journey to the Hook of Holland prepared you for this, Alex?" said Gus. "My last sea trip was to the Isle of Wight with Lydia. The sea was like a millpond that day. These waves are making me regret that fried breakfast at the hotel."

"Not long now, guv," said Alex. "I called Lydia from the bar last night after you turned in. They made little progress in finding Yuri Kovalev's current occupation. However, Lydia was waiting for a callback from the Hub this morning. Kovalev may be here in the UK."

"Should we keep an eye out for an old Vauxhall Zafira?" asked Gus.

"I'll text her and remind them to check the hire companies, guv. You never know. Did you ring DI Ferris last night?"

"First thing I did when I reached our room," said Gus. "The long day caught up with me sooner than for a young fellow like yourself. After that, I slept like a log."

"Don't I know it, guv," said Alex.

Alex drove them off the ferry and negotiated the streets of Douglas. Freddie Watt's pub, The Mariner, stood on a hillside two miles out of town. They parked in front of the tired-looking whitewashed building and went inside.

"It's quiet for August, guv," said Alex. "I imagined a lot more holidaymakers."

"There were plenty milling around in the town," said Gus. "This place is off the beaten tracks and doesn't have the kerb appeal of those in the tourist hotspot. Perhaps Keith Smith was right. Lofty's keener on lifting his elbow than serving customers. Where is everyone anyway?"

Gus rapped his knuckles on the counter.

"Wakey, wakey!"

"Hold your horses. I'm coming. What can I get you?"

"I'm DS Hardy from Wiltshire Police," said Alex. "Mr Watts is expecting us. Mr Freeman and I have come to interview him. Can we speak to him, please?"

"Freddie Watts, yeah, that's me. It was about Alan Duncan, wasn't it?"

"Close the door, Alex," said Gus. "We don't want any customers coming in while we speak to Mr Lambert."

The man on the other side of the bar seemed to crumble in front of his eyes. Gus beckoned to Lenny Lambert, inviting him to sit at a table near the window.

Alex studied the man sitting opposite and compared him to Watts's photos from almost fifteen years ago. Gus was right. This wasn't Freddie. Alan Duncan had removed the only picture of Lambert from Happy Valley. Bob and Elizabeth Duncan could give a brief description but nothing definite. When he and Gus spoke to Max Hughes and Keith Smith, Lenny Lambert's name came up quite often, but apart from Max saying Lenny was a porker, nobody produced a photograph.

"I think you had better explain," said Gus.

"Freddie spoke to me about his plans after he retired," said Lambert. "He'd had his eyes on this place for years. Freddie's parents brought him to the island when he was a kid. When he went for his annual medical three months before he retired, the medics told him he had cancer. They told him he had a year, tops. Physically, we had both changed over the years. He was still four inches taller than me, but I went on a diet and lost four stones. I needed to for my health. The older we got, the fewer the differences between us. I stayed close to him towards the end at the hospice and told him about my problem. We hatched a plan between us."

"You became Freddie Watts after he died," said Gus, "and moved here to take over the pub he'd always wanted."

"I didn't need a passport," said Lambert. "I was surprised by how simple it was in the end."

"Well, you were hardly going to make waves once you got here, were you?" said Gus. "The whole point was to hide away like Alan Duncan. It's quiet here. I don't imagine you advertise this place."

"So, what was the problem you shared with Freddie Watts?" asked Alex.

"Come on, Alex, keep up," said Gus. "Lenny and Alan

placed large bets on racecourses around the world. Nobody beats the bookies all the time. You got into debt with the wrong people, didn't you, Lenny?"

"It was when we were in Dubai in 2003," said Lenny. "It was my swansong. I was coming out within twelve months, and I had followed this trainer and his horses for months. I just knew they were holding back that horse for a killing. You see it all the time. They run in nothing races and tell the jockey to hold his horse in check, don't give the stewards any hint that you're not trying. Then when the season's almost over, you bring the horse out for one last run. She was nowhere in her last six races. Fifty-to-one she was that evening. I told Alan to pile on with everything he had. We both did."

"What happened?"

"Finished fifth in a field of six. I could have wept."

"How much were you in for?" asked Gus.

"The best part of ten grand each," said Lambert.

"When did Alan come up with the plan?" asked Gus.

"We met up for a drink in Glasgow between Christmas and Hogmanay," said Lambert.

"Alan proposed that he approached the Russians with information about this country's nuclear submarines," said Gus. "I assume he asked for twenty thousand?"

Lenny Lambert gave a wry smile.

"Here's me spilling my guts because I thought you knew everything already," he said. "You've got it all wrong."

"What happened then?" asked Gus.

"Alan would never have sold us out, and I wouldn't have let him. But Alan was a superb draughtsman. He produced drawings that passed muster when we handed them over to a contact he made on the Dark Web via the Tor browser. Alan exchanged the drawings for cash in

Moscow the following May. We got the bookies off our backs, I retired, and came here after winding up Freddie's affairs."

"When did you learn about Alan's murder?" asked Gus.

"When your bloke called to arrange this meeting. I was serving a customer when I heard my phone on Sunday lunchtime. I recognised the 01249 code from the mainland as being familiar. Alan and I swore never to get in touch again. We couldn't risk it. I wondered who it was calling and why, but they didn't try again, so I forgot about it."

"Bob Duncan still had a contact number for Freddie Watts in his diary," said Gus. "I guess he called, got no reply, and didn't want to leave a message. Did Alan know Freddie was dying?"

"No. Freddie didn't want the others fussing around him, pitying him. They were out on patrol when Freddie died. Also, keeping that quiet from Alan was part of the plan."

"Surely the Russians soon twigged you had conned them?" asked Alex.

"If it took them four years before they sent someone to find Alan, it doesn't say much for their Intelligence people. Alan thought unless they boarded one of our vessels, they couldn't be certain his drawings were anything but genuine. The longer I lived here without a problem, the more I thought we'd got away with it."

"Yuri Kovalev was the contact in Moscow, wasn't he?" asked Gus.

"I never met him," said Lenny. "Alan travelled to Moscow alone."

Alex showed Lenny Lambert the photograph of the Russian.

"Alan's killer," said Alex. "Kovalev knew what Alan looked like. Do you need to worry?"

"I can't see why," said Lenny. "That was the only time Alan met with him."

"We have colleagues on the mainland hunting for Kovalev," said Gus. "We heard last night that he might return to the country."

"Do you think he's after me?" asked Lambert. "Why would he wait ten years after he killed Alan? He can't possibly know who to look for."

"I hope you're right," said Gus.

"What happens now?" asked Lambert.

"Beats me," said Gus. "You got money under false pretences and assumed a dead man's identity. We'll file a report when we finish dealing with this case. What the authorities will decide to do with it, I don't have a clue. Come on, Alex. We've got a ferry to catch. At least we can get a drink there."

The journey home to Urchfont was a nightmare. There were hold-ups on the M6 and the M5. A contraflow was in operation on the M4, and they found a broken-down car transporter stuck at the traffic lights at Kingston St Michael.

Gus nodded off to sleep before they reached Avonmouth, so he missed most of the fun.

Alex dropped Gus at the bungalow and drove home to Chippenham.

Gus had reminded him not to worry about getting to work until lunchtime.

Wednesday, 8 August 2018

GUS WOKE at six o'clock for the third morning in succession. He hoped his body clock would quickly kick back into its regular routine. Then he remembered that in eight months, it would alter forever.

As he drifted to sleep in the car next to Alex yesterday evening, something was niggling at him. He'd come indoors to find Suzie asleep in front of the TV. They talked about everything except the case, and whatever was on his mind slipped out of his grasp. So what was it that disturbed his sleep last night? It had to be important.

Suzie was in the bathroom by seven; Gus went to the kitchen to get breakfast for one. After that, he wanted to get to the office. He had meant to call Luke last night to hear if any news had come from Bradford, but the trip from Liverpool had taken far too long.

Gus offered Suzie a cup of coffee when she surfaced. She took it and grimaced.

"It won't be for long," she said. "Mum had this with all three of us."

"I'm going in early," said Gus. "I gave Alex the morning off. He did the lion's share of the driving. I might come home and have a nap if things get quiet after lunch. I'll see you later."

Gus left Suzie, nursing her cup of coffee, sitting at the kitchen table. His Ford Focus seemed happy to see him back when he walked outside. It started the first time and trundled into Devizes without a complaint. Twenty minutes later, Gus was in the lift and heading for the office.

He glanced at the clock an hour later. Almost nine o'clock, The others should arrive soon. He'd updated his files. The Duncan murder case was as good as closed. The icing on the cake would be the arrest of Yuri Kovalev. Gus prayed that Lydia was right and the killer was back in the country. They might have half a chance.

Gus clicked his fingers.

"That was it," he shouted as Lydia, and the others exited the lift.

"Talking to yourself, guv?" said Neil. "That's the first sign of madness."

Gus was already on the phone. He hoped he wasn't too late.

Five minutes later, Gus sat back in his chair. He'd done all he could—time to switch back to the schedule for the day.

"What did I miss while we were away?" he asked.

"DCI Banks called yesterday afternoon, guv," said Luke.

"After exhaustive searches with various agencies, he said they had come to an inevitable conclusion," said Neil.

"Phil Banks started a search on scrubland near Digley Reservoir," said Luke. "That's about seven miles from the village of Marsden and twenty-five miles from the last sighting of Kyle Ellison."

"What, they're searching for a body?" said Gus. "Who has been posing as Kyle Ellison online all these years?"

"We wanted to see you before we left for Bradford, guv," said Neil. "We'll sit in on the interviews as you suggested. Phil Banks is happy for us to tag along."

"My guess would be the brother, guv," said Blessing, "Darren Forsyth. The language, the EDL affiliation, and his comments about the football read more like a man's words."

"Well, I suppose it's all going to come out in the next couple of days," said Gus. "If they find Ellison's remains."

"I didn't see that coming, did you, guv?" asked Neil.

"We knew Maddy Telfer was hiding something, Neil. I won't profess to have had that scenario in my head."

"We'll be on our way, guv," said Luke. "We'll call as soon as we have news."

"Thanks, Luke," said Gus. "Have a safe trip."

"Alex told me what happened on your trip, guv," said Lydia when the two detectives had left. "Where do we go from here?"

"Call the Hub, Lydia. Push them for sightings of Kovalev. We need to stop him from killing again."

"Sorry, guv," said Blessing. "Who's his target this time?"

"Lenny Lambert. Oddjob. The man was posing as Freddie Watts at The Mariner pub near Douglas on the Isle of Man. I've alerted the local police."

"Did we miss something, guv?" asked Lydia.

"No," said Gus. "I did. I should have kept digging into why that photograph was missing."

"The one from Happy Valley, guv?" asked Blessing.

"That's the one, Blessing—long story short, for now. You can read the full version in the Freeman Files later. Alan Duncan and Lenny Lambert appeared together in only one photo. Lenny was on several trips, but he knew he was overweight and chose to take the photos rather than appear in them. A few extra drinks and a Hawaiian shirt resulted in Lenny making his solitary appearance. Why did Alan remove that photo from his home? He recognised Kovalev at the Crown and near the duck pond. Alan knew the Russian had worked out that he'd conned him. He and Lambert had devised a plan to exchange valuable information about our nuclear submarines for money to settle their gambling debts. Kovalev only met Alan Duncan. He didn't know Lambert at all. Alan took that photo with him when he ran the night he died and tried to trade his life for Lambert's. No doubt he offered the eight and a half thousand pounds cash first, but Kovalev was under orders. Duncan had to die."

"If Kovalev had the photo, why didn't he go after this Lambert immediately," said Blessing.

"Lambert switched identities with Freddie Watts, who died of cancer in 2004. Lofty Watts was four inches taller, but after Lambert lost four stones, he looked nothing like the fat guy in that photo. But, of course, Alan Duncan didn't know about the weight loss, nor the switched identity."

"So what tipped off Kovalev now if we think he's looking for vengeance?" asked Lydia.

"We did," said Gus. "The Russians always watch our boats at Faslane from the Irish Sea. We visited the base and then took the ferry to Douglas. If Kovalev is here in the UK, it makes sense he was watching too. Did you find that hire car yet, Lydia? When you do, check CCTV evidence of it boarding a ferry."

"Blimey," said Lydia. She set to work.

Gus's phone rang.

"Freeman speaking. Good morning, Phil."

Lydia and Blessing paused what they were doing while Gus listened to DCI Banks.

"Thank you, Phil. My lads will be with you in around three hours. Good hunting."

Gus ended the call and puffed out his cheeks,

"Well, I never," he said.

"Did they find a body, guv?" asked Blessing.

"They found remains that appear to have been in the ground for around fifteen years. So Phil Banks has to wait for the autopsy to confirm that he's found Kyle Ellison at last."

"What prompted them to start searching there, guv?" asked Lydia.

"One of DCI Banks's officers called Mr and Mrs Forsyth to set up a meeting. Mary Forsyth asked why the police wanted to speak to her and her husband. The officer took a gamble and said it concerned Kyle Ellison's disappearance. Mary seemed relieved that it was over. She told the officer where to look."

"What was her role in it, guv?" asked Blessing.

"They don't know at this stage, Blessing. Luke and Neil will learn the tragic tale over the next day or two. I thought you or Lydia should accompany the detectives who arrested Maddy Telfer, but Phil Banks has already contacted London Road. DS Mercer is arranging for her to be taken into custody."

There wasn't much more to be said.

Epilogue

ON WEDNESDAY MORNING, Lydia continued the hunt for signs that Kovalev had hired a car somewhere in the country.

Divya rang from the Hub late at a quarter to twelve with the news.

"They've spotted him, guv," cried Lydia. "Kovalev boarded a ferry in Liverpool as a foot passenger this morning. He should land in Douglas at noon. That's fifteen minutes from now, guv."

"I'll call the local police on the Isle of Man," said Gus. "They can have people waiting for Kovalev to come ashore. They already have armed officers guarding the pub. So Lenny Lambert can rest easy tonight, at least."

Gus made the call. They were in luck. Yuri Kovalev walked from the ferry straight into the arms of the island police. The ramifications of the arrest would last far longer than the phone call.

Gus Freeman didn't concern himself with such matters. The Crime Review Team had identified Alan Duncan's killer. They had to rely on more senior officers at London Road and the Crown Prosecution Service to ensure justice was served. If Kovalev's paymasters in Moscow wanted him back, there were diplomatic ways and means. All Gus could do was live in hope.

"What shall we do for the rest of the day, guv?" asked Lydia.

"Make sure you update your parts of the Freeman Files," said Gus. "Clear the decks ready for the next case. Whatever Phil Banks uncovers will get dealt with by West Yorkshire. After that, Geoff Mercer can decide what to do about Bunny Campbell-Drake withholding evidence ten years ago. We deserve to take it easy and put our feet up after what we've achieved this week."

"And it's only Wednesday, guv," said Lydia.

"It's always Wednesday for Alan Duncan, Lydia," said Gus. "Never forget that."

Monday, 13 August 2018

LUKE AND NEIL were back in the Old Police Station office for the start of the new week.

"A quick catch-up then, lads," said Gus. "Then I'm off to London Road to collect the next cold case."

"We drove straight to Trafalgar House in Bradford, guv," said Neil. "They had transported the remains to the mortuary while we were on the motorway. We met DCI Banks and his team, and they put Luke and me into the viewing room. Phil Banks and DI Clemence carried out the interviews."

"Darren Forsyth served three months of his six-month

sentence for assault," said Luke. "When he came out, Dave Forsyth was still adamant that they needed to get Kyle Ellison out of Jennifer's life for good. He persuaded his daughter to contact Ellison and convince him she wanted to go back to him. Jennifer went to a bus stop late at night and sat on a bench. As they started talking, Ellison arrived on foot; Darren crept from behind the bus shelter and brained Ellison with a tyre lever. Dave Forsyth then drove up, and Jennifer and Darren helped get Ellison's body into the boot. Darren and his father buried the body half a mile from Digley Reservoir."

"Jennifer moved away from Marsden the following week, guv," said Neil. "Darren got himself a flat in Leeds. The stuff Blessing found on social media was all Darren's doing. He set up fake accounts to convince the locals Kyle had moved away to find work."

"Jennifer changed her name to Maddy Mills as soon as she reached Chippenham," said Luke. "Maddy told the truth when she said she kept her whereabouts from her family. They had no idea where she was living. Mary Forsyth took no part in the murder. She co-operated with Phil Banks throughout. Mary was only too happy to give evidence against her husband. Dave had made her life hell for years."

"What a mess, guv," said Blessing.

"A tragic mess, Blessing," said Gus. "Suzie accompanied Geoff Mercer to Redwing Avenue in Chippenham last Thursday evening to arrest Madeleine Telfer. Suzie told me the confusion on the faces of young Oliver and Emily as their mother left the house in handcuffs will live with her forever. Chris Telfer looked like a broken man. He had no idea what secrets his wife had kept buried for so long."

"Can you ask the ACC for something less gruelling later, guv," said Lydia.

"The Duncan case was a puzzle wrapped in an enigma," said Gus. "Churchill said that about Russia, didn't he? So perhaps it's no surprise that the man who led us to uncover Alan and Maddy's deepest secrets was a Russian."

vinci-books.com/genuinemistake

Secrets, suspects, and a detective's quest for truth.

The murder of Gerry Hogan, a respected businessman, has
remained unsolved for years. As Freeman and his team delve into
the past, interviewing friends and family, they uncover a web of
potential suspects that grows increasingly complex.

Turn the page for a free preview…

A Genuine Mistake: Chapter One

Monday, 13 August 2018

When Gus Freeman arrived in the Old Police Station's car park, he soon realised that the team was back to its full complement. Luke and Neil had returned from their trip to the Yorkshire city of Bradford and parts of that vast county's rugged countryside.

There were just two empty spaces. So Gus drove into one near the middle of the row Geoff Mercer had secured from the County Council. Gus knew Blessing Umeh would arrive in the next few minutes, and his young Detective Constable would appreciate the last space on the right-hand end.

It was small compensation for a wounded heart, but Blessing was a tough cookie. She would get over the loss of PC Dave Smith's affections in time.

Gus travelled alone in the lift. He found Luke Sherman and Neil Davis hard at work. Alex Hardy and Lydia Logan Barre were still preparing for the start of a new week.

Gus nodded to the couple and walked over to chat with Neil and Luke.

He heard the lift returning to the ground floor. Blessing was on her way.

"A quick catch-up, lads," he said. "Then, I'm off to London Road to collect the next cold case."

Neil and Luke brought Gus up to speed on the events of last week.

DCI Phil Banks called on Tuesday afternoon. His team had searched high and low for Jennifer Forsyth's former boyfriend, Kyle Ellison. They found no utility or council tax bills carrying Ellison's details. There was no evidence Kyle had worked or paid National Insurance and Income Tax in the past twenty-five years. The paper trail ended at the flat he'd rented in Leeds.

DCI Banks decided there was only one logical explanation, so he arranged interviews with the people who had wanted Ellison out of their daughter's life. He needed to narrow the search area. Luke reminded Gus that scrubland near Digley Reservoir was already under investigation last Tuesday afternoon. The Reservoir was seven miles from the village of Marsden, where the Forsyth family lived. It was twenty-five miles from Leeds and the last sighting of Kyle Ellison.

Luke had driven north with Neil later last Wednesday morning and reached Trafalgar House in Bradford at two o'clock. Detective Inspector Clemence took charge of the interviews with the male members of the Forsyth family. Neil and Luke watched from an observation room next door as Jennifer's father, Dave, and brother, Darren, adopted the 'no comment' tactic favoured by people who hoped to hide their guilt.

Neil and Luke learned that Jennifer's mother, Mary, had

been more forthcoming in an interview late Tuesday afternoon. It transpired there was no love lost between Mary and her husband.

"We drove to Digley Reservoir late on Wednesday afternoon, guv," said Luke. "Mary Forsyth overheard her husband describe an odd-shaped broom tree near where they dumped Ellison's body after Darren killed him. The remains were in the mortuary on Tuesday evening, but Clemence had kept a forensic team gathering evidence."

"It didn't take long to find the poor devil," said Gus.

"An hour, guv," said Neil. "There was plenty to do before they could close the case."

"Darren Forsyth served three months of his six-month sentence for assault," said Luke. "When he came out, Dave Forsyth was adamant that they needed to get Kyle Ellison out of Jennifer's life for good. He persuaded his daughter to contact Ellison and convince him she wanted to go back to him. Jennifer walked to a bus stop late at night and sat on a bench. As they talked, Ellison arrived on foot, and Darren crept from behind the bus shelter and brained Ellison with a tyre lever. Dave Forsyth then drove up, and Jennifer and Darren helped get Ellison's body into the boot. Darren and his father buried the body half a mile from Digley Reservoir."

"Jennifer moved away from Marsden to Chippenham the following week, guv," said Neil. "Darren got himself a flat in Leeds. The stuff Blessing found on social media was Darren's doing. He set up fake accounts to convince the locals Kyle had moved away to find work."

"Jennifer changed her name to Maddy Mills as soon as she reached Chippenham," said Luke. "Maddy told the truth when she said she kept her whereabouts from her family. They did not know where she was living. Mary

Forsyth took no part in the murder. She was happy to give evidence against her husband. Dave had made her life hell for years."

"Mary Forsyth told them everything she knew to save herself from prison," said Neil. "She didn't know Jennifer lured Ellison to his death on her father's orders. However, she realised what must have happened when Jennifer left home, Darren moved out, and Dave and Darren referred to the burial site in a drunken conversation during a family night in a pub."

"Mary Forsyth was an accessory after the fact," said Gus. "A person who knows something that might help secure an arrest for a serious offence must disclose that information."

"Clemence and his detectives, together with the forensic people, worked on the evidence from the burial site on Thursday and Friday morning," said Luke. "The coroner's report showed that the body was that of a male, aged between eighteen and twenty-four. The cause of death was a single blow to the back of the skull."

"The police had searched for DNA, dental records, and any item known to have belonged to Kyle without luck," said Neil. "So, proving the body was Ellison would be impossible without fresh evidence or a confession."

"Darren was the first to crack," said Luke. "The social media accounts he set up in Kyle Ellison's name sunk him. They have their version of the Hub at Trafalgar House, and the computer whiz kids soon unearthed the dummy email accounts, usernames, and passwords Darren had set up on his laptop. He changed passwords regularly, as the experts suggest you should, but he kept a note of every item in a cardboard box. Then, as Blessing discovered, Darren posted bits and pieces to fool people into thinking the accounts were active."

"It worked, too," said Blessing.

"Did he confess to the murder?" asked Gus.

"Not at first," said Neil. "When we arrived at our B&B on Thursday night, Luke and I thought things were slipping away, but on Friday morning, something from the Digley Reservoir site turned up trumps."

"Darren must have got splashed with Kyle's blood when he struck him with the tyre lever," said Luke. "The forensic team found a bandana lying under the remains. There was nothing to prove that the bloodstains on it were Kyle Ellison's, but they found traces of a second person's DNA."

"Darren Forsyth's?" asked Gus. "Did he wipe the blood from his clothes and face?"

"Yes, guv," said Luke.

"As soon as he saw the evidence bag with the bandana inside, Darren sang like a canary, guv," said Neil.

"Blaming everything on his father, no doubt," said Gus.

"He made me do it. His very words, guv," said Luke.

"What a mess, guv," said Blessing.

"A tragic mess, Blessing," said Gus. "Suzie accompanied Geoff Mercer to Redwing Avenue in Chippenham last Thursday evening to arrest Madeleine Telfer. Suzie told me the confusion on young Oliver's and Emily's faces as their mother left the house in handcuffs will live with her forever. Chris Telfer did not know what secrets his wife had kept buried for so long. He looked broken."

"Can you ask the ACC for something less gruelling later, guv," said Lydia.

"The Duncan case was a puzzle wrapped in an enigma," said Gus. "Churchill said that about Russia, didn't he?

Perhaps it's no surprise that the man who led us to uncover Alan and Maddy's deepest secrets was Russian."

"When did you two get back from Yorkshire?" asked Alex.

"We stayed until DI Clemence spoke with Dave Forsyth," said Neil. "Jennifer's father's supply of no comments ran out. There was a fair bit of swearing, but he realised the game was up. Clemence informed Forsyth as he left the interview room that his daughter was on her way to Bradford from Chippenham. All three would get charged in due course."

"I got home to Warminster at around eight o'clock," said Luke. "Nicky was livid."

"Squash court booked?" asked Lydia.

"No, souffle ruined," said Luke.

"Ouch," said Lydia. "Not a brilliant start to the weekend."

Gus was itching to leave for London Road.

"Has everyone updated their files?" he asked.

Each team member replied in the affirmative.

Gus flicked through the folder on his desk.

"Right, I'll be back in a couple of hours. Try not to miss me."

With that, Gus was in the lift and heading for the car park.

"Right, Luke," said Lydia, "spill the beans."

"We had a row," said Luke. "Not our first by any stretch of the imagination, but our latest cases have meant me working overtime and at weekends. Nicky works, too but sticks to what he calls normal hours. I had promised we'd have a full uninterrupted weekend for a change. How the Duncan case played out in different parts of the country altered that. I could do nothing, but Nicky thought it was symptomatic of my attitude to our relationship. I asked him to marry me six weeks ago, and we bought rings. We debated whether to honeymoon in the Caribbean or the Maldives. What have we done since?"

"You decorated part of the house when Gus gave you time off for good behaviour," said Alex.

"I don't think Nicky considered that a step towards us tying the knot," said Luke. "We were in a DIY store when I proposed. The refurbishments we planned were the catalyst. I suddenly realised that if we were shopping in B&Q, we were getting like our parents, conforming to type. Therefore, we should get married."

"What came out of this summit meeting?" asked Lydia.

"We decided on the Maldives for the honeymoon," said Luke. "As for the date, it will depend on our family's and friend's availability, but we're aiming for late March or early April next year."

"That's great," said Alex. "Cancel any souffle for this Friday night. I think Gus will want to arrange a night out for the Crime Review Team at the Waggon & Horses. We can add that to our list of things to celebrate."

"It's long overdue," said Neil. "If Gus mentions it later, I might call Rick Chalmers. He always enjoys a party."

"Is he married, Neil?" asked Blessing.

"Not these days," said Neil. "You're seeing someone, aren't you, Blessing?"

"Not now, Neil," said Blessing. "At least I'd have someone to chat to, although I didn't think we were compatible when I met him."

"What happened to Dave, your traffic cop?" asked Alex.

"He said he wasn't ready to settle down," sighed Blessing.

"Oh, Blessing," said Lydia. "Men can be dumb, can't they."

"I wouldn't go out with him, but Rick's a good copper," said Neil. "He was a great help on the Stacey Read case. Rick is used to working undercover. I wouldn't have fancied spending hour after hour watching for cars and faces out at the Honda factory. It was tough enough monitoring Rod Maidment's place, where the suspect was static for ten hours a night. He's good company, and that's what you need right now. Don't waste time brooding."

"Rick likes his beer and fast food," said Luke. "He's still one of the lads, even though he's a couple of years older than me. You deserve better, Blessing. Whatever you do, don't miss out on a night out with us if you haven't got a date. We're a team; we'll look after you."

"Thanks, Luke," said Blessing. "I'll be there. Divya might enjoy a night out if her husband is working at the hospital."

"Good thinking, Blessing," said Alex. "Divya worked with Rick and me in the Hub on the Burnside case."

"The Waggon & Horses won't know what hit it," laughed Neil.

Gus pootled through Seend, climbed Caen Hill, and followed a steady stream of traffic through Devizes. As he parked the Focus in the visitor's car park, he glanced towards the ACC's office window. Kenneth Truelove was nowhere in sight.

After signing in at Reception, Gus took the stairs to the mezzanine two at a time. Vera Butler had her eyes fixed on her computer screen. He could hear Kassie Trotter's distinctive voice advertising last weekend's baking products in the administration area. His unsolicited burst of energy had been a waste of effort.

"Is Kenneth in his office, Vera?"

Vera nodded.

Gus decided it wise to escape to the relative safety of the ACC's office. There was a chill wind blowing on the mezzanine floor this morning. He tapped on the door and entered.

"Geoff Mercer, what a surprise," he said. "Good morning to you too, sir. I bring glad tidings from the Old Police Station office."

"That's enough frivolity for this morning, Freeman," said Kenneth Truelove. "DS Mercer is available again for our weekly review. Thank goodness we can move forward knowing he's with us for the foreseeable future."

"I was going nowhere," said Geoff. "Glad tidings, you said. Did you pull a rabbit out of the hat again?"

"There was nothing magical, Geoff, just old-fashioned, solid police work," said Gus. "The Duncan case proved baffling. But as with several cases the team handled, the answers were there the first time if the detectives involved asked the right questions."

"Please tell me you haven't exposed weaknesses in the work of another respected officer, Freeman," said Kenneth.

"I don't blame Phil Banks, sir," said Gus. "He did what he thought was right. I wouldn't have done any different. If Mrs Campbell-Drake had told him everything she saw on the night of the murder, my team would never have needed to review the case."

"Phil, is it now, not DCI Banks?" asked Geoff.

"I found him easy to get on with, Geoff. You must have rubbed him up the wrong way."

"Take me through your potted version of the case, Free-man," said Kenneth. "I'll try to find time to study the contents of that folder later. Things are hectic here this week."

"I sensed a disquiet outside, sir," Gus said. "I hope it's not catching."

"So do I, Freeman," said Kenneth.

"Right, sir. Let's get on. A moving target is harder to hit. The Duncan murder case was as good as closed once Alex Hardy and I returned from the Isle of Man. The icing on the cake was the arrest of Yuri Kovalev on Wednesday lunchtime. Lydia Logan Barre was right; Duncan's killer was back in the country."

"I'm not entirely up to speed with this part of the case, Freeman," said Kenneth. "Who arrested this Kovalev chap, and what's happening to him?"

"Something bothered me as we drove south from Liver-pool," said Gus. "You know how it is, everything seems to have fallen into place, but you can't allow yourself to believe it's over. It kept me awake on Tuesday night, and when I reached the office in the morning, it hit me. The life of the man we left in a tranquil holiday pub on the Isle of Man was in danger. I called the local police and suggested they keep watch on the place. I mentioned your name, sir. That worked like a charm; you'll be pleased to hear. Once I knew that the bar owner was safe, I could relax."

"The fog is clearing, Freeman," said the ACC. "Slowly."

"Sorry, sir," said Gus. "I struggled from the outset with the background information on Alan Duncan and Maddy Mills. Everything pointed to them being in the wrong jobs based on their education and history, yet they seemed content. Phil Banks could never get a fix on the motive behind the murder. After the initial suggestion of suicide, he switched the hunt to find someone who wanted Alan

Duncan dead. He got nowhere. If Lady Davinia had described Kovalev to the officer who received the emergency call, the killer would have been behind bars in no time."

"What first put you on the track of this Russian chap's involvement?" asked Kenneth.

"Oh, that came late in the day, sir," said Gus. "We spent ages talking with people in Biddestone, Corsham, and Chippenham before Blessing Umeh stumbled on a photo of Alan Duncan taken in Moscow. The victim's mother had several photos in a drawer, including one of Yuri Kovalev, but Phil Banks never got to see them. It's not common to search the home of a murder victim's parents, where the said victim lived five miles away with a partner."

"I assume uniformed officers visited the parents to notify them of their son's death, confirmed they had an alibi, then left them to grieve?"

"Exactly, sir," said Gus. "At that point, it could still have been suicide. The next day, they had no reason to return to Corsham when the coroner reported strangulation as the cause of death."

"It was heartening to hear that the Hub helped to solve the case," said the ACC.

"We couldn't have done it without their help, sir," said Gus. "The answer lay in the photographs that Alan Duncan sent his parents. We had seen those early in the piece but didn't appreciate their significance. Maddy Mills was hiding a secret, and my attempts to uncover it delayed the deeper analysis of those photographs. The pictures from Moscow sped up the process because, at last, I could see a plausible reason for Duncan's murder. I suspected a submariner or a colleague not in those photos. Somebody that the men had in common."

"You got little right until the very end, did you, Gus?" said Geoff Mercer.

"Possibly not," said Gus, "but it wouldn't be the first time that a lightbulb moment saved the day in a case you handled, would it?"

"Fair comment," said Geoff.

"I can think of several," admitted the ACC.

"Duncan and Lambert enjoyed a bet on the horses," said Gus. "Nothing wrong with that in moderation, but they let things get out of hand. Rather than ask their colleagues to get them out of trouble, they hatched a plan to pretend to sell secrets to the Russians. I thought Duncan working as a draughtsman in a small company was odd, but although people mentioned he was a stickler for getting things right, nobody said he was a master at his craft. I can't imagine how tough it must have been to produce something that fooled Russian engineers for two decades. Ultimately, they realised their mistake and sent Kovalev to find Duncan and kill him."

"Lambert was Duncan's partner-in-crime, I take it?" said Geoff Mercer, "and the bar owner you referred to earlier."

"He was the group's so-called racing expert," said Gus. "Bob Duncan noticed a missing photograph taken at the Happy Valley racecourse in Hong Kong. Lambert appeared in just one of the group pictures. More often than not, he was behind the camera. I should have kept digging into why it went missing. Duncan took it with him from his parent's home on Sunday before he died. It was a desperate ploy. Kovalev wasn't interested in the cash that Duncan withdrew from the bank, nor in a photograph of Lambert. His mission was to kill Duncan."

"If Mrs Campbell-Drake had told the police everything,

you would never have discovered this Lambert character," said the ACC.

"True," said Gus, "nor would we have learned that Lambert tried to hide his connection to Duncan and the misleading drawings by assuming the identity of his dead colleague, Freddie Watts. That's another spin-off offence that resulted from this case. Add that to the eventual exposure of the secret that Maddy Mills, or Jennifer Forsyth, had buried for twenty-odd years; then it has to be one of the most complex and distressing cases I've handled."

"Distressing?" asked the ACC. "In what way?"

"I went to Chippenham with DI Ferris the other evening, sir," said Geoff Mercer. "We arrested Madeleine Telfer in her kitchen and then had to escort her through the hallway in front of her husband and two children. All three were innocents in this case."

"A tangled web, gentlemen," said the ACC. "What are the odds that Kovalev will stand trial here?"

"Slim," said Gus. "I haven't spoken with our colleagues in Douglas today. They still had Yuri Kovalev under lock and key on Friday. The Russians have no embassy on the island, and as a Crown Dependency, the Manx government can set some of its laws. They defer to the UK Government to handle their foreign affairs. So, as long as Kovalev remains on the island, it could be ages before the Russians can apply diplomatic pressure to release him."

"I remember a Polish criminal hiding on the island last year," said Geoff. "He had found out that European arrest warrants weren't valid there. With these smaller dependencies, the paperwork here on the mainland doesn't always account for every eventuality. The Ministry's pen-pushers often cover the things that might need a proper procedure."

"As my name appears to carry weight in Douglas, I

might suggest they liaise with you, Mercer," said the ACC. "A member of your team should take this case forward now that Freeman has done the groundwork."

"Good idea, sir," said Gus. "When you speak to the locals, Geoff, make sure that the second they hear from the Russians, they must spread the word. '*Russia bullies a tiny island in the Irish Sea.*' The negative publicity could encourage them to cut comrade Kovalev adrift."

"Leave it with me," said Geoff.

"Is there another cold case in your in-tray waiting to pounce, sir?" asked Gus. "My team wondered whether there was any chance of the next one being a piece of cake."

"I have a stack of case reviews on my desk, Freeman," said the ACC. "I grab the first one off the top every time. Your team will have to get used to taking pot luck."

Kenneth Truelove lifted the weighty file from the pile and perused it.

"This case is more recent," he said. "Only six years ago. Someone shot the poor devil on his doorstep on the outskirts of Trowbridge. Gerald Hogan was a fifty-four-year-old financial services professional who worked as a financial advisor, providing investment management and evaluating tax strategies for a range of clients. Gerry, as his friends and family called him, was playing snooker with his two sons, Sean and Byron, at their home on Trowle Common. Sean was eighteen and Byron sixteen. Gerry's partner, Rachel Cummins, a thirty-year-old personal trainer, was in the home gym."

"That could make for an interesting family dynamic," said Gus.

"Get your mind out of the gutter, Freeman," said the ACC.

"Sorry, sir. I'm sure whoever handled this case first asked the right questions. The murder file will highlight any shenanigans."

"The financial services game must pay well if Hogan had a large enough property to accommodate a snooker room," said Geoff Mercer.

"If I might finish the outline of the case, gentlemen," said Kenneth. "The attack occurred on Sunday, the sixth of May, at half-past six in the evening. Gerry and the boys were having a few frames before watching the World Championship final from The Crucible Theatre in Sheffield. The doorbell rang once, but nobody reacted in the games room. The boys hadn't heard it because they had the TV on for the build-up to the evening session. Rachel had to towel herself down and dash from the gym to the front door. On the doorstep, she found a man, half-turned away from her, who asked for Gerry Hogan. Rachel was annoyed at getting dragged away from her fitness routines. She left the man outside while she dashed towards the games room at the back of the house and shouted for her partner."

"Could she supply an accurate description of this man?" asked Gus.

"Rachel carried her towel to the front door," said the ACC. "She told the detectives she was more interested in covering her sweat-covered top half and not giving this guy or the neighbours a cheap thrill."

"The gunman didn't register then," said Gus.

"Ms Cummins said he was tall, white, and casually dressed. As she didn't get a look at his face, she couldn't give the police an accurate assessment of his age. As she said to DI Kirkpatrick in 2012, it was unusual for someone to turn up uninvited, but she never queried why this man wanted to speak to Gerry."

"What happened next?" asked Gus.

"Rachel returned to the gym. The sons told the police they carried on the game they were playing. All three were too far from the front door to hear anything that happened on the doorstep."

"What about the neighbours?" asked Gus. "Did nobody hear raised voices, sounds of a scuffle or an argument? The attack occurred early on a Sunday evening. You can guarantee there would be a dog walker somewhere in the vicinity. Couldn't the police find someone on their way to or from a church?"

"We know it was a sizeable property, Gus," said Geoff. "The name of the area where they lived suggests wide and open spaces surrounding it. So my first question would be, how did the killer get there? Was he on foot? Did Rachel Cummins see a car outside on the roadway?"

"A neighbour heard a motorcycle accelerating past his house that evening," said Kenneth. "He couldn't be sure of the time, but he heard it backfire, and then it buzzed past, sounding like an angry wasp. Ms Cummins said there was no car in their driveway. She was only at the door for a few seconds. The last thing she wanted to do was stand in a sports bra and lycra bottoms talking to a stranger."

"I doubt the motorcycle connected to the murder as it wasn't a high-powered machine," said Gus. "Perhaps the sort of moped a teenager might ride? What about the backfire the neighbour mentioned?"

"Let me run through the sequence of events we can verify," said the ACC. "The front doorbell rang at around six-thirty. Rachel Cummins answered the door, and only ten seconds later, she was hurrying to the back of the house to call her partner. Gerry left the games room to talk to the man on the doorstep. Rachel returned to the gym. Sean and Byron finished the frame of snooker they were playing when their father left. Sean opened the games room door at six-forty-five. The front door was half-open. Sean called out to his Dad that Ronnie O'Sullivan and Ali Carter would soon get introduced to the crowd. The boys were keen not to miss a ball getting potted. Rachel heard Sean shout and decided the interruptions to her exercising had destroyed the mood. She donned a t-shirt and went to the hallway to see what kept her partner. Rachel peered around the door to find Gerry lying on the gravel outside. He'd been shot in the head at close range. A single shot to the temple."

"Well, that changes everything," said Gus.

"Why?" asked Geoff Mercer. "The neighbour said he heard a backfire, and then a motorcycle went past his house."

"The man Rachel saw might not be our gunman," said Gus. "Would Gerry Hogan step outside to talk to a stranger who might have posed a threat? It's more likely he would stand inside his home with one hand on the door for security. He would want to get rid of the bloke quickly. Remember what Gerry and his sons had planned for the evening. If Gerry knew the man well, he might have invited him indoors. Then there's the conversation itself. Gerry was a financial professional. Did this casually dressed stranger want advice on which ISA to use or which stocks and shares were worth a look? Was everything Gerry Hogan dabbled in strictly legal? Few professionals conduct business on a Sunday evening. Did Gerry step outside, away from the house, to chat with the man? Maybe he didn't want Rachel to hear what they said."

"You're right, of course, Freeman," said the ACC. "The time lag between the doorbell ringing and the discovery of the body left things open for conjecture. DI Kirkpatrick treated the entire episode as an extended argument between Hogan and the killer. That may have been remiss of him."

"Kirkpatrick could have got it right," said Gus. "We'll need to explore both avenues. The two men could have had a brief conversation, and then the man left. Sean didn't shout for his father to remind him of the time until six forty-five. There was plenty of time for someone else to approach the property in the twelve or thirteen minutes between Gerry arriving at the open door and discovering his body. We can't know how long that gap was without finding the man who rang the bell at six-thirty."

"If there was another man," said the ACC.

"Nothing is ever straightforward, is it," said Geoff.

"I'll take the folder back to the office," said Gus. "Some-where in the volumes of material that they gathered, there has to be a clue as to motive. Who wanted Gerry Hogan dead, and why?

Gus drove left the London Road car park without further ado. There was no chance of a brief conversation with Vera and Kassie today. Grace Packenham stood on the far side of the room outside Rhys Evans's office, keeping watch.

When he drew up behind the Old Police Station, Gus took another look at the passenger seat's weighty folder.

"Who was Gerry Hogan?" he asked.

Gerry Hogan was born in the Royal United Hospital, Bath, on March the fifth, 1958. His parents were Peter and Jean Hogan, whose daughter, Belinda, had arrived three years earlier. The family lived in Bradford-on-Avon, a small town of around nine thousand people located six miles from the Roman city of Bath. Gerry attended Christchurch Primary and later Fitzmaurice Grammar School. His head-teacher at Fitzmaurice remembered him as well-mannered, good-natured, and intelligent.

Nick Barratt, a close friend throughout their schooling, remembered Gerry as a focused individual. Gerry had his goals mapped out from an early age. No way was he the sort of lad who'd get caught underage drinking, shoplifting, or getting involved with the wrong crowd. Gerry did his utmost to steer clear of trouble. After school, he went to Bristol University to study for a Business and Finance degree. He graduated in 1980 and, after a gap year in Australia, joined the newly formed Hargreaves Lansdown company.

While on his travels, Gerry met his first wife, Evelyn, a wildlife photographer. It was a whirlwind romance. The pair got engaged only weeks after meeting on Bondi Beach. When Gerry returned home to Bradford-on-Avon to start work, Evelyn stayed in New South Wales to complete an assignment at the Macquarie Pass National Park. One month later, she flew into Heathrow Airport and lived with Gerry and his family in Bradford-on-Avon until their registry office wedding in early 1982.

Evelyn continued her career in the UK, accepting commissions closer to home. She made regular trips to West Wales, Richmond Park in London, the Cairngorms in Scotland, and the Farne Islands off the Northumberland coast. The couple bought a place in Clifton, Bristol, that suited them, both for its proximity to Gerry's job and transport links for Evelyn but also for the nightlife they enjoyed as a young professional couple.

A decade later, Gerry wanted to branch out independently and find a family home closer to his parents. They had fallen in love with the Trowle Common property at first sight. It altered somewhat in the next ten years as Gerry's business prospered and Evelyn stopped travelling long enough to give birth to Sean and Byron. They extended the property to one side and at the rear. The sunroom was Evelyn's choice on the ground floor. The games room to the side of it was Gerry's pick for somewhere he could spend what free time he had with his boys.

Evelyn had transformed the spare bedroom into her studio. She explained to Gerry that the direction of the window made a huge difference in light quality. North-facing windows always have soft light because the sun never directly shines through them, while South-facing windows should expect direct sunlight for a good portion of the day. Gerry knew why his wife couldn't resist that dig. Evelyn missed the Australian sunshine.

Sean and Byron were aged eight and six and attending Fitzmaurice Primary in Bradford-on-Avon when Evelyn decided she'd exhausted the most lucrative assignments the UK could offer. The wanderlust was tough to get out of her system. Gerry's business went from strength to strength, so he let Evelyn fly back to Australia for a month with his full support. She returned to the Macquarie Pass National Park to follow up on the work she'd carried out in 1981.

Macquarie Pass is a five-mile-long section of the Illawarra Highway passing through the National Park. The pass links the town of Robertson to the coastal town of Albion Park, where Evelyn rented an apartment.

The pass descends via a narrow roadway with several single-lane sections. It's mostly two lanes with double lines showing no overtaking. This roadway section is very steep and contains many hairpin bends, resulting in buses and trucks needing to back up on some curves. The pass was notorious for accidents, requiring drivers and motorcycle riders to be cautious. After heavy rain, the Macquarie Pass could be closed because of flooding on its top half.

In early March 2002, Evelyn returned from a day photographing egrets, ibis, and herons. A motorcyclist came around a hairpin bend on the wrong side of the road, and she swerved to avoid it. Evelyn's rental car rolled over, somersaulted the safety barrier, and she was dead before the emergency services could arrive from Albion Park. Evelyn was just forty years old.

Gerry Hogan flew to Sydney and met Evelyn's parents for the first time since he and his wife got engaged. The couple couldn't afford to visit the UK for the wedding. Evelyn kept in touch by phone and letter in the intervening years, and Gerry kept promising they would fly out one day so that Sean and Byron could meet their grandparents.

Gerry knew that his in-laws didn't want their daughter to lie in a grave in England. He agreed they should scatter Evelyn's ashes in the Macquarie Pass National Park. When he flew home towards the end of March, he faced up to life looking after Sean and Byron alone.

His sister, Belinda, was always ready to offer a helping hand. When the police talked to her after Gerry's death, Belinda said he had been a brilliant father. He never complained about the cards life had dealt him. Instead, he wholeheartedly threw himself into being the best father to those two boys.

Gerry met Rachel Cummins five years later, in 2007. Belinda worried it was too soon. She was concerned that the boys would find it difficult to adjust. Sean was thirteen, and Byron was eleven by that time. They both attended St Laurence School in Bradford-on-Avon. Gerry and Rachel dated for several months before Gerry introduced her to the boys. They went on holiday to Portugal in the Algarve in the Spring of 2008. Rachel moved into the house on Trowle Common when they returned home.

Gus flicked through the folder to find anything on Rachel Cummins. Who was she? What first attracted her to the wealthy and successful business owner Gerry Hogan? That might be simple enough to fathom, but although Gerry Hogan was old enough to be her father, two teenage boys were in the mix to consider. Rachel might not be a gold-digger after all. Gus knew all too well that two people from different generations could fall in love.

The Rachel Cummins file was far slimmer, not unlike the lady herself, based on the photograph at the top of the first page.

Rachel was born in the first week of January 1982 in Haslemere, Surrey. Her parents were Jeffrey and Katherine Cummins, who lived and worked in the small town twelve miles from Guildford. Rachel's parents separated eighteen months after Rachel was born, and Katherine raised Rachel alone.

After leaving Woolmer Hill Technology College, Rachel continued her studies to gather a bundle of health, exercise, and fitness diplomas. Then, aged twenty, she started a business as a personal trainer. Rachel continued to live with her mother in Haslemere, driving to various sites across the county for group fitness sessions. She also secured one-to-one appointments with clients in their own homes to boost her earnings.

In 2005, Katherine Cummins reconnected with an old school friend through Facebook, and Rachel arrived home from a fitness session to learn that her mother was eager for Lawrence Wallace to move in.

Rachel thought Lawrence was a creep, but it was her mother's life. Perhaps it was time to plough her own furrow? Three months after Lawrence moved in and several rows with her mother, Rachel moved out. She did her best to find other trainers to accommodate her regulars, and after she was satisfied with her efforts, she moved to Bath. Rachel didn't know the city except by reputation, but her training and experience were transferable anywhere in the country.

After a rocky few weeks where she wondered whether

she had made the right decision, Rachel's business soon grew. Eighteen months after moving to Bath, Rachel ran one of her regular fitness classes in Bradford-on-Avon when Gerry Hogan arrived.

Gerry was forty-nine, a widower, and although he ran a successful business, he knew that two decades without regular exercise was playing havoc with his waistline. After the first occasion that he attended her class, they spoke briefly about what he wanted from the sessions. Gerry had told her he'd concentrated on caring for his two sons after losing his wife in a car accident. He needed to get fit for their sakes, and the hour at the gym with her would be the only social interaction he'd get without the boys tagging along.

Rachel had found herself thinking of Gerry during the following week and looked forward to seeing him again. She asked if he wanted to go for a drink after the following Thursday evening session. That was something she had never done before with any of her clients.

Rachel had had to fend off the odd amorous bloke who thought an appointment in his home promised something that was not on the published price list, but Gerry was different. She felt an instant attraction, and later that night, after the drink in the pub, Rachel discovered Gerry felt the same way.

It was the first time he'd been with a woman since his wife died. Despite Belinda's reservations, Gerry and Rachel grew closer, and after that foreign holiday in 2008, Rachel moved in, and for four years, everything was fine.

After Gerry's murder, some issues need sorting out. Gerry and Rachel had never married. Belinda received the money in the will, but the home on Trowle Common and the financial services business passed to Rachel. Gerry had altered his will after Evelyn's death so that if anything happened to him before the boys reached the age of majority, his sister, Belinda, would act as their guardian.

Gerry altered his will again in 2011. He and Rachel had lived together for three years by then, and there were no clouds on the horizon as far as he could see to stop them from staying together for many years. Sean was already almost seventeen, and the need for a guardian seemed superfluous. Although Byron was two years Sean's junior, what could go wrong?

"Eighteen is the age when minors cease to be considered such," he'd told Rachel. "They can assume control over their actions and decisions at that stage. I'm hoping we can see them married and with their own children before we worry over the provisions of my will again."

From the sixth of May 2012, that worry transferred to Rachel Cummins when her partner got killed. It soon became apparent that Belinda Hogan wished to challenge the will. She told friends she believed Rachel hired a hitman to kill Gerry. Belinda thought that was her plan all along; to live with him for a short period and then cash in.

Gus closed the file for now. This case had more angles than he'd imagined when the ACC walked through it earlier. He vaguely remembered a bloke in a suit coming to their home in Downton one evening to help him and Tess fill out a form. In the event of, and so on, but like Gerry Hogan, they'd thought nothing untoward would happen to them.

They expected to grow old gracefully, and the surviving spouse would inherit the lot when one of them died. That meant they carried on pretty much as before, like millions of other couples whose wills were simple and straightforward.

After Tess died and the usual rush of urgent official paperwork, Gus couldn't recall what he'd done with their will. He certainly hadn't thought it necessary to amend it. He was only fifty-eight. What was the rush?

As Gus sat in the Focus, staring at the back wall of the Old Police Station, he realised that he'd better find that brown envelope and start thinking about how the wording needed to change. Suzie might not be in a rush to become the second Mrs Freeman, but there was someone else to consider.

Gus grabbed the folder and travelled up in the lift.

"Welcome back, guv," said Lydia. "My word, that's a big one."

"Don't even think about saying anything, Neil," said Gus.

"Me, guv?" said Neil. "I'm pure in thought and mind. That was what the actress is supposed to have said to the bishop, too."

"We have the murder file here for a financial advisor, Gerald or Gerry Hogan," said Gus. "Hogan died on his doorstep at the beginning of May 2012."

"That we're looking at it now implies the original investigation got nowhere, I assume?" said Blessing Umeh.

"You've got it in one, Blessing," said Gus. "Right, the usual procedure, please. Get the crime scene photos up on the walls and whiteboards. We need photos of the key players and their backgrounds—a Trowbridge and Bradford-on-Avon map that allows us to focus on the murder site on Trowle Common. Luke, you can set up meetings with witnesses and the surviving family members. Alex, I want you to put Gerry Hogan's business life under the microscope. I'll run through the sequence of events in a moment, but if someone wanted Hogan dead badly enough to shoot him in the head in broad daylight, money probably figures in the affair somewhere."

Gus opened the large folder on Blessing's desk, and Lydia joined her colleague to sort through the items they needed.

"I was right. This file carries a lot more detail than we're used to," she said.

"At least someone had the decency to prepare an index," said Blessing. "We'll find the major items so much easier."

Gus returned to his desk and rang Geoff Mercer at London Road.

"Geoff, what happened to John Kirkpatrick?"

"He transferred to Portishead," said Geoff. "John Kirkpatrick's a Detective Chief Inspector with Avon & Somerset."

"I can see a pattern developing here," said Gus. "Every officer I need to contact has got promoted since handling a murder case that the ACC gives me. Is that the reward for failure these days?"

"Cheeky," said Geoff. "They could have had a decent clear-up rate for all you know. Not as stellar as yours, of course, Gus. You get to tackle the occasional blip in their careers."

"If you say so, Geoff," said Gus. "I suppose Victoria Bennison has moved on from being a Detective Sergeant?"

"Vicky Bennison left the police, Gus," said Geoff. "I can get her contact details to you if you need to speak to her, but I can't guarantee she'll cooperate. Vicky transferred to Thames Valley to work in Oxford a couple of years after the Hogan case. In June 2015, she joined officers policing an anti-austerity protest march on a Saturday afternoon in central London."

"One of those marches that started with good intentions but got infiltrated by anarchists, I imagine," said Gus.

"There were many undesirable elements that attached themselves to the peaceful protestors, and things turned nasty," said Geoff. "A male colleague went into the crowd to make an arrest. Vicky saw him quickly surrounded by four or five heavies and waded in to help. Someone behind her shoved Vicky hard in the back, and she hit the ground. While other officers struggled to control the situation ahead of where she fell, Vicky took a severe kicking from the thugs who remained. Every time she opened her eyes to identify her attackers, she saw a sea of mobile phones filming the attack. A dozen officers ended up in the hospital that afternoon. Her male colleague didn't return to duty for fifteen months."

"What about Vicky?" asked Gus.

"Like many other officers, she joined the police to protect the public," said Geoff. "When Vicky shouted for their help, all they did was laugh and keep filming. After the Chief Constable handed her a medal, she threw it in the nearest waste bin and walked away."

"Send me her details, Geoff," said Gus. "I'll tread with care if I ask for her opinions on the case. Thanks for the heads up."

Gus looked around the room. He hoped that none of the Crime Review Team ever suffered like Vicky Bennison. Whatever happened to respect for authority? If only they could rewind the clock to the days when he joined as a uniformed constable. Things were far from perfect in the mid-Seventies, but his old Sergeant would have kittens if he saw what the world was like today. Ah, well, time to move on. At least the walls and whiteboards carried everything they needed for the next few days.

"Right," he said. "A quick summary, and then I want your first impressions. Gerry Hogan lived in Bradford-on-Avon as a child. After university, he joined a well-known financial services firm in Bristol. Hogan married an Australian girl, Evelyn, in 1982 and set up his own business in 1992. They had two sons, Sean and Byron, born in 1994 and 1996. In 2002, Evelyn died in a traffic accident in Australia. She was a wildlife photographer who had worked in the UK throughout their marriage. Before leaving New South Wales, her last commission to live in the UK had been at the same location. The trip back home was to take photographs she could use to compare the wildlife volumes in the Macquarie Pass National Park after a twenty-year gap. The climate change fraternity was eager to see the results. Gerry Hogan didn't cut back on his business involvement but spent every spare minute of free time looking after his sons. His older sister, Belinda, did her best to support her brother. In 2007, Gerry Hogan met Rachel Cummins, a personal trainer. There was a significant age gap, but the couple stayed together, and the boys liked her. Everything seemed fine in the relationship. There were no problems with the business. Rachel Cummins continued to operate her business, holding fitness and exercise classes in and around Trowbridge and Bradford-on-Avon."

"I think I've seen her adverts in the local press," said Neil.

"You never thought of signing up?" asked Lydia.

"Can you picture me in lycra?" asked Neil.

"That's an image I'll never get out of my head now. Thanks a bunch," said Luke.

"Any sensible comments before I move on?" asked Gus.

"Sorry, guv," said Neil.

"On Sunday the sixth of May, six years ago, Gerry and the boys were in the games room at the right-hand rear of the house. Rachel was exercising in the gym on the left-hand side, on the ground floor and at the back. The door-bell rang at six-thirty in the evening, and Gerry and the boys stayed put, meaning Rachel had to stop what she was doing to answer the door. A man stood in the driveway, not facing her head-on but half-turned away. Rachel was in a rush. She opened the door, and the man asked for her partner by name, nothing more. Rachel pushed the door to and made for the games room. She shouted for Gerry and told him someone wanted to speak to him. Rachel returned to the gym. Gerry went to the doorstep to talk to the visitor. At a quarter to seven, Sean left the games room to look for his father. He called out, thinking he was outside in the driveway as the front door was still ajar. Rachel heard Sean call out and stopped exercising. She walked into the hallway, peered around the front door, and found Gerry dead on the gravel. Someone had shot him in the head."

"No known enemies," said Neil.

"A happy relationship," said Blessing.

"Hogan wasn't known to the police," said Luke.

"Déjà vu," said Alex, "all over again."

"It sounds like we've been here before, doesn't it?" said Gus. "We start our review with more information available than with some cases we've handled. The detective who was Senior Investigating Officer on the case now works at Portishead. DS Mercer has told me that DCI John Kirkpatrick will be available to clarify any of the methodologies they followed. His second-in-command, DS Bennison, has left the service. I'll track her down if we need her input and have a quiet chat."

"Vicky Bennison, guv?" said Neil Davis. "We joined around the same time. I remember when she got injured in London. Her head was never right after that. The physical wounds healed within a month, but the mental scars never left her."

"If you knew Vicky when you were both raw recruits, Neil, it makes sense for you to come along. A friendly face might persuade her to give us a helping hand."

"What lines of enquiry did the investigation follow, guv?" asked Alex Hardy.

"After interviews with family and neighbours on Monday and Tuesday following the murder, they were struggling," said Gus. "Nobody saw the man who rang the doorbell arrive or leave the house. Rachel couldn't give the police anything other than a vague description."

"That should have made the SIO suspicious, guv," said Lydia. "Once the sister started spreading the rumour that Rachel had hired a hitman."

"Belinda didn't raise her concerns with her friends until she learned of the provisions in her brother's will," said Gus. "After his wife's death, Gerry had written a new will. So if something happened to him, Belinda would become the boys' guardian until they reached eighteen."

"There must have been another will," said Neil. "If the will with Belinda in it was still valid, Rachel had nothing to gain by bumping off her partner."

"A year before his death, Gerry told Rachel he wanted to amend his will so that she inherited most of his estate. Gerry left money in a trust for the boys to receive when they reached twenty-five. He also made financial provisions for his sister, but Belinda would no longer need to look after his boys. All things being equal, they would be grown men with their own families by the time any will came into effect."

"True, Neil," said Alex. "Nobody could foresee the events of May the sixth. The murder file states that Gerry discussed the new will with Rachel in detail. They both agreed it was the right thing to do. At thirty, Rachel hadn't got around to making a will herself, and she admitted to Kirkpatrick and Bennison that although she and Gerry had lived together for four years, they were in no rush to get married. Rachel hoped it would happen in the future, but it wouldn't have damaged their relationship if it didn't. She loved him as much as she had within weeks of their meeting."

"Sean and Byron confirmed that their father's feelings for Rachel hadn't altered in the months before the murder," added Lydia. "Byron told DI Kirkpatrick, 'They were loved-up. We called her Rachel, not Mum. She never tried to take Mum's place, but she made Dad happy, and we all got on together. There were never any arguments.' Sean added that their Dad dealt with them when they had the odd teenage tantrum. Rachel never interfered, but when he was suffering after getting dumped by a girl he'd liked, Rachel had listened to him and offered him advice."

"The family situation appears idyllic," said Blessing. "The sister's claims don't seem to hold water, guv."

"Belinda Hogan might have been jealous of Rachel Cummins," said Neil. "After Gerry lost his wife, his sister was the first person he'd asked to look after the boys. She was single, with no children of her own, and for around five years, she assumed a mother's role. Gerry amended his will to accommodate that situation. She would have gotten the lot if he'd dropped dead of a heart attack in 2007. A year later, Gerry had a new girlfriend. The boys didn't need Auntie Belinda to look after them any longer. Belinda did not know that Gerry had amended his will yet again."

"But you can understand why he did what he did," said Alex. "It seems quite sensible. Gerry set money aside for the boys and stipulated that they shouldn't get their hands on it and squander it in their teens. So they would be better prepared to cope with a sudden financial windfall when they reached twenty-five. Belinda was also going to inherit a sum of money. Based on the sort of bloke that Gerry Hogan appeared to be, that would be a sum that reflected her input to the family after Evelyn's tragic death."

"Two hundred thousand pounds, Alex," said Gus.

"His financial services business *was* doing well," said Luke.

"In the vital first forty-eight to seventy-two hours of a murder case, the detective team did everything one might expect," said Gus. "The only neighbour that hinted at what might have happened lived half a mile away. He heard what he thought was an engine backfiring, followed by a motorcycle speeding past his house. Now, it's possible the murderer arrived on a motorcycle, argued with Gerry Hogan, shot him, and then escaped on the bike."

"Why only possible, guv?" asked Blessing. "It sounds plausible to me."

"I'm not saying it didn't happen that way, Blessing," said Gus. "When the ACC ran through the report this morning, I found the timing interesting. Rachel answered the door when it rang at six-thirty; she called Gerry, who went to see what the man wanted. Sean didn't leave the games room until six forty-five. The neighbour couldn't confirm the time that he heard the motorcycle. There was too much of a gap between Gerry reaching the front door and Rachel discovering the body a little after six forty-five. It's unlikely, I admit, but someone else could have visited the house after the first man left. The motorcycle needn't be involved in any way, shape, or form. The neighbour's recollection of a sound he heard on Sunday evening could have been anywhere between six o'clock and nine."

"When did Belinda learn about the new will?" asked Lydia.

"She contacted the family solicitors on Tuesday morning," Gus said. "In the will that Belinda believed was relevant, she was the sole executor. Belinda soon learned that another will existed where Rachel Cummins was now in charge of proceedings. That was when the proverbial hit the fan. John Kirkpatrick had Belinda in his ear every day, wanting to know why they weren't treating Rachel as a suspect. He told her they had considered whether the murder was carried out by a professional rather than a local with a grudge. They hadn't dismissed it out of hand, but several things didn't add up, so they shelved it until new evidence surfaced."

"The timing you mentioned didn't add up, guv," said Alex. "A hitman would have shot Gerry the second he was on the doorstep, not stand around arguing the toss for almost a quarter of an hour."

"Whoever it was," said Neil, "they carried a gun to the house. They were prepared to kill, but the extended conversation could suggest they went to negotiate, not assassinate."

"Negotiate what, though, Neil?" asked Blessing. "Gerry Hogan ran a successful business giving financial advice to fellow professionals. The vague description of the man on the doorstep didn't sound like the sort of person Gerry Hogan would represent, even allowing that it was a Sunday evening. But, as my father says, there's casual, and then there's casual."

"What type of gun was it, guv?" asked Luke.

"A semi-automatic pocket pistol," said Gus. "A Beretta Tomcat."

"How do we know that?" asked Luke.

"It turned up in the autumn of 2012," said Gus. "Matthew Knight, a local councillor, got fed up with local people moaning about drains getting blocked by falling leaves and standing water on several roads across the Common. After a phone call and a flea in the head of the Environmental Protection Department's ear, a road sweeper visited Trowle Common and cleared the drains and gullies. It was common for the sweeper operator to find shoes, coins, mobile phones, and watches. When he spotted the small gun drop out, he thought it was a novelty cigarette lighter. It wasn't much bigger than the palm of his hand."

"How far from the house was the gun found?" asked Alex.

"Over a mile," said Gus. "Yes, questions were asked why they hadn't found it in May. John Kirkpatrick had limited resources, and as each day passed, the trail grew colder. They confined the search area to several hundred yards around the property. Finally, the Beretta went for a forensic examination and proved to be the murder weapon. There were no fingerprints. The pistol had sat in a drain for five months, and every criminal worth his salt removes every trace of DNA before discarding a weapon."

"So, the detectives had a body and the murder weapon," said Lydia, "but no motive."

"That about sums it up," said Gus. "I reckon we should call it a day for today. We start looking for that motive in the morning."

Grab your copy…
vinci-books.com/genuinemistake